Runaway Grandma Reviews

Ann McCauley's new novel *Runaway Grandma* will make you laugh and it will make you cry. One thing is certain - you will not be able to put it down. Widowed Olivia Hampton tries to escape from the demands of her scheming children and find some well-deserved freedom, but life has a funny way of refusing to let her be. If you've ever wanted to run away yourself, escape into the pages of *Runaway Grandma*. This novel's memorable characters, witty dialogue and unexpected plot twists will make you glad you did.

—**Linda Underhill**, author of *The Unequal Hours*

Fearful that her adult children intend to take control of her life and finances, Olivia Hampton takes drastic measures to insure that she is the one in charge of her own destiny. Ann McCauley's *Runaway Grandma* is the story of Olivia's journey with its highs and lows and how her decision impacts the lives of others, both the family and friends she left behind as well as her new friends. You can not help but be drawn into the story of this warm, brave woman who makes a brand new life for herself at the age of seventy.

—**Karen J. Gause**, Librarian

Olivia feels that her son will try to have her declared incompetent and take control of her assets, so she carefully devises a plan to disappear. She ends up living in a different part of the country where she meets an older gentleman and they become great friends. This book reveals an unusual solution to a family problem. I highly recommend *Runaway Grandma*. RATING: **4 Flames-*Rare Find***

—**Wilma Frana**, Reviewer for WordMuseum.com

Everyone comes to a place where the looming question of what to do next confronts us. Olivia Hampton, faced this dilemma when she believed her children were going to have her declared incompetent and she would lose her freedom. Instead of risking this possibility, she faked her own death, left everything behind and found a new life. The novel brings out some important truths the least not being that if life doesn't turn out the way we plan, plan something else.

—**Patti Lawson**, author of *The Dog Diet, A Memoir*

This is a story that anyone who ever thought about cutting and running would enjoy. Ms. McCauley has captured our dreams, our fears and our imaginations as her heroine Olivia steps out of all that is familiar and ventures into the unknown. Olivia proves it's never too late to begin again. I couldn't put this book down until I finished it.

—**Ronald A. Schmidt**, Book Reviewer, Scottsdale, AZ

Disillusioned with her grown children, Olivia Hampton fakes her death, changes her name and sets out to start a new life—at age seventy! But has she made the right decision? *Runaway Grandma* is a tender tale about friendships, regrets—and ultimately, hope. Once again, Ann McCauley has penned an insightful, thought provoking glimpse into relationships.

—**Lauren Nichols**, author of seven romance novels

Runaway Grandma

Ann McCauley

Enjoy!

Ann McCauley

Also by Ann McCauley:

Mother Love

Printed in the United States of America

ISBN: 978-0-9798726-0-0

Acknowledgements

WRITING CAN BE A solitary profession, and without my family and friends who help me stay connected to the real world... I don't know where I'd be, let alone this book!

I commend my writing friends: Susan Anderson, Edie Hanes and Barbara Kennedy, for their continued support and critiques.

Special thanks to my dear friend and first reader, Ingrid Fokstuen for your comments and encouragement. To Maureen Johnson for excellent editorial advice and Lynn Graham for invaluable proofreading expertise. And special thanks to the Office of Aging staff and our local police department for their patience as they answered my numerous and often vague questions.

Of course, my constant sources of inspiration are our five children, their mates and our ten grandchildren. And my best friend and husband, Widad, who helps keep my stories on track. I'd be lost without you!

Many thanks to all of you with my continued heartfelt gratitude.

Ann McCauley

CONTENTS

Prologue

Runaway Grandma leaves readers searching their souls for attitudes and biases about the elderly; while pondering life's heavy questions. Such as can anyone truly escape their past and start over? When does strong personal determination cross the line into stubborn pride? Unexpected plot twists and quirky characters keep the pages turning.

Olivia is an atypical character but there may be a tiny spark of her spirit in most grandmothers. After all, who among us has *never* had an urge to run away? This is an escape story that takes you away without leaving the comfort of your own home and then makes you glad you never left it.

It will promote lively thought-provoking reading group discussions. Runaway Grandma is a serious novel that deals with quality of life issues as well as the right to dignity and autonomy in our twilight years.

Dedication

I dedicate RUNAWAY GRANDMA to grandmothers who have *always* been there for their families. Grandmothers who sometimes feel they have just a glint of a notion that they'd maybe like to run off and try their luck somewhere new, somewhere they just might be a tad more appreciated…

So sit back and enjoy the adventure in the comfort of your home. And remember what your grandmother told you, "The grass isn't really any greener on the other side of the fence!"

CHAPTER ONE

The Escape

OLIVIA

AUGUST 2000

I LOADED MY THINGS INTO the trunk of Luella's car as she sat there crying silently. "Are you sure about this, Olivia? We can always just go back home and no one would ever be the wiser."

I slid into the passenger's seat. "Drive the damn car, Luella! I've never been more certain of anything in my life."

Luella sighed deeply; both hands gripped the steering wheel. The steady flow of the Platte River broke the deadly silence as the Buick slowly purred its way down the service road toward the highway. Her voice cracked with emotion. "I don't know what I'm going to do without you, Ollie."

I answered softly. "We've already talked about this and you said you understood; I can't bear to live that life anymore. I just feel there's got to be more out there for me than Andrea and Alex with their constant demands and efforts to control my life. They can fight over what I've left behind; the rest is for me to use as I please."

Suddenly I was crying, and I hated myself for it. "Oh Jesus, God and, sweet Mary, sometimes I get so scared thinking about a life without you. I'm going to miss you so much, my dear. We've been best friends for more than sixty years... but you still have Hank and you managed to raise good kids. I know you'll be all right...I'll be okay too. I *really* will."

I think I was trying to convince myself as much as Luella with my brave words. I'm seventy, sound in mind and body and dammit, nothing and no one is going to stop me from starting a new life.

Our subdued sniffles broke the silence as we drove east on Interstate 80 for the next three hours. We stopped for lunch in Grand Island, Nebraska, and then drove another two hours. By evening we were tired; after all we're not spring chicks anymore. We stopped at a Motel Six, clean beds, a bath and a great price. What more could a couple of old ladies want? On our way back from a quick dinner at Bob Evans, I noticed the car dealerships.

"Look at that, Luella, I think it's time for me to buy a car." I took a deep breath, "I'll see what kind of deal I can get for myself."

I got out of the car when she stopped at a traffic light. "I'll call you at the room when I need a ride."

Luella nodded and smiled regretfully. "Good luck, old girl!"

When the light changed, she drove away.

I knew I wanted a good used ordinary SUV. Something reliable. I expected it would take a chunk of my money. The second sales lot had a dark blue four-year old Chevy Blazer. We agreed on a price. I felt like a bootlegger as the surprised salesman counted the cash. It was the first test of my new identification papers and I was relieved to sail through without a hitch. We agreed that I'd pick up the SUV at eleven the next morning. I called Luella for a ride from a pay phone in the lounge.

Despite our weariness, we talked through the night. As the hour of our final good-byes drew closer, the more we ignored our fatigue.

As I checked out, ambivalent feelings flooded my soul. Luella and I settled for a pancake breakfast. After our second cup of coffee and our second trip to the restroom, it was time to pick up my 'new' SUV. She waited in a nearby parking lot.

Everything went like clock work. I pulled up beside her and she heaved my bags onto the back seat of my new Blazer.

"I just can't believe I'll never see you again. Please be safe and have many healthy years ahead of you, dear Olivia," Luella said, wiping tears from her cheeks. "I'll think of you everyday and I'll pray for you too. Just leaving like this doesn't mean you can escape me; I'll be with you in spirit everyday."

I hugged my best friend. "I'll call you after the dust settles, I really will. You know I'll always love you."

She gently squeezed my shoulder. "Be safe, my friend."

I clasped her hand one last time. "Godspeed."

I pulled onto the highway followed by Luella. We honked loud final goodbyes as I drove onto the eastbound ramp, and Luella entered the westbound ramp of Interstate 80 to return to the only life we've ever known.

I began to wonder if I could really follow through with this decision I'd made, my constantly misting eyes made driving difficult for the first hour but I was determined not to turn back.

I'd packed a few things that won't even be missed when they go through the house. They'll be certain they waited too long to act on their incompetent old mother when they find I withdrew my entire pension. But by then I'll be long gone; I chose freedom with uncertainty over secure entrapment.

A month ago it hit me; I'd outlived my little sister. Poor Eloise. She hadn't even been buried as I watched her quibbling offspring and their greedy spouses bicker about how much was she worth and who would get what. It made me sick with disgust…as well as stop and think.

And I'd tried to help my late husband's dear sister, Evelyn, as much as I could through her last years, but it was excruciatingly painful. Her two sons were determined to get their 'rightful inheritance' while they were still young enough to enjoy it. They set out and succeeded to prove their own mother incompetent, which was overturned by the court a year later. Two months after the competency reversal an untreatable brain malignancy was diagnosed. She died six months later at the Hospice Care Center, her sons nowhere in sight. In the meantime, they'd squandered her life savings and she was left with barely enough to pay for her funeral.

So, I made my annual trip to New York City a few months earlier than usual to attend the theaters. I'd always been fascinated by the foreign ambiance of Forty Seventh St. I managed to become acquainted with Isaac, a nice young diamond dealer who sold me a small bag of diamonds with the proceeds of my pension and investments. And he agreed to buy them back from me as I needed cash. It was my ticket to freedom. Of course, I set aside some starter cash.

I also found a good counterfeiter, thanks to a tip from Isaac, and obtained my two sets of false identities. Damn those kids. No matter what, they've never been satisfied. Their voracity is insatiable. I decided to break free before Alexander's veiled threats about my incompetence became my reality. I need one last adventure and that's just what I'm going to do. Have me an adventure.

My sleepless night caught up with me and by early afternoon I checked in at a cozy bed and breakfast in Auburn, Iowa. Mrs. Tuft, the sixty-something proprietor, didn't ask too many questions and readily accepted cash. I appreciated that.

I took my overnight bag to my room and went for a walk. A brief afternoon shower had created an ambience of refreshing peacefulness. I bought a large-print paperback mystery at a convenience store three blocks from the B & B. Then I stopped at a small corner restaurant and enjoyed a light early dinner. It was a nice place to visit, but I didn't feel an urge to stay more than one night.

The next day I drove east for six hours. I'd studied the atlas and decided to avoid the fast food restaurants that abounded at nearly every exit. I was under no time constraints except when I felt the urgency for a restroom - more often than I liked to admit. I made a list of where I'd like to stop for lunch, B & B and dinners. I trusted my instincts that I'd know what I was looking for when I found it.

That evening I drove to another small town looking for a B &B. The only one I found appeared to be in operation, but no one answered the door. I decided they probably only accepted advance reservations.

So I ended up at a motel, the kind of place my late husband would never have considered hanging his hat. I ate a tasteless sandwich at a small restaurant across the street from the motel. It was overcast and drizzling and not the kind of town or weather that made me feel like going for a walk. I felt secure only after sliding a small cabinet in front of the locked door and propping a chair against the cabinet. I was glad I'd enrolled in the shooting range classes after Melvin died and learned how to handle a revolver. It was in my purse with my money, diamonds, pepper spray, comb, compact, lipstick, and a small bottle of Tylenol. I put on my flannel pajamas and got as comfortable as I could on the lumpy mattress, with my new mystery book and my purse tucked under the blankets beside me.

The next morning I awoke to howling wind and rain pounding on the motel window. I felt surprisingly rested but dreaded driving very far in that weather. I opened my atlas and saw that I was only about two hours from Davenport. I decided to leave immediately and eat breakfast a bit later. I just wanted that town behind me. And soon it was.

The older I get, the more I notice an insidious change in the way people respond to me. It's like I'm becoming an invisible person. Waitresses and clerks only half listen to my requests and become irritated when I inform them, "That's not what I ordered."

More than a few angry young service workers have rolled their eyes and groaned dramatically. "Well, why didn't you tell me that in the first place!?"

I've learned to hold my own by simply stating, "I did. And why didn't you listen?"

By the time I was in my early fifties, I was already a widow, but I still felt vibrant and alive. I was successful in my work and the children were grown and living on their own.

Our family physician retired and the new one was younger than my children. I'm a healthy seventy. My only medications are vitamins and calcium tablets and an occasional Tylenol tablet or two. But I watched my poor sister Eloise suffer. I can't help but wonder if she might still be with us, if she'd have been given the correct diagnosis when she first complained of discomfort, instead of, 'At your age, what can you expect?' After all, Mother and Father lived till they were eighty-seven and eighty-nine.

And car shopping used to be a nightmare for me. I'd actually have to ask for a salesman who then proceeded to treat me like I had only half a brain. Alexander went with me to buy my first car after his father died. He'd been a cocky twenty-two year old, fresh out of college with a business degree and he treated me worse than the salesman. That was the last time I ever shopped with Alexander for anything.

Melvin and I had lived a frugal lifestyle in order to give the children their educations and seed money to get started in life. Nothing was ever enough to make them happy. Andrea still resents her State

University degree and holds a grudge against me for not sacrificing more to send her to an Ivy League university. She works part time in her husband's law office. There have been times I've felt sorry for him as he struggles for success while Andrea flaunts her designer clothes, country club membership and Mercedes.

Andrea had the gall to say. "Mother, why shouldn't you take responsibility for the children's college educations? I mean really, what on earth could you possibly do with all that money in your pension? Your home is paid for, you have no bills and you never do anything, well, except those trips to New York City. What's that all about anyway!? Tiffany and Thomas deserve the best, and since they're your grandchildren…well, it was just a thought I wanted to share with you."

I was furious by the time she left. She dropped that bomb three days before Eloise died. Her children may be my grandchildren, but they have no manners and possess an even greater sense of entitlement than their mother. Andrea and her husband make no effort to save any money. Their lifestyle is way beyond their means. I've bailed them out on two previous occasions. I couldn't help resenting their way of life when they don't try to help themselves. Somewhere in my efforts, I'd crossed the line and instead of being a helper I became an enabler. Enough is enough.

Both my children are totally self-absorbed. They cannot fathom that perhaps I had a life before they were born and may even have a life exclusive of them now. It's simply never occurred to them to ask me about anything, except my money.

Alexander is even more pretentious than Andrea. He earned an MBA from Wharton and feels he's much too clever and important to waste time talking with a retired school teacher even if I am his mother. He's been married and divorced twice. He has one child, Cassie, with his first wife, who moved to California when Cassie was only two. She's seventeen years old now and I've seen her maybe eight times since the divorce. I used to call her when she was small, but it's very hard to carry on a phone conversation with an uninterested child who'd rather be doing almost anything besides talking on the phone. I've sent birthday and Christmas gifts and many letters with self-addressed stamped envelopes and phone cards. Never once has the child contacted me. In the beginning I rationalized she was too small to write if her mother didn't help her. But especially the last five years I've come to accept the fact Cassie is not interested in a relationship with me.

I must take responsibility for the creation of these people who call me Mother. Melvin and I wanted them to excel and we always told them they were special...I guess we went overboard. I know they're not the kind of adults we'd hoped they'd grow up to be.

For the last six months Alex has become fixated on my pension fund and has brought me three separate sets of papers to sign to roll it over to a fund his firm could manage for me. Each time I've told him, "I'll think it over and get back to you."

He didn't even know about my stock portfolio. And he'll never learn about it from me! In the past I'd trusted him with several smaller investments and each time all had been lost. He responded with a snicker. "Good thing you still have that good old Social Security to fall back on, Mother."

I just felt certain if I didn't do something I'd end up in some small apartment living the life of a destitute recluse. I'm healthy and contrary to my children's opinion, I do have my wits about me. So here I am, the new Alice Smith, (and I've got the driver's license, Social Security card and other identity papers to prove it), driving down Interstate 80, looking for my future.

Whatever my future holds it can't be any worse than these last six years have been. And I've made a change I desperately needed; Olivia's gone and I'm Alice Smith...it's going to take some doing to get used to that.

Chapter Two

Where's Mother?

Andrea and Alexander

"MOTHER, FOR GOD'S SAKE, pick up the phone!" Andrea paced impatiently across the kitchen. Glancing at the clock, she left a stern message, "Mother, please call me as soon as possible. I must talk to you. It's really quite urgent."

Andrea's frequent annoyance with her mother surfaced again. "Where could she be? That's the fourth message in two days. Even for Mother, this is unusual."

The phone rang as she was about to leave to pick Tiffany up from dance class and Thomas from chess club.

Alexander's voice was tremulous as he struggled to maintain his composure. "They found her car, Andrea. They found…"

"Whose car did they find, Alex?"

"Mother's."

"Take a deep breath and please explain just what the hell you're talking about."

"The State Police called; they found the Chrysler with her purse and keys lying on the front seat. No sign of any struggle. It was parked on a bluff high above the North Platte River, down state near Bridgeport. They suspect suicide." He cried softly.

"Oh, my God!" Andrea collapsed to the floor sobbing in shock and grief.

"I'm coming over. Call Joel." Alexander gulped a quick shot of whiskey and then drove to his sister's home in a record twenty minutes.

He walked in the back door. "Andrea, where are you?"

He followed the resonance of muted sniveling to the far side of the kitchen island and found Andrea sitting on the floor with the phone beside her.

He sat down beside her and gently touched her cheek. "Did you call Joel?"

She shook her head and whispered. "Not yet."

Alex dialed his brother-in-law's cell phone. "Do you want to talk?"

She nodded and reached for the phone. "Joel, Mother's gone."

She broke down again in a flood of deep painful tears.

Alex took the phone. "I'm here with her, Joel."

"What's happened to Mother Hampton?"

Alex told Joel. "…her purse and keys were on the car seat. No trace of her and no sign of any struggle, they suspect *suicide*. Her driver's license and seventy-seven dollars were still in her purse."

Slowly Joel managed to respond in a subdued voice. "I'd never have thought Mother Hampton was the suicide type. You'll stay with Andrea till I get home?"

"Of course, Joel, is there anyone I can call for the children to stay with for the night? I don't think Andrea is up to caring for them."

"I'll make a couple calls while I'm driving home."

Alex stood up and reached for his sister's hands. "Come on, Andrea. Do you want something to drink? We've got to talk. Have you noticed any changes in Mother's behavior?"

She reluctantly stood. "Nothing unusual. I think Aunt Eloise's death coming so soon after Aunt Evelyn's may have been harder on her than we realized, but then she still took that trip to New York City. I thought that was kind of strange, so soon after the funeral. But Mother never was one to ask my approval of her actions. She's always been such a private person."

Alex fixed them each a cup of hot tea with a touch of vodka. "Drink this, Andrea; it'll help you get through. Trust me."

They sat together at the kitchen table. "I can't think of anything out of the ordinary either. I'm calling Luella; maybe she can shed some light on this mess."

Luella answered on the third ring. She didn't want to appear too eager so she never answered on less than three rings. It was all a matter of class. And everyone knew Luella had class. "Hello."

"Hello, Luella. This is Alex Hampton. Please sit down, I have bad news... Mother's missing; the State Police found her car abandoned down state and they say it looks like a suicide.

"Have you noticed any odd attitudes or behavior the last few weeks?"

Luella gasped as if in shock. "Absolutely not! I can't believe Olivia would do such a thing. She even managed to get through the tragic but unnecessary passing of poor Eloise and so soon after Evelyn. She told me she'd had a good trip to New York City. She's always loved the theater."

"When did you talk to her last? What did she say?"

Luella managed a tearful answer and crossed her fingers as she lied. "We talked nearly every day. But I was away at a church retreat and haven't talked to her for nearly three days; I...I just can't believe this."

"If you can think of anything, Luella, please call me. I'm truly sorry to call you out of the blue and dump this on you." Alex managed to stay official and dignified. He did not want people to know he could be emotional.

Luella wept as she quietly replied in a choked tight voice. "Alex, if I can do anything for you or Andrea, please call. Your Mother was my oldest and dearest friend. This is such a shock, so...so unbelievable."

"Thanks, Luella, we'll be in touch." He hung up the phone as tears trickled down his cheeks again.

"What did she say? Can she make any sense out of this?"

Alex answered. "She said she just can't believe it, she'd been away at a church retreat, and hasn't talked to Mother for three days."

Andrea spoke softly, "Do you think Mother suddenly became a depressed psychotic and committed suicide without any warning signs? I've read about these things happening, but without a word to us? This is totally... surreal."

"Somehow I can't picture our mother as depressed or psychotic. But she definitely seems to be gone and there are no signs of foul play.

Let's go over to the house and see if things look normal there."

"Okay. But not till Joel gets home. When was the last time you talked to her, Alex?"

"I've been trying to remember; it's not easy in my position to keep up with all the small talk that made up Mother's world. I know I talked to her after Aunt Eloise's funeral; she was making plans for her annual trip to New York City and choosing the shows she'd see. I hate to admit it but I was impatient and I told her. "Have fun if you can so soon after your sister's funeral. After all I really don't care what shows you see. I'm a very busy man."

"Oh, Alex. You must feel terrible about talking to her like that. I'm sorry."

"Don't feel sorry for me. I spoke the truth. Still, if I'd have known it'd be my last conversation with her, I might have been a bit easier on her.

"So, Andrea, when did you last talk to Mother?"

"I've been trying to remember. I talked to her every two or three days, but only short, superficial conversations. 'Hello Mother, how are you today? Any plans?' She'd ask about the children, Joel and me. Then sometimes she'd ask me to go out to lunch with her." She sighed sadly. "Can you imagine with all my commitments, having time to go to lunch with Mother!? I always had to give her my regrets. She kept me at such a distance. I just never felt I could make it into her inner circle. There were times I felt like an intruder with my own mother."

"Andrea, in hindsight do you wish you'd have taken time to go out to lunch with her occasionally?"

"For heavens sake, Alex, be real. You know what it's been like since she retired. I thought she'd be a more interested grandmother, but no. All she did was criticize Tiffany and Thomas. It's not like she doesn't know children after all those years of teaching. But she always seemed to care more for strangers than she did her own children and grandchildren."

Andrea bit her lower lip as if trying to stop the flow of negativity that was beginning to erupt from deep within her soul.

"I know; I tried to help her manage her pension funds and she just kept brushing me off. It was like she had no confidence in me, her own son."

Andrea gave her brother a piercing stare. "Well, I guess you're entitled to managing half her pension fund now. I wonder how much there is?"

"When we go over to her house, I'll look through her papers and see if I can find some information. It takes awhile to settle estates, you know."

"I'm aware of that. But I want to see whatever you find with my own eyes."

Suddenly there was an unwelcome, almost hostile feeling between them. Then as if fate determined they'd be allies, they heard a car in the driveway.

Andrea glanced out the window. "Thank God, Joel's home."

Joel rushed into the kitchen and affectionately embraced his wife, before giving his brother-in-law an empathetic hug. "Andie, Baby, I'm so sorry. Alex, what can I say? This is tragic. Your mother was one great lady, a real class act. We're all going to miss her."

Andrea asked about the children.

Joel answered. "Tiffany went home with her dance teacher for the night. Thomas is staying with the Kemmer family. They'll be okay. They don't know about their grandmother yet. Both families agreed to let us break the news to them tomorrow."

They told Joel all they knew about their missing mother. They agreed to go check out Olivia's home for clues and then stop for a quick bite to eat.

Half an hour later they entered their mother's home. There was an eerie silence about the house. The kitchen was tidy as usual and there was nothing out of the ordinary about the living room, dining room, laundry or sewing room. The family room was so clean it looked like she'd been expecting company. Maybe she was. It was odd not to see a stack of books by her chair.

Upstairs the two guest rooms were spotless, but the master bedroom was a surprise. Drawers were half open on both dressers. The bed was unmade and the adjoining bathroom had two towels lying on the floor and again drawers were half opened.

Andrea spoke softly with a sincere sadness in her voice. "I've never in my whole life seen Mother's bedroom or bathroom look like this.

Something is really wrong. She never allowed us out of the house without putting the lid on the toothpaste. And since when did she change to Colgate. She *always* insisted 'Crest is best'." The lid was nowhere in sight.

Alex, annoyed with his sister, bristled. "Well, of course something's wrong. That's why we're here. Remember the car, the police report? Something a whole lot more important than Mother's brand of toothpaste is wrong!"

Joel walked between them and put an arm on each of their shoulders. "Come on, you two, you're both under a hell of a lot of stress. Let's go take a look at her study."

Together the three of them walked down the hall to the small room that long ago had been a nursery for both Andrea and Alex. But it had been a study for more than thirty years now. They'd all been impressed when Olivia became proficient on the computer after she retired.

"I don't think I ever told Mother how proud I was of her computer skills." Alex wiped his eyes on his sleeve and said in an unusually soft voice. He felt like he was on an emotional roller coaster. "I wish I had."

"Look at this." Andrea picked up the envelopes and gave her brother the one with his name on it; feeling a bit unsteady, she sat down and slowly opened her envelope. Alex dropped beside her on the small sofa and opened his.

My Dearest Andrea,
I know this is going to be hard for you. Please believe me… I felt I had no choice but to end things this way. I've always loved you.
Mother

Alex received the same vague letter. His voice trembled. "I just don't get it. Why didn't we see some warning signs?"

"Maybe they were there and we were too busy to notice them." Andrea cried quietly.

Joel sat at Olivia's desk and shook his head. "I've known your Mother for eighteen years and she *never* seemed like the suicidal type. There's something strange about all this. I can't put my finger on it, but something just doesn't add up."

Alex stared at his brother in law. "What are you saying? That she didn't commit suicide? Then why this note, the car, purse...and where is she?"

"Where is she? That's the question we need answered. No doubt about it." Joel answered.

Andrea glared at her husband. "What do you mean, where? The police told us she jumped into the river. My God. Where?" She continued to shout. "Have you no compassion!"

Joel answered in his calming condescending attorney voice that always made Andrea furious. "Andrea, they cannot declare a death without a body. Not without going to court and that takes time. Where your mother is, is indeed very important."

Alex listened intently. "My God. Do you think she might still be alive and..."

"Well, the coroner cannot sign a death certificate until they have a body. That's just a simple fact of law. Look, I'm really sorry about all this." Joel wearily turned his back to them with his elbows on the desk, put his face in his hands and rubbed his forehead. It had been an exceptionally hard day even before Alex called.

A few long silent minutes later he noticed a large brown envelope carefully placed under a four-day-old newspaper. He moved the newspaper. "You two better look at this..."

Alex hurried to the desk, and read in his Mother's careful script. "To be opened by Alexander and Alicia in the event of my death."

And it was dated four days ago.

Joel muttered. "This just keeps getting weirder."

Andrea sat solemnly on the sofa. "Open it, Alex."

He pulled out the title to his Mother's two-year-old Chrysler and a bound legal document. "She deeded the house to us, Andrea. She did it a month ago. And the car title is in both our names, too."

Andrea's tension escalated. "I don't understand why she didn't tell us about the deed and title. If she needed to talk, I would've listened."

Joel said, "It looks like she didn't want you to pay inheritance taxes. Obviously she didn't expect to need her car or house anymore."

"Is there anything else on the desk we need to look at?" Andrea asked.

The two men carefully looked over the other envelopes and Joel answered, "Looks like you've got the two most important things for today."

Alex opened the top desk drawer and removed the key for the locked files. "I might as well check her investment status since we're here anyway."

Joel sighed, sat down beside his wife and tenderly put his arm around her shoulders. He thought how small and vulnerable Andrea felt.

He'd have been shocked if he could've known the anguished fury that was slowly awakening inside her.

Alex pulled out the Investment File; he opened it with a flutter of anticipation. After all, his mother had a forty-two year teacher's pension as well as a thrifty lifestyle and their father's pension. "Well, I'll be damned! It's all gone. All accounts were closed out a month ago. A small note from their mother was attached to the top page…

Andrea & Alexander,
I'm sorry, but I felt this was my only way out.
I knew you'd *never* understand.
Mother

Andrea sobbed as she shouted. "Her only way out? What did she do with the money? It can't be gone! What in God's name is she talking about!?"

Alex sat there as if in a daze staring at the closed out accounts. "I'll call Richard at the bank tomorrow morning to see if he can shed any light on these closed accounts. Something is very peculiar about all this."

Andrea, Joel and Alex solemnly left Olivia's house, each lost in their thoughts, trying to make some sense of the events of the day. Though, no one had an appetite, they still stopped by The Scotts Club for a late dinner.

CHAPTER THREE

Starting Over

OLIVIA

FOUR WEEKS LATER AND I was still traveling, visiting one small town after another. Still searching, I knew I'd know the right place when I got there. I didn't know how, but I'd know. I sold the Chevy Blazer three weeks ago for far less than I paid for it. I purchased a smaller and even more discreet SUV. I pulled out another set of identity papers for that purchase; and became Dorothy Myers.

As I drove down the highway I kept repeating, "I mustn't forget; my name is Dorothy Myers. Dorothy Myers. Dorothy Myers…"

Ten days later, I drove into a lovely small town in western Pennsylvania, far from the beaten path of Interstate 80. The late afternoon sun hit the hills that surrounded the town like an artist's palette of reds, oranges, yellows and browns. It was the most glorious array of nature's colors I'd ever seen. It was almost like a huge welcoming banner just for me. It seemed like a possible sign…

I stopped in front of the silver facade of the Route 66 Diner. I ordered the special and pulled out a book to pretend to read as I listened to the easy banter of the obvious regulars. The other diners all seemed to share the same dinner conversation even though they sat at different tables and booths around the small restaurant. I was impressed with their strong sense of community. I soon realized I was sitting in the midst of a Republican stronghold, but decided to give the place a chance anyway. Besides, my dinner was delicious.

An hour and a half after arriving in Harmonyville, I checked into a lovely bed & breakfast. The owners were retired from military life and had decorated their home with treasures they'd collected from their world travels. They were warm and gracious hosts and the most personable folks I'd encountered during my weeks of solo traveling. I felt like I was visiting the home of old friends, so I checked in for three days, the longest I'd stayed anywhere since I started my journey. I felt safe and secure as I drifted off to sleep in the comfort of the four-poster bed in the picture perfect guest room of the Hewitt's Bed and Breakfast with my purse close beside me under the comforter.

After a late and leisurely breakfast, I went for a walk down Main Street. It was a brisk, sunny, autumn morning. I felt alive and strangely at home.

There were so many gorgeous old Victorian mansions lining both sides of the street that I lost count and couldn't decide which one was the most beautiful. An hour later I stopped by the Route 66 Diner again for a cup of late morning tea. It was almost deserted except for three older men at the table in the corner. This became my routine for my first two days in town.

The third day as I was enjoying the feisty editorial page of the Harmonyville Daily News, I was startled to hear a pleasant male voice say, "Mornin' Mam, would ya like some company? Mighty hard to make any new friends when ya always hidin' behind somebody else's words like ya been doin' every time ya come in here."

I slowly looked up at him. He was a large elderly man with thinning white hair and his light blue eyes had a lively spark that made him easy to look at. "Excuse me, but what makes you think I want to make friends?"

He folded his arms and squinted impishly as he scratched his chin. "Well, it seems to me a nice lookin' lady shouldn't have to be eatin' by herself even if ya are new to town."

"I'm just passing through and making new friends is not on my itinerary. Now if you'll excuse me." I tried to go back to reading the local newspaper. But the big man did not budge.

The waitress came over. "Is everything okay here, Mam?"

"Oh yes, of course. I think this gentleman is going to join me for a cup of coffee. Could you freshen my tea and bring him coffee?" I smiled and winked at the waitress.

"Now that's mighty friendly of ya. I'm Ray Clinger, pleased to meet ya." And he sat right down at my table.

I used my most official sounding voice. "I'm Dorothy Myers, nice to meet you, Mr. Clinger. Which section of the morning paper would you like?"

"Everybody jes calls me Ray. Nice o' ya to invite me for a cup o' coffee. I already read today's paper. Where ya headin', Dorothy Myers? An where ya from?"

I couldn't resist teasing him. "Well, I didn't have much choice but to ask you to sit down since I was trying to read the paper and you were blocking my light; I'm from out west and decided to move east to finish my retirement."

"Out west covers a lot o' territory, an' where in the east are ya headin'?"

"Where I'm from in the west doesn't matter. I left the past behind. And I haven't decided where I'll put down roots for the rest of my days."

He gave me a skeptical look. "Well, looks sure can be deceivin'. You must be one feisty dame to make a move like that. I don't think I ever met anyone in our age bracket who'd jes' up n' move on. Did ya hate your old life that much?"

I stared at him and with an intentionally icy edge to my voice, I answered. "Mr. Clinger, when I left my old life I closed the door and threw away the key. It's over and I'd rather not talk about it."

Ray looked like his feelings were a bit wounded. "Sorry. So, where do ya go from here?"

"Why back to the Bed & Breakfast, of course. I like the Hewitts very much. I've been here three days and I think I'll stay a few more. This is such a beautiful little town. I've been traveling for weeks and your village seems to be just the break I needed."

"Ya picked a good place to rest awhile. May I...huh, may I invite ya to dinner tonight here at the diner at six p.m? I'd be honored, Miss Dorothy."

I was totally surprised. I hesitated, then finally answered, "Well, I...I don't know."

"So why not? Jes dinner, nothin' more. I'm a lonely ol' man an' I like talking to ya."

I smiled and thought, why not? "All right, Ray, I'll meet you here at six."

The Hewitt's were delighted that I decided to stay a few more days and invited me for a cup of tea in their private kitchen area. And then I told them about meeting Ray Clinger.

Mary Hewitt smiled and shook her head slowly, "Well, well, that's a surprise. Ray's a good person, but he's been a lost soul since Sophie died about four years ago. Lots of the local widows had their sights set on him, but he made it clear he wasn't interested. All he's done is rehash his life with his Sophie. They were married for more than fifty years. Something about you must've somehow pulled him out of his shell. And that's needed to be done."

After lunch I went exploring again in the outlying areas around the town. The crisp autumn colors gave the hillside an enchanted glow. The obvious pride the local country folks had in their homes impressed me well beyond any of the other communities I'd visited during my last few weeks of traveling. I began to seriously ponder, "Could this be the place I've been looking for?"

Ray was sitting on a bench in front of the diner waiting. When he saw me walking towards him, he gallantly stood up and bowed slightly. "Good evenin', Miss Dorothy, nice to see ya agin. I hope yur hungry, 'cause there's been mighty grand aromas comin' outa there." He nodded toward the diner. "Sure did get my appetite worked right up."

I was starting to feel like an excited school girl... "It's nice to see you too, Mr. Clinger. And yes I believe I am hungry. It's seems like ages since I ate lunch."

"Now jes wait a minute here, I told ya to call me Ray. No more o' this Mr. Clinger."

I couldn't help smiling. "Okay, okay, Ray it is. Now could we eat, please?"

We found an empty booth and the waitress hurried over to clean the table and claim her tip. "How you two doin' tonight? Specials are on the board, except'n we already sold outa barbecue ribs. Still got some chicken n' biscuits. What you'in's fancyin' tonite?"

Ray said, "Now, slow down there, Darlene. We ain't goin to no fire.

Jes' bring two glasses o' water and give us a minute to decide."

Darlene stopped, took a deep breath and sighed as she smiled at Ray. "Okay, Uncle Ray, two glasses o' water comin' right up."

"Your niece is a lovely girl though she seems a bit frazzled."

"Ah, Darlene's not my kin, lot o' the young'ins in town call me Uncle Ray. I don't rightly recall when or why it started, but I ain't got no problem with it. Darlene oughta look done in. She's raisin two little babies, her man run off with a barmaid from that tavern out on the edge o' town and now Darlene's goin' to school by day to learn nursin'. Her Mama and Daddy help her take care o' the twins an' she works part-time for gas n' diaper money. She's a damn nice girl, smart too. She'll be okay."

He looked up and smiled, "Well, speak o' the devil, here she is."

"Hey, Uncle Ray you gotta give a girl a little respect! Have you'in's decided yet?"

Ray said, "Darlene I'll be havin' a large helpin' o' the chicken n' biscuits. Miss Dorothy, I can highly recommend it."

"I'll have the same. Also, a cup of tea."

"Make that two teas." Ray added.

I smiled and sighed. "After traveling alone for several weeks, it is rather a pleasant change to have someone to share dinner with. Have you lived here all your life?"

"Yes Mam, I'm proud to say I have. Just like my Dad and his dad did before him. My Granddaddy came across from Germany to make a better life for himself an' that's jes what he did. All my people loved this area...except my own boy. He's another story. Doesn't have a lick o' sense. Jes keeps movin' around like a rollin' stone. He damn near broke his dear Mother's heart." His eyes began to get watery.

"I'm sorry, Ray, I didn't mean to upset you. Sometimes it's very hard for parents to accept their adult children's life choices."

Ray gave me a curious look. "Not your fault, I gotta learn to let go o' him."

I spoke softly. "I've heard that sometimes the only way to hold on to someone is to let go."

Ray stared at her hard. "Sounds like yur words of wisdom might jes be comin' from experience."

"Yes and no. I was a teacher for forty-five years and I've seen all kinds of family dynamics. Trust me on that."

"So what's a nice retired school teacher doin' travelin' all over the country by herself?"

"I already answered that question this morning and I told you the subject was closed to further discussion. It was a beautiful day. I went out exploring and the hillsides were glorious in the splendor of their colors. I've never seen a lovelier place in my whole life."

"I think I'm eatin' dinner with one stubborn lady. But ya got good taste to say somethin' like that about my hometown. I gotta give ya credit for that."

I couldn't help smiling again. "Well, thank you, I do appreciate your generosity, Ray."

"Miss Dorothy, do you know what I like about yur face?"

I blushed and stared at my teacup. "I have no idea what you're about to say. But I must admit I am curious. Do tell."

"My Granny always said the eyes are the window to the soul. An' the lines on an agin' face is a history of the life led by the person on the other side o' the face."

I grinned, "I think I'd have liked your Grandmother. She sounds like a wise woman. So what does my face tell you about me?"

Ray pretended to examine my face as if looking into a crystal ball. "Ah yeah, my Granny was a wise one, all right. Let's see...I like the fact ya have laugh lines instead o' frown lines. An' ya don't seem to give a damn if ya look your age... which I'd guess is about sixty-eight."

"Well, thank you again, sir, I think!" I was relieved when Darlene interrupted us with our dinners. It'd been more than fifteen years since I'd had dinner with a man and never before, alone, with a stranger.

"This is the best chicken and biscuits I've had in years. You've got a real gold mine with this little diner. Everything I've eaten here has been extremely good."

"Yep, that's why we all keep comin' back for more. Good food an' good prices. And tonight, good company, too."

I felt myself blushing which embarrassed me all the more. I answered softly. "You do flatter me, Ray. But I'll have to agree with you on all three counts."

We took our time with dinner and even stayed for a scrumptious dessert of homemade banana cream pie.

"Good thing I don't eat like this everyday or I'd have to join a health club just to stay in the same size clothing. This pie is sinfully good."

While trying to conceal it from each other, we each left Darlene a ten dollar tip. Ray scowled as he ask, "Miss Dorothy, why would ya go and leave a big tip like that for?"

I raised my eyebrows, smiled and answered in my best school teacher voice. "Perhaps for the same reason you did, 'Uncle Ray'."

Dusk was already starting to set in when we left the diner two hours after we'd started our dinners. I'd truly enjoyed the evening.

"Would ya like a ride back, Miss Dorothy?"

"Goodness, no, but thanks for the offer. After all that food, I really need to walk and it's such a beautiful evening. I can see quite well from the street lights. Thank you for my dinner. It was kind of you, I've enjoyed the evening very much."

"Well, then the least I can do is walk a lady home." He gallantly extended his arm with the charm of a true gentleman.

For the second time within the last hour I felt my face blush and I was glad we were outside with little light. I timidly placed my hand on his arm and was surprised to feel the strength of his muscles through his long sleeved plaid shirt.

When we reached Hewitt's' B& B, I said, "I don't know when I've enjoyed an evening quite so much, Ray. Thank you and good night." I turned and started to walk up the stairs toward the front door.

"Miss Dorothy, jes wait a darn minute...ah, I really enjoyed the evening, too. I jes wanna thank ya. It was awful nice talkin' with ya. Haven't really talked with a lady since my Sophie passed on near four years ago. Well, that's all I got to say, maybe I'll see ya around town. Good night now."

I smiled. "Good night."

Ray turned to walk back down the street to his pick up truck and he couldn't stop grinning. He was glad it was too dark for anyone to see him out and about, makin' a darn fool outa himself.

The next morning I wore a navy pullover and khaki slacks with my black walking shoes. Mary Hewitt met me in the foyer and insisted I join her in the kitchen for breakfast. "Good morning, Dorothy. I want you to meet our grandson Joey. He's visiting us for a few days before he leaves for Army basic training. Besides you were our only guest last night."

"Well, I wouldn't want to interfere with your visit with your grandson."

"Nonsense. Joey, this is Dorothy Myers. We only met her a few days ago and already she feels like an old friend."

A tall, handsome, young man walked over and extended his hand. "Glad to meet you, Ms. Myers."

"Likewise, I'm sure." His tough hands indicated he wasn't a stranger to work and his grip was strong. I admired the relationship Mary obviously shared with this striking young man.

"Well, let's eat. Breakfast is almost ready. Ahh, there goes the oven timer. Joey would you please find your Granddad and tell him breakfast is ready."

I followed her to the kitchen. "Something certainly smells delicious; I really appreciate being included in your family breakfast."

Mary turned and put her arm around my shoulders. "You know, moving around as much as we did, I got used to making friends quickly. John and I were talking and we're going to give you every other night free for as long as you want to stay with us."

I rarely found myself speechless but this was one of those times. John and Joey walked in through the back door.

John said, "Breakfast sure smells good."

He pulled out a chair for me. "Please have a seat and join us. Mary tells me you've decided to stay awhile longer. Good decision. If we're lucky, you'll make Harmonyville your new hometown. We think it's the best place in the world to put down roots, right, Mary?"

She smiled at her husband, the kind of smile that only true intimates can share, and nodded. "Absolutely."

I managed to answer. "I don't know what to say, I'm most flattered, but..."

Joey laughed easily and said, "Let's start with pass the biscuits, please."

I relaxed and enjoyed a delicious breakfast with my new friends. "So Joey, do you think you may make the Army a career like your grandfather?"

He shrugged. "Too soon to tell, but I could do far worse than follow in Granddad's footsteps. I know that I want to eventually be a crime scene investigator; after boot camp I'll be going to Military Police training in Missouri. Who knows?"

After my second cup of coffee, I excused myself and thanked them again for their kind hospitality. The baked omelet and fresh cinnamon rolls were an excellent start for the day.

Later in the morning I went for a long walk, and contemplated if maybe this was just the place I've been looking for. I continued my walk around the small picturesque lake in the center of town.

I bought the Harmonyville Daily and sat down on a street bench to check what apartments might be available here. It was another glorious sunny autumn day. I sighed and marveled at the peace I felt with my new found freedom. Liberation felt wonderful.

I ended up back at the diner about one, having missed the lunch crowd. Before my food was even served, Ray walked through the front door. He was obviously surprised to see me there since he blushed from his neck to the top of his balding head. "Well, I'll be, ahh, Good Day to ya, Miss Dorothy."

"And Good Day to you, Ray. How are you? Would you like to join me for lunch? I just ordered."

He stood there considering the offer for a few seconds and then pulled out a chair across the table from me. "Thank you. I think that's jes too good an offer for an old codger like me to pass up."

"I went walking around the lake and all around town today. It's so lovely here. You've been fortunate to have lived your life in such a place."

The waitress served my lunch and took Ray's order. I sipped my ice tea and Ray nursed his coffee. He appeared to be deep in thought.

"Well, thank ya. I never could find a reason to leave. Sophie an' me started spoonin' when we were sixteen years old an' married when we were jes nineteen. I was lucky to have found a good woman on my first try. We had fifty-three good years together. Ya woulda liked my Sophie, she was a real sweetheart. My God, I still miss her. 'Specially in the evenings, it gets darn awful lonesome without her."

"It sounds like Sophie and you were both very lucky to have had so many good years together." I hesitated, unsure of how much I should say about my real past. "I know what you mean about loneliness. The evenings are always the worst. My husband died eighteen years ago. I kept myself busy and tried to adjust to being alone; but there's always that emptiness."

"So, Miss Dorothy, why didn't a nice lookin' woman like ya ever marry again? Ya must o' had lots o' offers."

I couldn't help smiling. "I've not turned down any worthwhile offers. You know, Ray, last night was the first time in fifteen years I've had dinner alone with a man, and I enjoyed it."

"Well, I'll be darned. There must be a hell o' alotta fools in this world. Miss Dorothy, did ya know the whole room lights up when ya smile. I'd be honored to have the pleasure of yur company for dinner agin' tonight."

I felt myself blushing again. And without thinking I bit my lip, contemplating if I should have dinner with a man two nights in a row and then slowly answered. "I think...I'd like that very much, Ray."

We chatted amicably throughout the rest of our lunch. I felt so at ease with this big man with the patch of white hair and the warm blue eyes. We agreed to meet in front of the diner at six again that evening.

I spoke briefly with Mary before going up to my room to read and rest. I decided to wear a skirt and jacket that night. The Hewitt's nodded approvingly at my spruced up look, as questions danced in their eyes.

I smiled and said, "Okay, okay, I'm having dinner at the diner with Ray again tonight."

"Have a good time, Dorothy. And don't do anything we wouldn't do!"

Joey sat on the front porch reading a novel. "Hey, Ms. Myers, good to see you again. How was your day?"

"Good. A little confusing. How was yours?" I looked at my watch and realized I was ready fifteen minutes early. "Mind if I sit with you? I'm meeting someone for dinner and I seem to have a few extra minutes. I don't want to appear too anxious."

"Sure, have a seat. I always have a great time when I visit my grandparents. I'll miss my family when I go to the Army. So...what was so confusing about your day?"

I looked at this nineteen-year-old boy/man. I have to admit I was impressed by his candor and concern. "Oh, nothing serious, just me being a silly old woman."

He looked at me intently. "I don't think *you* could be a silly old woman if you tried. So what's up? Are you uncomfortable having a male friend?"

"Excuse me!" I stood up and started to walk away.

"Ms. Myers, I'm sorry. I didn't mean to offend you. Gram and Granddad told me about you and Uncle Ray. He's a good man, real salt of the earth. I've known him since I was twelve." He closed his book and gazed at me intently. "Neither one of you should have to spend the rest of your lives alone if you don't want to and it's okay if you like to spend time together. Really it is."

I sat back down beside the young philosopher soon to be soldier. "No offense taken. How did a kid like you come to be so smart anyway?"

He gave me a wicked grin. "Oh, you know, by hanging out with my grandparents and Uncle Ray."

After chatting awhile longer, I looked at my watch. I stood to leave and bid young Joey good by. Then I turned went back and kissed his cheek. "Thank you, young man. I actually do feel a bit less confused now, thanks to your words of wisdom."

"Have a nice evening, Ms. Myers, you both deserve it." A smiling Joey went back to his reading.

As I expected, Ray was sitting on the bench in front of the diner. When he saw me he stood up and bowed dramatically. "Well, looky at ya. If yur not a sight for sore eyes, nothin' is!"

"It's nice to see you too, Ray." He impressed me as an authentic gentle man.

We walked into the diner together and several heads looked our way and then quickly turned and continued hushed conversations. There was no community discussion that night. We sat at a corner booth. A few minutes later Darlene brought us each a glass of water and stood there waiting with a big grin.

"Well, what the hell, girl, yur standin' around grinnin' like a cat that swallowed the canary. Where're the menus anyway?"

"No menus for you, Uncle Ray, till you introduce me to your

friend." She turned to me and extended her hand. "Hi, I'm Darlene. I've seen you in here before. Thanks for that tip last night. It was right kind o' both o' ya. Just give me a wave when you're ready to order."

I shook her hand. "It's good to meet you, Darlene. I'm Dorothy Myers. I hear you have lovely one-year-old twins. I'd love to meet them sometime."

She smiled. "Yea, sure, that'd be fun. I think they're pretty special. Nice to meet you too, Ms. Myers. Word sure does get around in a small town, doesn't it?"

Before walking away she smiled at Ray. "Since when do you need a menu? The specials are on the board. And so far tonight we're not outa' anything."

I gave Ray a puzzled look and asked, "What was that all about?"

He shrugged. "Everybody's talking about ol' Ray hookin' up with a strange new woman who come into town."

I played innocent. "Why Ray, I'm shocked at you, and here I was starting to feel pretty special!"

Ray blushed again. "Darn it, woman, ya are special to me and ya know it. I ain't looked at another woman since my Sophie passed on. And not since I was sixteen 'afore that. These people jes' better get used to lettin' people live their own lives around here. An' that's all I got to say about that."

He motioned for Darlene; we both ordered the roast beef special and ate in a comfortable silence. During after-dinner tea I said, "This may shock you, Ray, but I like your town so much and I've met such wonderful people here that I think this just might be where I'm supposed to be. What do you think?"

Ray looked absolutely stunned and stared into his tea cup. I didn't have a clue of what he might have been thinking.

Then he looked at me through misty eyes and quietly answered. "I was hopin' ya would, but I didn' know how to bring it up with ya bein' so secretive about yur past an' all. That's 'bout the best news I've heard in the last four years."

"I'm so relieved, Ray. This is all new territory for me geographically as well as personally. I really enjoy spending time with you. And just because I don't want to talk about my past doesn't necessarily make me secretive. I simply prefer to live in the present. And I'm happy to have you as my friend. What else can I say?"

Darlene freshened our after-dinner teas and offered us dessert. We both declined. Ray insisted on paying for my dinner again and we both left a tip. It was starting to drizzle when we left the diner.

Ray said, "I think ya best let me drive you back to the Hewitt's tonight. We got some more talkin' to do an' this ain't no kinda' weather for walkin' an' talkin'."

I couldn't argue with that, so he guided me across the street to his pick-up and opened the passenger door for me. I was impressed with the tidy interior; I never could stand messy personal spaces.

"Nice truck. Oh, I almost forgot to tell you, Joey Hewitt said to tell you hello. He's visiting his grandparents for a few days before he goes to Army basic training. He's a nice boy and seems to know exactly what he wants out of life."

"Yep, Joey's a good kid, a chip off the old Hewitt block. They never believed in coddlin' their kids or grandkids, an' the results sure look like they knew what the hell they were doin'. Please tell Joey to come around an' see me before he goes off to the Army. Glad you like my ol' truck. She's been a dependable piece o' transportation. An' I like that."

I felt a chill and shivered. "It's surprising how quickly the weather has cooled off with the rain. What else did you want to talk about Ray?"

"The weather's like that in this part o' the country. Well, I was jes' wanderin' if ya'd wanna' come by my place tomorrow an' maybe I could fix us a bite o' lunch. I'd like to show ya my home."

I answered without really thinking, "That sounds delightful, I'd like that, Ray. But I'll need directions."

"I'll drive ya' out by there right now. If you're not sure tomorrow, jes ask one o' the Hewitt's."

He cautiously pulled the truck out of the parking space. I could tell driving at night in the rain was not easy for him. "I'll never remember anything from the drive tonight. Why don't you just drop me at the bed & breakfast? I'll get directions from Mary and Bob in the morning. It'll be easier for me to find your place during the day."

It was raining quite hard by then and he seemed relieved. He parked in front of the Hewitt's. I reached over and covered his hand with mine and gently squeezed it. "Thanks, Ray. I enjoyed the evening with you and I look forward to seeing you tomorrow. Can I bring anything for lunch?"

He lifted my hand to his lips, and softly kissed the back of my hand. No one had ever kissed my hand before! Chills raced through me. "Jes ya bring yurself around about one o'clock. Good night, Miss Dorothy."

I didn't even notice the rain as I floated, I mean walked, up the steps to the bed & breakfast. I couldn't stop smiling as I wondered if I wasn't far too old for such feelings and goings on.

Then I decided I should pack my bag and get out of town, fast. But I heard a small voice in the back of my mind, the one that kept that smile on my face say, "No way, you stay, girl!"

So of course, I stayed. And I slept like a contented baby all night long.

The next morning Mary had a wicked grin on her face as she gave me directions to Ray's home.

I told her, "It's just a lunch, for heavens sake."

Mary called after me as I was leaving. "Well, you two have fun and enjoy your just lunch'."

I found Ray's place without difficulty. It was a windy, rainy day and most of the leaves had fallen from the trees. The ground was freshly covered with a luster of wet color and the barren trees were stark and grey - such a contrast to just a few days ago.

Ray's home was a Cape Cod style log bungalow with dormer windows on the second floor; it was set in a clearing in a wooded area. He kept a tidy home.

He hung my wet coat. A fire crackled in the fireplace which was the focal point of the large but cozy room. It appeared to be a living/ dining room combination. Lunch was a real treat, flavorful potato chowder with crackers and salad as well as Boston cream pie for dessert.

"Ray, this is delicious. I'm so impressed. You're a wonderful cook."

"I'm pleased ya liked it. I always enjoyed helpin' Sophie in the kitchen, but it ain't much fun to cook for one. So I mostly eat at the diner these days. Lucky for me I do, else I probably wouldn't o' met ya'."

"I'm happy I met you too, Ray. Your home is lovely. Nice n' cozy, just the right size."

"Glad ya' like my place, I like it too. I gotta' tell ya somethin'. That Boston cream pie, I bought that at the bakery this mornin'. I did make the chowder and salad though. Jes' didn't want to be deceivin' ya'. How about an after-lunch tea?"

"That sounds perfect. And don't worry about the dessert. I didn't realize there was any other way to come by Boston cream pie except buying it at the bakery. So what do you do on rainy cold afternoons?"

"I never liked watchin' television much. Sometimes I'll take in a good movie when they play the old ones. Ya know, back when they knew how to make good picture shows. I play chess an' checkers. An' I like to play a little poker from time to time. Do ya know how to play Pinochle? I have to admit I'm a pretty darn good card player."

"So put your cards on the table, Ray. Let's see just how good you are."

The afternoon passed quickly. I gave him a run for his money, but he did win two more games than me. Cards can become almost addictive when two highly competitive Pinochle players go at it in a cozy cottage on a rainy afternoon. I laughed as Ray gloated over his victories.

I told him, "Just wait till next time, I'll show you who the real card player is!"

"Lordy, do ya realize it's already six thirty? We're late for dinner. Wanna' go eat at the diner?"

I hesitated a few moments and then asked, "Well, isn't there enough chowder to warm up? I could make us each a small salad and we could top it off with the delicious Boston cream pie. I hate to go out in the rain twice if not necessary."

So we ate leftovers together. I felt comfortable with Ray and I think he did with me too. We watched the evening news after dinner and then he turned off the television. "Can't see any sense in watchin' the television when I got me a nice lady to talk to."

"I don't know where this day has gone. I've enjoyed myself more today than any other day for more years than I'd like to admit. Thank you, Ray, it's been delightful, but I think I should head back to the Hewitt's."

He asked with a big grin, "Well, how 'bout another go at Pinochle before ya leave? Or maybe yur afraid o' losin' to the great card shark agin'?"

"Lord have mercy! I'm afraid if we started another round I might end up being here all night."

"Well, now that sounds like an interestin' proposition to me. Miss Dorothy, you're most welcome to stay. "

I thought he was probably teasing me, but still I felt myself turning red. I was really quite flustered. "How you talk, Mr. Ray Clinger. Of course I'm not staying!"

He was laughing, laughing at me. I stood up abruptly. He continued to laugh quietly and held my rain coat for me, "Here's your coat, what's your hurry?"

I put my arms into the coat and couldn't help noticing his hands remained on the sleeve after I had it on. He slowly turned me toward him and held my chin with his right hand. "Thank you, lovely lady that ya are, for sharin' yur laughter an' joy with me today. It's been the best time I've had in years."

A few tears slipped from my eyes. I reached up and cradled Ray's well-worn distinguished face in my hands and slowly shook my head. "You know Ray, you're really something."

And then I embraced him before I even realized what I was doing. It just seemed like the most natural thing in the world to do at that moment.

And he hugged me back. Just like that, so normal and yet so strange. I could feel his face in my hair as he quietly said. "Dorothy, I want ya to seriously think about havin' some kind o' future with me. I know it may seem like we're movin' a tad fast, but at our age we don't have all the time in the world. Please think about it."

I stepped back and studied him closely. "I will Ray, I will. Now I must go."

The wind howled and the rain continued to pelt the earth. I shivered as I slid into the Bronco. I didn't know if it was my uncertainty or the weather that gave me the chills.

CHAPTER FOUR

Decisions

OLIVIA

THE TRIP BACK TO town seemed to be a long one that night. I had to drive extra cautiously as the torrential rain pounded on the Bronco in the near total darkness. I didn't see one other vehicle on the road. I thought I surely must be the only fool out driving.

I wanted to talk to Luella so bad I almost ached, but I knew I couldn't call her, not yet. I couldn't risk Alex and Andrea tracing calls to her...and then finding me. They'd have a field day trying to prove my incompetence during my last few weeks of freedom. Even though I *know* I've been completely rational. I'd carefully planned out all the details of my escape and new identity. Of course, there'd be those who'd say every thing I've done since I decided to leave my old life is clear evidence of my incompetence. And I didn't want to go there with my children or anyone else for that matter. So I took a few deep breaths and I didn't call Luella.

When Melvin died I'd invested a chunk of the life insurance in the stock market. I'd never told my financially zealous children about this. They believed my income sources were exclusively from Social Security, their father's pension and my teacher's pension. I always had all my stock dividends reinvested. When I cashed in the stocks three months ago, it had multiplied fifty times the original investment. I'd been lucky, no doubt about it. There were stiff penalties when I cashed in both pensions as I knew there would be.

I had to give up my Medicare, Blue Cross Supplementary policy as well as my Social Security when I left with my new identity. I decided to take the chance of being uninsured. I'd been blessed with a legacy of good genes from my parents. I've paid outrageous health insurance premiums since I retired and I've never made one claim. Besides medical care hadn't helped my sister any. When her time was up, it was up. I took over the counter vitamins and cold medicines when I got a cold. I rarely even needed a Tylenol and I know first aid from my years as a teacher. I believed I could take care of myself.

Of course, I was aware of the potential dangers. I made that trip to New York City and bought the diamonds which I sewed into the lining of my good leather handbag and kept one hundred thousand dollars, (most of which was also carefully sewn into the purse lining), to get me through the first year or so. There are those who'd say, "That's too much risk to keep all your valuables in one place."

I understand. I had some qualms about it at first. Then I remembered all the times I've been ignored, like I was invisible. So I bought a large good quality sturdy leather purse and I carried it with me everywhere I went just like I always have and no one was the wiser. Heavens, I carried it for three weeks before I left and no one in Scottsbluff even noticed I had a new purse.

I'm as careful as possible. I have to keep reminding myself what my choices were. This seemed like the best option for me so I just had to take the chance. I keep a low profile and I'm cautious.

Having bought two vehicles and taken a sizable loss on the first one while spending cash for every night of sleep, well, I wasn't really worried, but I knew I had to be a bit careful. I planned to settle close enough New York City to be able to drive in for long week ends once a year to see the shows and, more importantly, sell diamonds as I needed cash. I didn't want a bank account; I wanted no numbers associated with my new name. And then, an unexpected turn of events! I found myself beginning to feel like I could become part of a community again with new friends. Was it really possible that I could have this option to make a new life with Ray...at my age? He does have a point about us not having all the time in the world.

I parked in the Hewitt's driveway and Mary opened the backdoor and shouted, "Come in this door, it's too nasty to go around front tonight."

I ran for the open door and shivered as I entered her warm home. "So, how was the lunch? You look cold. How about a cup of hot tea to warm you up a bit?" Mary hung my coat in their family coat room to dry.

I nodded. "Oh, Mary that would be grand, if it's decaffeinated. I had a delightful afternoon. We just sat by the fire and played Pinochle for hours. We're both very competitive card players. I had fun. It's been years since I've enjoyed myself as much as I have the past few days here in Harmonyville. How was your day? Did you have a chance to spend some time with Joey?"

"Oh yes, he helped me with a few chores. Then we looked at old photo albums and reminisced, a perfect activity for a rainy day visit. I gave him the address book I'd made for him with phone numbers and addresses of all the relatives to take with him when he goes to basic training." Mary glowed as she described her day with her grandson. "He really appreciated it. We're lucky to have such a fine young man as our grandson. You know, we'd like him even if he wasn't related to us!"

I smiled, "Mary, if I hadn't met Joey myself, I'd have assumed you were a typical proud, bragging grandmother! But since I've met him, I understand exactly what you mean. He's not my grandson and I like him too. This tea was just what I needed. That's very nasty weather out there tonight."

We chatted a while longer, then I excused myself to go up to my room to relax, read and hopefully sleep early. I was exhausted. The down comforter felt extraordinarily comforting and warm. My mind felt surprisingly at peace and that night I slept like the contented soul that I was.

The storm continued the next day. I stayed at the B& B all day; I purposely avoided the diner and facing Ray. I felt more confused than when I went to bed the night before. I guess a good night's sleep had caused me to doubt my judgment. Mary graciously invited me to join them for lunch and dinner. She loaned me several books to read and was very tactful not to pry into my affairs. I appreciated that.

The following day I was awakened by brilliant sunshine beaming through the curtains. I slid out of bed and dressed in black slacks and a bulky light blue sweater. I looked out the window and the sun made every surface it touched glisten. And I thought of Ray.

I decided not to avoid the diner and hoped I'd see Ray. I knew we needed to talk before we could decide about having any kind of future together.

After breakfast I visited the Laundromat. It was either that or another shopping spree. Mary had offered to do my laundry, but I've always done my own and didn't want to take any further advantage of her gracious hospitality. After I finished the laundry, I stopped by the diner for lunch.

I was almost done when Ray walked in; he saw me and smiled sheepishly. "Well, fancy seein' ya here, Dorothy." He sat down across the table from me without asking or being invited and I didn't even care. He was no longer a stranger to me.

"Hi, Ray, how are you today? I've been thinking about you. I had such a nice time on Tuesday."

He smiled and began to blush. "I been thinkin' about ya too, Dorothy. Tuesday was a good day for me. Best since my Sophie passed on. Anyway, I got a proposition for ya to consider..."

Just then the waitress came over to bring my check and get Ray's order; I decided to stay a bit longer, so I ordered another cup of tea and dessert. Ray ordered a hot roast beef sandwich and salad with a cup of coffee.

I looked at him and smiled. "Okay, I'm listening..."

He grinned and shook his head. "Interruptions! Damn it all, where was I?"

I smiled and answered, "Proposition to consider..."

"Okay, here's an idea I came up with yesterday. I have this nice little apartment behind my garage an' workshop out behind my house. Ain't nobody lived there for years. It jes needs some cleanin' an' a fresh coat o' paint. Well, Miss Dorothy, I'd be happy to move out there if ya'd live in my house. Don't give me an answer now. I jes want ya to think it over."

I was stunned. Then I stammered, "Ray? I. . . I can't."

He held up his hand as if to stop traffic, "Don't even try to answer me now. I jes want ya to think about my idea, Miss Dorothy. I gotta go now."

He stood up and smiled, then hesitated before leaving. "Nice o' ya to stay while I ate my lunch. Would ya do me the honor o' havin' dinner with me tonight?"

I answered slowly, "Well, I guess I could do that. Should I meet you here at six?"

"Not tonight. I'll pick ya up at five thirty and take ya to a fancier place than this. I think ya'll like it jes fine."

I raised my eyebrows and considered the invitation. "This sounds very interesting. I'll see you at five-thirty."

As I drove back to the Bed & Breakfast I felt like reality was hitting me over the head with a thud. I fetched the shoebox from the Bronco's back seat floor. I hadn't opened it since packing it full of photos before leaving home. I'd systematically gone through all the photo albums and made copies of all the pictures that I wanted to take with me. I put the copies in the albums and frames and kept the originals for myself. I felt it was unlikely anyone would even notice the switch and if they did, I'd admire the observation skills of whoever it might be. For the first time since beginning my adventure I questioned if I'd done the right thing. I decided tomorrow I'll go to the library to check the local newspapers back home on the internet for the weeks since I'd been gone. I needed to know if I'd been declared dead and if there were any splashes about Andrea or Alexander. Just looking at all the old photos made me feel nostalgic.

Mary knocked on my door about four o'clock. "Would you like a cup of tea, Dorothy? I was about to fix one for myself and could make two just as easy."

I answered, "That's a wonderful idea. I'll be down in five minutes."

Immediately, I gathered the photos and carefully deposited them back in the shoebox. As I was about to open the door I noticed one picture lying on the floor by the bed. I bent to pick it up; it was a photo of Andrea and Alexander when they were five and eight years old. They'd been such beautiful children, no wonder we'd spoiled them so badly...I found myself sniffling and had to wipe tears from my eyes before joining Mary for tea.

As I closed the door to my room, the delicious smell from Mary's oven floated up the stairs. When I reached the downstairs hallway, she smiled. "Come sit with me at the kitchen table."

It was set with casual elegance for our afternoon tea. "Here you go, my friend. Have a cookie still warm from the oven. So, how's your day going, Dorothy?"

"So far it's been a good day. I've been resting all afternoon; this morning I did my laundry. Oh, I know you said you'd do my laundry or I could use your washer, but I didn't want to impose on your hospitality."

"I'd say that you are one stubborn lady, Dorothy Myers!"

"Why thank you. I'll take that as a compliment. These cookies hit the spot. They're delicious. Mary, I don't know how you stay so trim with all this cooking and baking you do."

She replied with a smile, "Part of its' metabolism. My family never did have much trouble with weight, and of course, the cooking and baking don't put on the weight, it's the overeating that causes the problems."

We chatted like a couple of old friends. I briefly had an urge to tell her who I really was and how I came to be a guest in her Bed & Breakfast. But I didn't. I couldn't take the chance. I stood up suddenly when I looked at her kitchen clock. It was ten after five. "Oh my goodness, where has the time gone? Ray will be here to pick me up in twenty minutes. We're going to a nice restaurant tonight so I must go change. Thanks so much for the tea, cookies and your good company."

Mary had an amused expression as I hurried out of the kitchen. She called after me, "You kids have fun tonight!"

I wore my new gray wool skirt, white blouse and burgundy blazer with a pair of black pumps. I decided to take my raincoat along just in case the evening cooled off too much for comfort with just a blazer. Before I knew it there was a tap on my door.

John said, "Dorothy, Ray's here. We'll keep him company until you're ready."

I answered through the door, "Thanks, John, I'll be right down." But first I went to the closet and put the shoe box inside my luggage and carefully locked it. I knew I had to be careful with my secrets. I liked Mary and John very much, but sometimes I felt they were maybe becoming a little too curious about me.

As I descended the stairs I could hear Mary, John, Joey and Ray involved in an amiable conversation. I walked into the living room, "Hi everyone."

Ray stood up immediately and gave a low whistle. "Now aren't ya a sight for sore old eyes. Ya look simply lovely tonight, Miss Dorothy." He seemed to have forgotten there were others in the room with us.

I felt myself turn crimson. "Well, thank you, Ray. You don't look so bad yourself."

He turned to the smiling Hewitts and said, "Pardon us, but I have reservations for six at The Barlow Club. So, I'll bid you fine folks good night. If I don't see ya before ya leave, Joey, good luck. You'll make a hell of an M.P."

After we left, the Hewitts looked at each other and smiled knowingly. John said, "If that's not a smitten couple, then I don't know what one would look like!"

———

Mary and he wrapped their arms around each other as they watched Ray open his pick up door for Dorothy to get in.

Joey stood there, mystified, as he watched out the window beside his smooching grandparents. "I've seen about everything now!"

Mary and John turned to him and laughed; his grandmother replied, "I think you'll see a lot more of life by the time you're our age, but this was a special thing for you to see today and I'm glad you were here to see it. Love is *not* an exclusive possession of the young."

———

Ray and I chatted briefly about the weather and the national news, but mostly just rode along in a comfortable silence. Fifteen minutes later he turned onto a secondary road and we passed several large estates and then an expansive lush golf course. This was an area I'd missed on my exploratory drives. Then he made a sudden turn to the left. I noticed a small indiscreet bronze sign with hunter green trim hanging from a black iron post. (*The Barlow Club...established 1875*). We entered the long narrow paved driveway nestled quietly between towering pines with classic landscape lamps tucked discreetly between the trees. The ride between the shadowy pines gave an illusion of early dusk.

Then he drove out of the pines into an expansive opening and before us was one of the grandest buildings I've ever seen. I couldn't believe this Tudor style stone castle was really in rural Pennsylvania. The landscaping was quietly elegant with clusters of chrysanthemums, and regal evergreens, as well as oaks and white ash, enveloping The Barlow Club in an aura of graceful country charm.

I looked at Ray. "It almost takes my breath away. It's simply magnificent!"

He smiled, "Jes wait till ya see the inside. Round here we all take a bunch o' pride in this place."

There were at least fifty cars in that remote country parking lot, a few very expensive imports and even more pickups and late model mid priced cars. A doorman gallantly held the main door for us as we walked in.

I was speechless as I looked around the elegant, but sturdy interior. A rustic slate entry floor led to the stately polished wood floors of the lounge and beyond to the formal dining rooms. The doors were opened to two smaller carpeted rooms on the right. I counted four huge fieldstone fireplaces as we were guided to our table by a uniformed waiter. There were large Persian carpets tastefully covering parts of the floors. Heavy dark wood paneling covered the lower half of the walls, while the top half was painted a dark hunter green; the large windows were dressed with lush burgundy velvet draperies. Several classic paintings were hung throughout the interior. All the furniture was very thick heavy dark wood as one might expect in exclusive men's clubs. Crisp white damask linens covered the tables, which were all set in formal place settings.

We were seated near a large window over-looking the golf course. The view was beautiful even though the trees were barren of color except for the evergreens. Several golfers straggled toward The Club as twilight settled in.

Ray ordered two glasses of champagne and a plate of house appetizers. The service was extraordinary.

Ray grinned. "So, Dorothy, what do ya think o' our Club?"

"It's fabulous; almost takes my breath away. I don't understand how a small community can support such a place. And champagne? You are full of surprises."

Ray grinned again. "Well, for starters, I'm a dues payin' member here."

I couldn't help smiling at him as I began to relax and enjoy the evening. "No offense, Ray, but I think it would take a great deal more than your dues to keep a place like this alive and well, and it certainly appears to be healthy."

The waiter brought house appetizers and drinks to the table, and before he had a chance to ask us, Ray said, "Johnny, we're in no hurry tonight. We'll jes take our time before we order dinner."

"Certainly, Uncle Ray. Just give me a signal when you're ready."

I asked, "Do you know everyone in the county?"

He contemplated his answer and then slowly replied. "I doubt it, but I know a lot of 'em."

"Well…please tell me how your town came to have a place like this."

"There used to be big money families 'round here. Lumber an' oil mostly. But some jes made their money off the ones that hit big. Some were dumber than deadwood and jes plain lucky. Anyways, most o' the new generations moved west or south over the years. But, two families stayed here with each generation bein' as good as the first. They're the only ones o' the crop that didn't hand everything to their children. An' the proof is in the puddin'. They taught 'em the importance o' roots an' givin' back to the community, that havin' wealth has big responsibilities." Ray humbly glanced around the beautiful lodge. "Yep, the McKee's and Frampton's have kept this town goin'. And you won't find a slacker among 'em. They set this club up for the people o' the town by setting a slidin' scale membership fee so everyone who wanted to could belong. You'd be damn right if ya figure we're jes a bit proud o' this place."

"I'm truly impressed; I never knew any thing existed like this except in movies. Do you golf too, Ray?"

"I've golfed a few times. Can't really see much sense in gettin' excited about hittin' or chasin' a little white ball all over them green fields out there. I have plenty o' things goin' on to keep me busy an' jes don't have much time left for the game o' golf."

Dinner was absolutely perfect. The whole evening was. Then over dessert Ray asks me, "Well, have ya thought about my proposition, Dorothy?"

I looked at him, his deep laugh lines and his kind blue eyes that seemed more like the eyes of an excited child than those of an elderly man. "Of course, I've thought about your offer. I've thought of little else."

"So, what's your answer, Dorothy?"

"Well, it's yes and no. No, I couldn't possibly move into the home you shared with your dear wife all those years. And yes, I'd be interested in renting your garage apartment. I think it'll be great fun having you as my neighbor and getting to know you better each day as a friend."

His eyes flickered as he stared at me without a trace of his familiar smile. "Damn it, woman, I never offered ya the garage apartment. It's not set up for the likes o' a lady like ya."

I held my ground. "Perhaps we should establish something right now. I'll decide what's best for me. We'll get along much better if that's understood."

We stared at each other for a few seconds and then I nervously fidgeted with my hair and looked out the window at the dark golf course. There were a few night lights on around the building which accented the beauty of The Club even at night.

"Ya know ya jes don't seem like a Dorothy to me. Maybe a Cynthia, Gloria or Olivia, but not a Dorothy."

I stopped fidgeting my hair and quickly gave him a wary glance. "Excuse me? Just what does that have to do with this discussion? You suddenly realized you don't like my name?"

"Don't get all fussed up on me. I only meant it as a compliment that ya seem like a fancier lady to me than a Dorothy. Damn it, woman, I like ya and if ya insist on the apartment rather than acceptin' my good intentions of offerin' ya my house, so be it. I been awful damn lonely since my Sophie's been gone. I like spendin' time with ya an' I know ya gotta do what ya believe is right for yourself."

Johnny approached the table. "Uncle Ray, may I interest you and your friend in after dinner tea or coffee?"

Ray gave me a questioning look. I smiled and nodded. Then I

looked at Johnny and asked, "Do you have decaf tea?"

He answered. "Of course, Mam."

Ray said, "We'll each have a cup of decaf tea. Thanks, Johnny."

When we were alone again I asked, "Ray, did we almost have an argument?"

He grinned. "Miss Dorothy, we weren't even close!"

I shrugged and smiled. "Well, you could've fooled me. I thought it felt a bit tense."

"I'll say one thing for sure, ya gotta be one o' the most stubborn people I ever met."

"You've mentioned that before. So, when do I get to see the apartment? May I pick out the paint since I'm the one who'll be living in it and how many rooms does it have?"

Ray held up his hand as if to stop traffic. "Hold on a minute. I think the best thing to do is for ya to come see the place tomorrow morning an' see if it looks like somethin' ya can live with. It's a one bedroom apartment with some useable ol' furniture."

"Yes, I'd like to take a look, I'm traveling light and I'll have to buy some things. But I knew that when I started cross country."

"Dorothy ya sure are an adventurous lady of mystery. Ya sure are."

"Ray, you flatter me. No one else in the whole world would call someone adventurous who taught in the same school for forty-five years! That doesn't have an adventurous or mysterious ring to it at all."

He leaned back in his chair with his arms folded and a crooked smile on his face. "Well, I'm somebody the last I knew, an' ya brought adventure an' intrigue into *my* life. I feel more alive than I have in years."

I lifted my tea cup and toasted my new friend, Ray. "Till tomorrow."

He lifted his and joined me. "For many tomorrows."

CHAPTER FIVE

The Search

ANDREA AND ALEXANDER

IN THE THREE MONTHS since their mother had disappeared, Andrea had experienced a range of emotions she wouldn't have believed herself capable of prior to her mother's … death. Anger, resentment, grief, embarrassment, abandonment and a very deep sadness were only the tip of her emotional iceberg.

They'd had a Memorial Service for her at the Methodist Church two months after Olivia's disappearance; the obituary had been posted in the newspaper. Many of her former students crammed into the church as well as long lost relatives. Mother had always been one to keep in touch and of course, her fellow church members and neighbors came. Rev. Morris gave a generic eulogy since he'd only been at the church for four months and didn't really know much about Olivia. Then friends, former students, cousins, and even Alexander shared favorite memories. Andrea couldn't bring herself to stand and say anything at all. Even though she had a family of her own and Alexander, she felt like an orphan without her mother. And since they'd never found her body, she had a hidden hope that maybe, just maybe…

She found herself gravitating towards Luella and wanting to learn more about her mother. One evening as she and Joel laid together in bed she said before turning out the light, "I'm amazed that Luella has not been more distraught without Mother. They'd always been so close. Maybe they're just from a more stoic generation."

"I've wondered about that myself. But, from what I see with my clients at work, their generation has the same emotional reactions to life as anyone else. Could it be she knows something we don't about your mother's passing?"

Andrea sat up in bed abruptly, "Joel, what do you mean by that?"

"I keep rehashing all that's happened and it feels like we're missing something ...I can't quite put my finger on it, but something just doesn't feel right about the facts as we have them."

Soon after he'd turned out the light, the phone rang. It was Alexander. As usual he ignored pleasantries and said, "Joel, you're not going to believe this. I was talking to Mildred Gustafson this evening. You remember her; she taught school with Mother for years. Anyway, she says, 'I'm so sorry about the loss of your dear Mother, etc and etc.', you know how those old ladies can go on. So I asked her when she last saw Mother. She says, 'Luella and I had lunch with her the day before she ah...died.' Joel, do you see what I see here? One big discrepancy. That's not the story we got from Luella. Not at all."

Joel turned the light on and sat up in bed. "Do you think Luella could've just forgotten when she last saw your mother?"

Alexander huffed. "Come on, Joel, you're the lawyer in the family. We talked to Luella the day after...it happened. She said she'd been at some retreat and hadn't seen or talked to Mother for three days. She's definitely hiding something."

"Maybe you're onto something, Alex. Do you want to check up on that church retreat story she gave us? I'll tell Andrea about it and we'll talk to you tomorrow."

Joel relayed Alex's news to Andrea. She said, "I can't think Luella would lie intentionally. She's not the type. Besides she and Mother were like sisters..."

Joel turned out the light as they lay back down in bed and they said their good nights again.

Several minutes later, Andrea whispered, "Joel, are you still awake?"

A drowsy voice answered, "Yeah."

She asked, "Do you think Luella could be covering up something as a favor to Mother? They wouldn't do something like that...would they?"

An even sleepier voice answered her, "I don't think so. But maybe she would. We'll talk about it tomorrow."

She soon heard him snoring softly. It was a sound that usually made her feel safe and secure. That night it annoyed her. Doubting questions nagged at her, Could Mother possibly still be alive? And hiding from us? But why? Andrea's mind raced from one scenario to another. "It's ironic I'm spending more time thinking about Mother now that she's gone than I did when she lived twenty minutes away." Sleep was as elusive to Andrea as was her mother that night.

She moaned as the radio alarm went off at six-thirty and forced herself to get out of bed. The children seemed to bicker even more than usual as they rushed about getting ready for school. She turned on the kitchen radio and prepared their breakfasts, but still the sounds of their morning squabble drifted down to the kitchen. She shook her head and wondered, "What do they find to fight about? They each have their own bedroom and bath. They don't have to share anything! My God. When Alex and I were kids we had to share one bath with Mother, Dad and each other."

Thirteen-year-old Thomas, self assured like his father, could be so aggravating with his haughty condescending remarks. One thing for sure, no one would call him Tommy, at least not twice! He has an air about him that sometimes made him seem like he truly did know more than everyone else. Yet Joel rarely had any difficulty interacting with him. Thomas definitely related better with men.

Andrea remembered asking Joel's mother when Thomas was eleven, "Does he remind you of Joel when he was this age?"

Joel's mother tactfully answered. "Today children are so different that it's hard to compare. These kids are electronic game and computer experts almost before they can read and somehow all that makes them seem...older. Certain facial expressions do remind me of Joel as a boy. There's just been so much water under the bridge since then that I really can't say."

Their arguing continued, but Andrea was preoccupied with a bittersweet memory of a discussion with her mother...one she had deeply resented at the time. "Andrea, your children are spoiled. They are overindulged, and therefore do not appreciate anything. They've developed attitudes of entitlement. I hate to say this about my grandchildren, but their behaviors are obnoxious more often than not."

Andrea remembered feeling so angry with her at the time that she simply refused to even consider there might be a grain of truth to her statement...

Her thoughts were interrupted by Tiffany's tearful complaint, "Mommy! Make Thomas give me my notebook. Please!"

Reality set in. "Thomas, give your sister her notebook. Now."

Joel pecked Andrea's cheek as he walked into the kitchen, and poured himself a cup of coffee. "Good morning, my loves. What's all the fuss about?"

Thomas raced in, slammed Tiffany's notebook on the table and grabbed a bowl for his cereal.

Andrea asked, "Does anyone want eggs this morning?"

Joel answered, "Sorry, no time. Hurry up, kids, if you want a ride to school. I'll call you later this morning on your cell, Andrea, and we'll finish talking about last night."

"Sorry, but I'll be tied up in meetings until after one. We're making the final plans for the Annual Hospital Charity Dance and you know how time consuming all those details can be..."

"Mommy, Thomas took all the milk and now there isn't any for my cereal!"

Andrea checked the refrigerator and sure enough she'd forgotten to buy more milk. "Damn. Well, how about a Pop Tart? I have one left in the cabinet. I promise I'll get an order of groceries today."

Thomas chimed in. "That's not fair. I'd rather have had a Pop Tart. Why do you always give Tiffany the special treats?"

Tiffany opened the tart and sneered at her brother as she slowly savored each bite.

Andrea and Joel gave each other hopeless glances. Then he resumed reading the morning paper as he sipped his coffee, totally oblivious to the confusion around him. Andrea knew her lack of sleep likely triggered her escalating agitation. She stifled ugly homicidal thoughts and silently counted the minutes before they'd all leave the house which couldn't happen soon enough. She realized her mother had been right about these children.

Andrea seethed and said between clenched teeth. "That's enough out of you two! Just eat your breakfasts and don't even think about saying another word."

Joel gave her another peck on the cheek as he went out the door. "We'll talk about it tonight. Have a good day, honey."

She patted her children's behinds as they followed their dad out the door. "You all have a good day now. Joel, please don't be late tonight, I'm counting on us talking."

She closed the door with a sigh. "And these are the good old days?!" That's what the older women who served on her various committees always told her. She couldn't help but shudder at the thought…"Sweet Jesus, if this is as good as it gets, I hate to think what the future holds."

Alexander called as she was dumping the fresh scrambled eggs into the garbage disposal and tidying up the kitchen. She put a seasoned chicken in the slow cooker for the evening meal as she listened to him in disbelief.

"Morning, Andrea, you're not going to believe this, but Luella didn't go to that church retreat. In fact, her church secretary always books the retreats and told me Luella's never gone on one. Yet her husband John swears she goes to a week end retreat every year in the middle of August."

"Maybe I'll just pay Luella a visit this morning. It doesn't make sense. Are you sure you talked to the right church? She goes to First Baptist. Oh, ah…have you had any news from the realtor about Mother's house? And what about the car?"

"Yeah, last week I finally unloaded the car. I've got a copy of the bill of sales for you and a check for your half. We made an extra thousand by holding out for the book value. The realtor has been showing the house and thinks he may have some serious interest now. He wants us to empty it as soon as possible. Will you have any time this week end?"

"I never have time unless I steal it from a previously obligated commitment." Andrea quickly checked her schedule. "I could meet you there at twelve-thirty Sunday afternoon. Bring packing boxes. Okay?"

"Sunday afternoon it is and we'll see how much we can accomplish. I'm afraid it's going to take us several trips to go through all Mother's things.

"Hey, Andrea, let me know how your visit with Luella goes."

Quick good byes were said. Andrea hung up the phone feeling that familiar, sick feeling she always did when she had to talk business with Alex. He was her brother; yet there was something about him that caused her to experience a free floating anxiety, caused by a deep gut feeling of distrust.

Twenty minutes later Andrea was sitting at Luella's kitchen table with a mug of tea.

Luella smiled at her. "It's always good to see you, my dear, but you surely must have something on your mind to come this early. Is something wrong, Andrea?"

She answered timidly. "Maybe. I need to ask you a personal question. Of course, it's up to you if you decide to answer or not."

Luella's grey eyes locked on her with a steely gaze. "So, what's your question?"

Andrea spoke softly as she stared at the shining kitchen floor. "You know the weekend back in August when mother, ah… disappeared? You told us at the time that you usually talk to her every day, but hadn't spoken to her for three days because you'd gone on a church retreat. Well…Alexander ran into Mildred Gustafson yesterday and she told him that you, Mother and she had lunch together that last Friday afternoon."

Luella huffed and turned to glare out the window, speaking hesitantly… "I miss your Mother more than anyone could ever imagine. We were closer than sisters, yes we were. All our lives. Hell, we told each other when we were pregnant with each of our babies before we told our families or even our husbands. That damn Mildred always did talk too much! Yes, I had lunch with your mother that day. Then I left for my retreat. What difference could it possibly make now anyway?"

"Well, what happened to our mother does matter to us. We're just trying to put the pieces together. It's a puzzle that doesn't make any sense. And Luella, Alex talked to your church secretary. She told him you've never gone on the church retreats. Please tell me the truth, Luella."

Luella continued to stare in silence.

Andrea sat at the table watching her Mother's oldest friend. And waiting.

Luella finally turned to her with an air of darkness Andrea had never seen in her before. "That secretary shouldn't have told anyone if I was or wasn't at the retreats. I don't know where or if your mother is still living. I do know as long as I live she'll always be my dearest friend."

"I don't understand, Luella. John swears you go to the retreat every year…"

Luella stepped forward, pointing her finger in Andrea's face, anger permeating her voice. "There are some things you will not understand. But you and your brother had better stay away from my John! Andrea, you've surely been married long enough to know that wives do not tell husbands everything. You, and your brother, just stay the hell out of my marriage! Speaking of that brother of yours, why don't you ask him about his last few visits with your mother?"

"I'm sorry, Luella, I didn't mean to upset you."

A tearful shaking Luella responded through a clenched jaw. "You've worn out your welcome and should just go…now."

Andrea let herself out; she trembled as she sat in her car and wondered, what had just happened in there. She looked back at the house and saw Luella glaring at her through the window, her face still distorted by the sudden anger. She decided she was definitely not up to committee meetings that day.

She drove to Joel's office, calling his cell phone after parking the car. Andrea's voice quivered. "Joel, I really need to talk to you!"

"What happened? You sound terrible. Where are you? I thought you had meetings all day…"

"I'm parked in front of the building. I'm too upset to come in…"

"I'll be right out." He closed his cell phone and told his secretary he'd be out for awhile.

Joel went straight to the driver's side and Andrea scooted over the console to the passenger seat. He stroked her cheek gently. "What's happened, Andie?"

She motioned for him to drive away from his office. And then, through her tears she proceeded to tell him about her strange visit with Luella following Alexander's morning phone call.

After driving around for an hour, he stopped outside of town at a small country restaurant for lunch. He ordered two grilled chicken salads and turned to her. "My thoughts are so convoluted that I don't know what to think or say. I'm sure Luella will call and apologize when she realizes how she attacked you. Let me think on it this afternoon. I'll be home for dinner and we'll talk about the whole thing then. Probably a good idea not to talk with your brother this afternoon. We don't want him to get all riled up and go raising cane with poor old Luella."

Andrea answered in a low voice. "Poor old Luella? She's not going to call and apologize. She thought I was out of line...I don't know, maybe I was. But you didn't see her. I did. Trust me. She won't be apologizing."

He reached across the small table and covered her hand with his. She smiled ruefully. "Don't worry. Alex is about the last person I feel like talking to this afternoon. This is all so distressing. I just couldn't handle the details of planning a charity dance today so I called Jen and made excuses for all my scheduled meetings. Do you think they'll fire me?"

"They'd be crazy to ever let you go." He glanced at his watch. "Are you ready, Andrea? I really should get back to the office."

He put his arm around her shoulders as they walked to the car. "It's good to see a trace of a smile on your beautiful face again. I know these last three months have been really tough for you."

"Sometimes you're a damn nice guy to have around, Joel. Who's driving?"

He tossed her the keys. "Sometimes, huh?"

Alexander left three messages on his sister's home phone and four on her cell phone. "Damn. Where is she? Why doesn't she pick up?"

His secretary, Jackie, buzzed him. "Alex, you have a call from a Lori in California."

"Okay, I'll take it. Thanks Jackie."

"Hey Lori, how's it going? How's Cassie?"

"We're okay. Sorry about your mother. She always treated me good.

A lot better than her son, that's for sure."

"I'm really not in the mood for your crap, so please just get to the point. I did not appreciate you refusing to send Cassie to her grandmother's memorial service last month. So, what do you want?"

"Oh, for God's sake, Alexander! I didn't refuse to send her. She was in soccer playoffs and she didn't want to come. She doesn't know your family; she didn't really know your mother and funerals are such downers. Give the kid a break."

"Well, it's a shame she missed it, there was a big crowd. Mother touched so many lives and everyone loved her. I gave an exceptional tribute to her; she was one of a kind."

"Well, that's sort of why I called. How much did you inherit? I'm really getting tired of sharing my car with Cass. I think you should buy your daughter a good car. Maybe one of those smaller BMWs. How about it, Dad?"

Alexander took a deep breath before answering his ex-wife, and wondered how in the world he'd ever ended up married to her? He concluded such stupidity deserved whatever she threw his way.

"I plan to take Cassie car shopping and buy her a car when I come out for her graduation next summer. End of discussion. I have to go now. Please tell Cassie to call me."

He covered his face with his hands after hanging up the phone. His mind raced with worry, he muttered to himself. "Between the child support and two spousal support payments each month...how will I ever be able to swing college tuition for four years plus buy a car for Cassie? A BMW! My God, Lori should know better than to put ideas like that in the girl's head. But Lori always did like to see me squirm. She's such a bitch."

Jackie knocked on the office door. "Whenever you're ready Alex, your two o'clock appointment is here."

"Thanks, just send him in." Alex pulled the Piscatelli folder from the cabinet beside his desk.

Alex walked over, shook the paunchy older man's hand and closed the office door behind them, as Ralph Piscatelli sat down. "So how am I doin' these days? Can I buy me an' the wife a fancy vacation condo in Florida?"

Alex smiled. "Well, Ralph I'd say that was up to you and Mrs. Piscatelli. Your portfolio is doing quite well…"

Alex cleverly suggested a few changes just to earn some extra commission fees. Ralph studied the numbers as Alex used a flip chart to cautiously predict future earnings and projected retirement income from his current investments.

Alexander smoothly flipped to a more aggressive plan that would provide twenty five percent return on all investments based on the last five years growth of the listed stocks. He watched Mr. Piscatelli's eyes and knew the greed for more would lead to another sale.

"Ralph, I know how hard you've worked for your money and I've got to warn you, there's no guarantee this investment will bring you what it did for these other investors over the last five years. There is a certain amount of risk involved, that's why it's called aggressive investments. It's not for the faint-hearted."

"Ah, come on, Alex, since when have ya ever known a faint-hearted Piscatelli? Are ya trying to keep me out jus' to make more profit for yourself?"

"Ralph, I just don't feel right about this. At least go home and talk it over with your wife and call me in the morning if you still want to buy and sell to make the changes in your investments."

Predictably Ralph's agitation exerted itself. "My God, I should jus' open me one o' them Ameritrade accounts and then I wouldn't have to ask permission to do what I wanna do with my own money. An' since when does a Piscatelli have to ask his woman's permission to make a money decision? Sometimes ya really piss me off, Alex!"

He stomped toward the door and turned. "I'm callin' ya in the mornin' and ya better be ready to deal."

Alex smiled to himself as he listened to the sound of his very smug customer leave. He muttered, "If Piscatelli loses money and he probably will; he can't blame me. After all I warned him. It works every time. I could be a professional poker player the way I can read faces…but damn, I couldn't get Mother to open up her purse strings for me. She was so damn tight with her money. It was almost like she didn't trust me, her own son!"

Jackie knocked on his door again. "Your two-thirty appointment is here, Alex."

"Thanks, please send her in." He pulled the Levin file from the stack beside his desk.

Mrs. Levin walked in, the widow of a well-heeled attorney. They'd both known his parents when he was growing up. She was an attractive elderly lady, who carried herself with an air of confidence, the kind that comes from a lifetime of security and she was very cautious with her investments. He decided not to use the flip charts with her.

"Alexander, I was so sorry to hear about your mother. Poor Olivia, and so soon after Eloise. It's hard to understand why things happen as they do. How are you and Andrea coping with it all?"

"Thanks for asking. We're doing about as well as a person could under the circumstances. Now, what can I do for you today?"

"Well, I'd like to sell some of my stocks. I need seventy-five thousand dollars. Based on previous transactions, I'll expect my money no later than seven days. Correct?"

"That's a rather large amount to withdraw at one time, are you sure about this, Mrs. Levin?"

Her tone changed and she gave him a defiant glare. "Now let's think about this, I wouldn't be here if I wasn't sure, would I, Alexander?"

Somehow her reaction was reminiscent of a few conversations he'd had with his mother. He cautiously continued. "Of course, please forgive me. Would you like to have it sent directly to your home or sent here and delivered in person?"

"I'd like to pick it up from the office myself, so please just call me when the check arrives. Thank you, Alexander."

As she left he couldn't help feeling like a reprimanded school boy. And the afternoon dragged on with a different client every half hour. Their paper work was sandwiched in between. It had turned into a very profitable day. The steady flow of clients helped him forget about Andrea, his mother, Lori and Cassie... the whole damn family mess. For that Alex was grateful. He worked until eight-thirty and then stopped at his favorite restaurant where he ate a late and lonely dinner.

CHAPTER SIX

Nesting

OLIVIA

THE FIRST TIME I saw the garage apartment I was completely charmed. I hadn't even noticed it sitting off behind Ray's house the day I'd gone for lunch. It was log cabin style like his house, with a two-car garage in front; the apartment attached directly behind the garage. In fact, the main entry was through the garage and the kitchen had a back door that opened onto a small deck facing the wooded area that surrounded Ray's backyard. There was a narrow staircase in the garage leading to a large unfinished loft area that was used for storage. No one had lived in the one bedroom apartment for more than twenty years, since Ray's son Billy...when he was first discharged from the army.

Ray said, "Ya must be a little crazy besides bein' stubborn as a mule, if ya think this dump is charmin'."

I smiled, "Just you wait and see."

I had such a sense of purpose and felt more alive than I had in years. I took an inventory of the garage furniture and cleared all my ideas for changing things with Ray.

Ray and his friends, Harry and Walter, started the painting two days later. They graciously let me chose the colors. I worked in the garage, sanding and painting the kitchen table and four chairs a subtle cornflower blue, while the men painted in the apartment. We agreed to just sand and varnish the few cabinets in the kitchen. I cleaned the kitchen range and oven; Harry gave Ray a late model refrigerator and Ray insisted on installing a new dishwasher. Who was I to argue with a landlord who wanted to install a dishwasher?

The fieldstone fireplace would be the focal point of the living room. I bought a new sofa, chair and lamps as well as a bedroom suite. Also, two sets of sheets, a down comforter and cover with coordinated draperies and window shades. I also bought a supply of bath towels and a small microwave. I refinished a long-abandoned coffee table and lamp tables. I felt like an excited child as I prepared my 'nest'.

Ray insisted he'd pay for the carpet since he was the landlord. Again, he kindly allowed me to choose the floor coverings.

The day we finished the apartment, I gave Ray two envelopes of cash.

I wasn't surprised when he said, "I don't need your money, Miss Dorothy, an' this apartment needed to be cleaned up for a long time. Ya did me a favor by motivatin' me to get at it."

"I was afraid you might feel like that, Ray Clinger. But, I will not move in if you do not accept rent. I checked with the local realtor and this is a fair rent for an apartment this size in Harmonyville. You'll find one month security deposit and one month rent. I bought you a booklet of receipts and I'd appreciate you writing me out a receipt. I will pay rent on the fifth of each month. This will be our arrangement or the deals off."

Three days later I moved in. The Hewitt's sent me a beautiful floral arrangement as a housewarming gift. Life was good. I continued to collect the things I needed to create my new home. The following week I invited the Hewitts, Harry, Walter and their wives...oh yes, and Ray, for a buffet dinner. Most of the dishes and pans for the dinner were borrowed from Ray's kitchen. We feasted on Swedish meatballs, seafood stew and home-fried potatoes, tossed salad and for dessert... Boston cream pie, from the bakery, of course.

Ray kept the fireplace going throughout the evening. The men played cards at the kitchen table after dinner and we ladies enjoyed a friendly visit in the living room. I'd never met Walter's wife, Irene, or Harry's wife, Joyce, before. Walter and Irene had recently celebrated their fifty-fourth wedding anniversary. They'd both grown up in Harmonyville just like Ray and Sophie.

Irene said, "Sophie was my dearest friend. And I know she'd be glad Ray and you are friends now. It's good to see him full of life again. I'm glad you've decided to stay. Do you have any family out west?"

I answered carefully. "None to speak of, I taught school for forty-five years. And then I decided to come east and make a new start, so here I am three months later. From everything I've heard about Sophie, she was a lovely person."

Irene smiled. "Indeed she was. And she always said, 'life is for the living.' Dorothy you're no slouch yourself...pulling up stakes and taking off like you did. My word, I don't think I'd ever have had the courage to do that, especially not at our age."

I returned her smile. "I never thought of myself as courageous, but I'll take that as a compliment."

I brought the tea pot in. "Who's ready for more tea?"

Mary said. "I love your apartment, Dorothy. It is cozy and perfect for you. I can't believe how homey it is already. You certainly have a knack for nesting, my dear."

Joyce asked, "Do you have everything you need? Harry and I have only been married for five years; we had two households to combine and we never did get around to having a garage sale. We have overflow stored in the garage, attic and basement. It's shameful really! All our kids were settled and adamantly refused any of our old junk. So it's just been sitting around gathering cobwebs. We've been too busy having a good time to bother with it."

I looked at her skeptically; she appeared to be serious and I was touched by her generosity. "That's very kind of you, Joyce. I'll give you a call before I head out to shop if there's anything else I need."

Joyce quickly opened her purse and pulled out a pen and small notepad and we exchanged phone numbers. "Well, you better give me a call even if you don't need anything! I'd love to have lunch with you one day next week."

The evening passed quickly with friendly relaxed conversation; we were all surprised at the time when Irene looked at her watch and said, "I can't believe it's after eleven already!"

The three couples left soon after Irene announced the time. They'd all enjoyed the evening and the food and promised we'd do it again soon in one of their homes. Ray lingered by the fire.

I plopped down on the sofa, feeling exhausted in a very warm and contented way.

Ray grinned. "I think ya' 'bout outdid yourself tonight, Miss Dorothy. Ya look downright done in. Do ya' want me to stoke the fire down an' go home so ya' can get right to bed?"

"No thanks. I think I'll just sit here and relax for awhile; you're welcome to sit with me if you'd like. I'm tired but still wound up too tight from the evening to sleep. I'm quite out of practice at socializing, you know."

He stood up and stretched, then looked at me with those mesmerizing eyes. "Well, no one woulda guessed ya were outa' practice on anythin' tonight. Ya gave a damn nice little party. The food was delicious and everyone had a good time. Can't ask for more than that, can ya?"

He sat down beside me on the sofa and we sat watching the fire. It had a mellowing effect on me.

Ray looked around and smiled. "I'd o' never believed this apartment coulda looked like this. Amazin', jes plain amazin' that's what it is. So how'd ya like Irene and Joyce?"

I answered carefully. "They're both lovely, kind ladies. I felt Irene wasn't real comfortable with me 'replacing' Sophie...which I'm definitely not doing. But she was very polite and certainly didn't offend me. I couldn't help but feel a bit more comfortable with Joyce and Mary, of course."

"Irene and Sophie were best friends all through school. Heck, that's how Walter an' me got to be buddies...jes taggin' along after our women all those years." He stared at the fire in deep thought for a couple minutes before responding. "Don't take Irene the wrong way. She's got a heart o' gold and you're probably right about this not bein' an easy evenin' for her."

"Oh ...I wasn't complaining, just being honest with you about your friends. I thought Joyce was delightful. And I will enjoy counting all of them among my new friends."

"I'm glad to hear that, Dorothy. I know we're all feelin' darn lucky havin' ya as our new friend."

I turned to him and smiled. "Ray, you're truly a sweet man. I'm glad you talked to me in the diner that day...or I might still be driving down some highway wondering where to stop and spend the winter..."

He turned to me with a concerned expression. "Ya know, Dorothy, sometimes ya' seem like a lost soul... Well, I'm goin' home now. Sleep well. Want me to close this fireplace up for the night?"

"Yes, I'd appreciate that, Ray. I'm going to bed, too. Thanks for all your help tonight. I really enjoyed the evening and I love my new home. It's absolutely perfect for me. Thank you for everything."

As he was leaving, I walked over and gave him an affectionate hug. "Good night, my friend. Sleep well."

He leaned down, gently embraced me and lightly kissed my cheek. "Good night to ya, dear heart. I'll see you tomorrow."

Before opening the door he looked back at me and almost whispered. "I'm mighty glad I stopped by yur table at the diner, too. Ya know that was real hard for me to git up enough courage to do. Ya' sleep well now." And he quietly closed the door behind him.

I locked up and went to bed.

The next morning I heard Ray out in the garage when I shuffled sleepily into the kitchen. I made a pot of tea and decided to watch the morning news show on television.

As I finished my breakfast I heard Ray leaving in his pick-up and I went for a walk. The sky was an ominous gray, there wasn't a trace of sunshine and the smell of winter was in the air. The wind was picking up, and by the time I'd walked two miles, a few large snow flakes gently floated to the ground. I felt invigorated and cold when I returned to the apartment. I started a fire in the fireplace, made myself a cup of hot chocolate and curled up on the sofa with an interesting book. Life was good, better than I'd expected it to be. New friends and a new home...then I thought of Andrea, Alexander and Luella. And I was flooded with remorse and homesickness. I told myself, what's done is done.

But the more I thought of them, the more difficult it was to concentrate on my book. I decided to go to the library that afternoon to use a computer to see what was happening back home.

I'd warmed up. Unable to concentrate, I closed the book. I sat watching the fire, knowing I wouldn't dare leave it for at least half an hour. Crackling fires have always soothed me. I decided to look at my box of photos again. I pulled the almost empty luggage out from under my bed, unlocked it and carefully lifted the shoebox as if it was the Holy Grail. I returned to the living room and slowly covered the coffee table with my past. It had a sentimental effect on me. And again I wondered if I'd made the right decision; maybe I really do have a past that's worthy of some recognition.

I sat there so long that the fire died out; I didn't even notice until I took a chill, then I realized my blouse was damp from the tears that had sneaked down my cheeks. I studied the pictures as I slowly packed them back into the box.

I decided to keep an eight by ten out, buy a frame when I went to town and set it on my bedroom dresser. The one of Andrea and Alexander when they were young, it had always been my favorite photo of them.

My reminiscing was broken by sounds from the garage and I knew Ray must have returned. I put the box back into the luggage, locked it and pushed it back under the bed. When I returned to the living room I saw the photo I planned to frame lying on the coffee table, I quickly tucked it inside my book just as I heard a knock on the door. Before answering, I hurried back to the bedroom and laid the book on my bed. I quickly slipped a cardigan on, wiped my eyes with a tissue and took a deep breath.

Ray had hung his coat in the garage. He was like a child when it came to the first snow of winter. He had a bag of deli boxes with him and announced. "Did ya see that snow this mornin'? It was beautiful! I could never live anywhere that didn't have a change o' seasons.

"Lunch is on me. Oh, I know ya got enough leftovers for a couple days, but ya can always freeze it. When I smelled this here roasted chicken I knew I had to bring it home. Are ya hungry yet?"

I couldn't help smiling at the big silly old man, who was quickly becoming my protector as well as landlord and friend. "I wasn't hungry till you walked in; the smell from your deli packages perked my appetite right up. I'll set out some plates and silverware. How were things in town today?"

"Walter and Harry both said they an' their wives had a real good time out here last night. My other buddies were all beggin' for invitations, too, when they heard'm talkin'. To hear'm go on you'd think we were takin' reservations!"

"They were just teasing you...weren't they?" I asked tentatively. I knew I didn't want to spend the rest of my life providing free food and entertainment to an endless stream of old geezers!

Ray noticed my cool response. "O' course they were only foolin'. They like to tease ol Ray. Guess I got it comin' cause o' how I been teasin' the lot o' 'em for years. Don't ya worry, Miss Dorothy, nobody's gonna take advantage o' ya. Are ya ready to eat?"

I marveled at his quick perception or was I just too easy to read?

"I was wonderin', Dorothy, if ya'd be wantin' a mailbox. I know ya' mus' be gettin' your mail at the Post Office, but if ya'd rather get it delivered jes' say the word."

"I don't know, I'll think about it and get back to you." And I pondered; it's not like I'll be getting any mail, not even Social Security. Olivia Hampton had received Social Security, but she's gone. As Dorothy Myers with my fake papers, well, I have my freedom and that's it. Should I open a post office box or have a mailbox? I didn't want to arouse any more suspicions than I already have. I couldn't help but feel trust already runs shallow and curiosity runs deep regarding me among some of the town folks. And I don't blame them. If I were in their place, I'd be suspicious too. 'A stranger with no past...is she trying to fleece our Ray?' Well, of course I'm not, but how can they know that. Only time will allay their fears.

I decided to check out the magazine section at the library and find a few mail-in cards to subscribe to a few magazines so that I'd actually have something to be delivered to my mailbox.

After lunch I announced, "Thanks for lunch, Ray - that was the best roast chicken I've had in ages. You're spoiling me! But now, if you'll excuse me, I've got some errands to do in town."

"You're welcome for lunch. Better dress warm, it's gettin' darn cold out there. I gotta see a man about gettin' us some firewood in for the winter."

He stood up to leave and turned back as he was about to go out the door. "Ya have yourself a good afternoon."

"I will and you have a good afternoon as well."

I tidied the kitchen and boxed up Ray's plates and pans which I left on the kitchen table for later. I was just about to leave as the phone rang. That hadn't happened very often since I didn't have many friends here yet.

"Hello, Dorothy, this is Joyce. We simply had a grand time last night and I wanted to thank you again."

"Joyce, how nice of you to call...I'd heard so much about you from Ray and Harry when we were painting and fixing up the apartment that I felt I almost knew you, so I was especially happy to finally meet you last night. I'm glad you both enjoyed the evening. I did too and that's a good sign when the hostess enjoys her own party."

"Dorothy, I can tell you're a gem, an original! And I wanted to remind you I wasn't kidding about having so much extra stuff over here. There must be some things you still need that I could fix you up with."

"Well...actually I could use some pans and dishes. I borrowed from Ray's kitchen for last night."

"Why don't you and Ray come for lunch tomorrow? We can play a few hands of cards after you pick out what you want. How's that sound?"

Though a retired nurse, Joyce seemed to be stuck in high gear. Her unabashed love of life prevented her from slowing down. "That sounds very nice. I'll talk to Ray later and call you back tonight. Thanks Joyce."

I tuned in the local radio station after I started the SUV and luckily caught the weather report as I drove the two miles into town. The skies still had a menacing overcast and the wind had picked up, but the snow flurries had stopped. Four inches of snow were predicted within the next few hours.

Lynne Shanely, the librarian, assured me even for Harmonyville, this was an extraordinarily early snow. One computer terminal was available. I immediately clicked on to the Scottsbluff Daily Review. I read local highlights for the last four months. I read about my disappearance, the abandoned car, the investigations and the missing person report filed by Andrea and Alexander. A photo of them leaving the courthouse flooded me with unfamiliar feelings of ... regret? Homesickness? I didn't know; I just knew I was beginning to feel very sad. Even though the local people have been so kind to me, I couldn't stop thinking about home...and the distraught expressions on the faces of my children in that grainy newspaper photo.

An hour later, Lynne tapped me on the shoulder, "Dorothy, I'm sorry but there is a thirty minute limit per sitting at the computer. That way everyone gets a chance to use it. Sorry."

"Oh my, I didn't realize I'd been here so long. I'm sorry." I quickly closed the site on the computer and tried in vain to delete the trail.

"Don't worry about it, dear, it wasn't like someone was waiting in line for it and besides almost everyone loses tract of time when using the computers."

Sorely embarrassed, I went directly to the magazine section and made myself comfortable in a wooden rocking chair after collecting six of my favorite magazines to browse through, looking for subscription cards that I discreetly tucked in my jacket pocket. Soon I'd be receiving my own copies of *Newsweek, Guidepost, Readers Digest, Ladies Home Journal, AARP* and *National Geographic*.

Then I left the library. Oh, how I wanted to talk to Luella. Or even write her a letter... I knew I had to pull myself out of the fog I was edging into. I sat in my car studying my *AAA Road Atlas* trying to decide which larger city would be best to do a day trip and use a computer cafe with perhaps more privacy than a public library...I couldn't get Andrea's face in that photo out of my mind. Such total despair! Did I do that to my own daughter? Had I misread her all these years? Did she really care about me after all? I even felt an urge to call her.

I decided Pittsburgh would be my city of choice. With all those universities, there had to be a few computer cafes where I could anonymously pay for as much time as I needed.

Snow flurries were suddenly swirling around the SUV. I decided two more stops would be plenty and then I'd head back to the apartment. First, I stopped at the hardware and bought a mailbox and an eight by ten photo frame. Then I dashed into the Post Office and registered for my new mailing address. Before leaving the Post Office, I filled out all six cards and checked 'bill me later'. Well, I was glad that was taken care of. On Sunday I'd filled out an address card at church. When the mail slowly starts to arrive, maybe people would look at me with less curiosity.

I was surprised to see the roads were already covered with a light layer of snow. Traffic was moving very slowly and that suited me just fine.

I set the new mailbox against the wall near my door. Ray wasn't home yet.

It was four-thirty, I said to myself. "If there's ever been a time that was right for a cozy fire, it's now."

I carried in a stack of logs, opened the flue and used my handy starter logs. I noticed the busier I kept myself the less nostalgic I felt. I heard Ray's truck pull in the garage.

I opened my front door and smiled. "Hi, would you like to join me for some leftovers after while?"

His face lit up. "I'd love to! Can ya believe this weather? Roads are already gettin' bad. But the trees look so pretty, especially the pines. I think the first snow o' each winter is 'bout one o' the prettiest sights in the whole world. So, what time's dinner?"

"About an hour."

"Okay, I'll see ya then. I got some things I gotta tend to first." And he walked across the lawn to his home.

Later we feasted by the fire on the ample leftovers as we watched the snow continue to fall. I couldn't help but feel cozy.

"I got us two cords o' firewood to be delivered this week. I'll have them stack it right outside the garage door. That should be nice an' handy for both o' us."

I smiled at him for several seconds. "Now, Ray please tell me how that'll be handy for you to have to come clear out to the garage when you want to build a fire? And how much do I owe for my share of the firewood?"

He looked at me intently as he answered. "I figure your share will be about twenty dollars. I still got me a good sized stack outside my back door left over from last year. Besides, maybe ya need to take another look at my house; it's pretty darn close to this apartment an' garage so it would be no big deal to haul wood in from out here if I needed to."

"Well, I'd like to have the name and phone number of this wood cutter who's selling firewood at twenty dollars a cord. I think I'll be able to get him lots of business. And he stacks it too? What a deal!"

Ray squirmed. "Damn it, woman, I ain't givin' ya his name, that's my price for ya. It ain't his regular price an' ya know it. He owed me some favors."

I stared at the fire. "Ray, I appreciate everything you've done for me. But you don't have to worry, I'm okay, and I can certainly pay my own way."

"Yur the most stubborn woman I ever met. I'd really like to know what made ya the way ya are...but I doubt I ever will. I'm jes darn glad we're friends an' yur livin' here." He covered my wrinkled hand with his own weathered hand...what a pair we made.

I smiled. "Oh, I almost forgot to tell you, Joyce called and invited us for lunch tomorrow. Will you be available? She's going to give me a few dishes and pans. Oh, and I have yours packed in the box on the kitchen table. She said we could play a few games of cards in the afternoon. I told her I'd call her back tonight after I talked to you."

"Dorothy, ya can keep those things in the box. I have plenty. An' sure, it sounds like a good time if we play cards with Joyce and Harry."

"I better give her a call before I forget..."

"Dorothy, there's something I've gotta tell ya. I got a call this evenin' before I came over here. My boy, Billy, is comin' home for awhile."

"Ray, that's wonderful news, you must be excited! When will he arrive?"

Ray stared at the fire. His gloomy expression made him look weary and old.

I put another log on the fire and stoked the embers.

Finally, Ray said in a low flat voice. "I stopped feelin' excited about Billy a long time ago. Dreaded anticipation would more accurately describe my feelins'. Sophie never gave up on him; ah, maybe I still hold a glimmer o' hope for him jes' cause he's my boy. But Billy sure as hell ain't given me no reason to expect better o' him."

"Is there anything I can do to help, Ray?"

He answered softly. "Jes don't hold anything he says or does agins' me. I don't know when he'll come. Could be any time within the next month, but then he may not show up at all. Billy marches to the beat o' his own drum, always has."

We played a few games of cards while listening to the radio. I beat

Ray at every hand. It was obvious his mind was not on the game. Finally he stood. "I think I'll head home. See ya in the mornin'."

If there was ever a time someone needed a hug, it was that moment. I stood and walked to the door with him. I reached up and held his face in my hands. "Ray, it'll be okay. You get some rest now, my friend."

He embraced me as a drowning man might grab hold of a life preserver. "I hope so...good night, Miss Dorothy."

I noticed the flowers the Hewitt's had sent, suddenly looked very gloomy. I thought it ironic that the flowers' wilt matched my own underlying sadness. I double checked to make sure my doors were locked and closed the blinds and draperies. I felt like this was as good a time as any to check my cash fund. I pulled out envelopes and wrote the months on them for the next eighteen months; then, I put the monthly rent in each one and carefully folded them shut. I kept out next month's rent and placed the rest inside an old black zippered bank deposit bag. I went into my bedroom and pushed the mattress off the bed and on its side against the wall. Then I slid the box springs up against the mattress. I used my new craft scissors, glue gun and sticky Velcro to make a safe hole on the under side of the box springs to slip my rent bag deposit into. I also slipped an extra twenty thousand dollars into a separate envelope and placed it inside the worn deposit bag. Then I carefully slid the box springs onto the frame, followed by the bed skirt and mattress. I was determined to not use any banking services. I didn't want my identity to be scrutinized.

After fixing the bed for sleeping, I decided to put the photograph in the new frame and to place ten thousand dollars behind the photo. I thought it was a good and somewhat handier savings place than under the box springs. And I still had five thousand dollars as well as the diamonds in the lining of my purse. Yes, I was okay for now. But if I got sick...well, I had better stay healthy.

I sat down to relax with my book, but instead of reading the words, I kept seeing the grainy newspaper photo of Andrea and Alexander. Oh what a tangled web I'd woven...I wrote a short note and folded it before I put it inside the zipped pocket inside my purse. The note stated:

"In the event of my death, please send this purse and all its contents to, 'Mrs. Andrea Silvis, 358 Jackson Ave., Scottsbluff, Nebraska.' Also, she is to inherit any assets accumulated by Dorothy Myers. Thank you.' Dorothy Myers."

Somehow that gesture of closure made me feel a bit better. I thought; this is not how I ever dreamed I'd live out my golden years. Hiding from my own children...My word! I'd have never believed it.

And I wiped away a few stray tears with the sleeve of my sweater.

CHAPTER SEVEN

Acceptance

ANDREA AND ALEXANDER

A NDREA HELD HER HANDS over her ears to block out the annoying sound of the phone. Still it continued to ring, as if the caller knew she'd break down and answer if it rang persistently. And the caller was right.

There was nothing perky in her sluggish almost slurred, "Hello."

At first Luella didn't recognize Andrea's voice, then she asked, "Andrea, are you all right? You don't sound like yourself. I've been trying to call you for days."

Andrea answered in an uncharacteristically monotone voice. "I'm fine Luella. What do you want?"

"Well, I…huh, Andrea, I want to apologize to you for my wretched behavior when you came to see me. I've been so upset about all this; your mother was my closest friend. I never wanted to lash out at you like I did. You lost your mother and you didn't deserve to be attacked and worse yet by someone you trusted. Please forgive me, dear."

Andrea replied flatly. "Okay, I forgive you; does that make you feel better?"

"Andrea, may I stop by to talk to you face to face?"

Silence.

"Please…Andrea."

In a voice void of emotion, "Okay Luella, when?"

"I'll come whenever it suits you, Andrea. I know how hectic your schedule is."

She answered hesitantly. "I'm home this morning."

"I'll be right over. Thank you, dear, I'll see you in a few minutes." Luella clicked off her phone and with a sense of trepidation put on her coat and left for Andrea's house.

Ten minutes later she rang the door bell, once, twice and finally on the third ring a disheveled Andrea opened the door. Dark circles under red puffy eyes betrayed her usual efforts to portray the affluent volunteer vivacious soccer mom, as she greeted Luella. Andrea gestured with her right arm, and said, "Come in if you must." Then she quickly closed the door as if it would block out the world.

Andrea stared at the floor.

Luella glanced around the once beautifully organized home that had fallen into disarray and spoke softly, as she reached out and cradled the younger woman's face in her hands. "My God, Andie, how long have you been living like this? I'm going to fix us each a cup of tea and then we'll talk."

Silence. Andrea continued to stare at the floor.

A few minutes later, Luella cleared a space on the coffee table for their tea. She spoke in a kind yet firm voice. "What on earth has happened to you? Is there trouble between you and Joel? The children? *Talk* to me, girl!"

Andrea slouched amidst newspapers strewn on the side chair in a detached manner.

Luella moved a pile of old mail and magazines to make room to sit on the sofa. "Andrea, your mother would never have wanted you to mourn her like this. It's not the Hampton way."

Andrea glared at her mother's old friend; she spoke softly with an unfamiliar edge to her voice. "Joel's okay, he works all the time. I don't know if he's even noticed the mess I've become or the house for that matter. Tiffany and Thomas are, well…they're just kids. So what if I've taken some time off for awhile?

"And what about Mother's suicide or did she just get tired of all of us and run away…was that the Hampton way?"

Slowly but steadily her sobs bubbled to the surface; she slowly spoke in a raspy voice. "I miss her so much. I really do. I wish I'd have made more time for her when she was here. I feel like such an idiot. And I can't help hoping against hope that she's still out there somewhere. If I could only look into her eyes and tell her I'm sorry I wasn't a better daughter, I guess I won't truly believe she's dead until they find her body."

Luella sighed as she offered comfort to her best friend's daughter. Part of her wanted to tell Andrea the real story about her mother, but she knew she was duty-bound to honor her promise to Olivia.

"I understand, Andrea, I miss your mother so very much. She was one of a kind. Yes, she surely was. My favorite memory of her is that look of determination and merriment that would overtake her at times. I captured that expression on this photograph I took a few years ago when she was in a quandary..." She pulled it out of her purse to show Andrea.

She held it gently in her hands and her breathing became normal as her tears continued to fall. "It's beautiful. Incredible how you've captured her very essence."

Luella answered, "I want you to keep it, dear."

"Thank you, Luella...I'll frame it and put it right here on the coffee table." Andrea leaned back in the chair and slowly sipped her tea.

"Luella, why were you so angry with me? You threw me a curve ball; I didn't know what to make of it. I only asked you a few questions to clarify some lose ends, trying to make some sense out of Mother's ... presumed death. I never expected the reaction I got from you."

"Andie, I've felt so guilty about lashing out like I did. You didn't deserve it." Luella took a deep breath and carefully continued. "I've always kept a few secrets from Hank. I reckon he's kept a few from me, too, and I'm okay with that. I was so damned drained with Olivia's passing that I lashed out at the one who needed comforting as much or maybe even more than I did."

Andrea shrugged and spoke softly. "Whatever. I hold no spite against you."

Luella leaned back on the sofa as they finished their tea in a comfortable silence.

Finally she said, "You know I'm sure Joel's noticed your slide into despondency. Why don't you go take a relaxing bath and I'll tidy up the kitchen and family room. I think it'll make you feel better."

An hour later the dishwasher was humming softly in the background and the two rooms were closer to their normal state of organization. Andrea walked in with an air of confidence that she'd been sorely missing for the last few weeks. She glanced around admiring the re-established order.

She looked at Luella, tears stinging her eyes, and quietly said, "Thanks, Luella, you're a lifesaver. Could you stay for lunch?"

"I can't because I'm taking you out for lunch. I don't want to see your nice clean kitchen get messy. Besides it'll do you good to get some fresh air and a change of scene."

Andrea looked stricken and stood like a wooden figure. "I...huh, I don't know if I can do that."

Luella put her arm around Andrea's thin shoulders. "Of course you can. Where's the powerhouse committee woman who always called my best friend 'Mother'?"

Andrea continued to hesitate. "But Joel calls me every day around lunch time. He'll worry if I don't answer."

Luella handed Andrea the phone. "So call him and ask him to join us. We can meet him at one of the restaurants downtown near his office."

Luella thought if he's been calling her every day, he must be worried. 'It'll be good to see them together and get a feel for any underlying currents.'

Andrea walked into the family room and returned a few minutes later. Her face was slightly flushed. "Joel said he'd be happy to meet us for lunch. He's making a reservation at the Steak House next to his office for one o'clock."

It was a brisk, sunny, November day. Since they were having a later lunch, they stopped and walked through the park before meeting Joel. Luella observed Andrea carefully. After thirty years of nursing with fifteen of them in psychiatric, it was nearly impossible for her not to.

She knew flying off the handle at her like that hadn't helped matters any. The more Andrea acted like her old self, the more Luella's guilt was allayed. If only Olivia had found some other way to stay free...but she did what she felt had to be done.

Joel was kind and attentive to his wife during lunch, when Andrea went to the ladies room it gave Luella the opportunity she'd been hoping for.

"Joel, how long has this been going on? I called and apologized to Andrea this morning and then insisted on visiting. I feel I owe you an apology, too, for causing Andrea additional pain with my outburst last month. I'm really very sorry about that. When I saw her this morning and your home in such disorder, well, I'm afraid I treated her like I would've one of my own daughters. After apologizing and drinking a cup of tea with her, I told her to take a bath while I tidied up the family room and the kitchen. Then I insisted she come to lunch with me."

Joel spoke quietly. "I've been worried about her. This is the first time I've ever seen her so completely down. But then she never lost her mother before, I didn't know what to do. I've actually picked up the phone to call you, but after the fiasco of her last visit with you, well, I was afraid that might only make things worse."

They watched Andrea start across the restaurant to their table when two well-dressed women greeted her with hugs and small talk.

Joel added. "Thanks for coming today."

"How are the children? And have you been working long hours, Joel?"

He frowned. "The kids are a handful, they always have been and it sure hasn't become any easier with puberty. I'm working about the same as usual. I'm home by six almost every evening. Why do you ask?"

"Something Andrea said this morning about you always working. She hasn't been keeping up with her usual volunteer work, has she?"

He looked sad as he answered. "I don't think she's even bothered to get dressed or take a shower most days for the last month."

Luella nodded. "Well, that answers my next question. She's not been into the office to help out then either. No wonder she thinks you work long hours, if she's just sitting home every day brooding."

"I feel bad for the children...she's been so short fused lately. Sometimes it seems like she almost hates them."

"Listen to me, Joel; you must get her into counseling. She needs help. This has been a very difficult time for her, coming out for lunch today will not fix it."

Andrea sat down smiling, very much like her old self. "Hey, am I interrupting something here? I just ran into Jackie and Pam and they told me what a terrible time they've had without my help. They begged me to start back to my committee meetings, like yesterday! So, what have you two been so deeply absorbed in discussing?"

Joel looked stricken, as if he'd been caught with his hand in the cookie jar.

Luella answered. "I was just about to tell Joel my personal opinion... you two need at least a week away *together alone.* Your choice of destinations. But go. I'm sure Alex could stay at your house for a week with the children. If he needs a little extra help I could pitch in an evening or two. Please don't just think about it. Do it! And in my professional opinion, Andrea, honey, you've been through such a terrible time; I believe you should see a counselor for at least a few weeks to help you come out of the darkness that's trapped you for the last few weeks."

The smile vanished from Andrea's face. "You think I need a shrink!?"

"I think you need to talk out all your anxieties...your mother would never have wanted you to fall into such a funk. You have a husband who loves you and children who need you." Luella reached across the table and she gently caressed Andrea's trembling hands. "Andrea, this afternoon is just a sample of the life you had and is waiting for you to come back to it. Please think about it, there is no shame in getting help when you need it."

Andrea started to calm down. She replied in a controlled tight voice. "Okay...I'll think about it."

Luella smiled, "Good." Then she glanced at her watch. "My land's, I can't believe the time. I'm late for an appointment. Lunch is on me. Please call me anytime, either one of you. And I'll be calling you to find out where you've decided to go for your little escape week." She lightly kissed their cheeks, left a tip on the table and hustled to the register to pay the lunch bill.

Andrea looked at Joel. "And I suppose you think I need therapy, too. Is that what Luella's visit was all about?"

He shrugged. "I had nothing to do with it. She's your mother's friend, you tell me. Do you think counseling could help you? I do think she's onto something about you and me going away together. We've never really had a vacation alone since we've had the children. And I think it'd be good for Alex to spend some real bonding time with them. What about it, Andrea?"

Andrea stared at the table and then looked at him. "Can we afford it?"

He smiled back and nodded affirmatively.

Andrea gave him a smoldering smile. "So, where would you like to go? And when?"

"Andie, the sooner the better. I think we both need a vacation."

Andrea volunteered. "I'll stop by the travel agency and get a few brochures this afternoon. Then I'll call Alex and see how the idea flies with him."

As they were leaving the restaurant Andrea remembered she'd come with Luella. "I can't believe this. She brings me to lunch and then just leaves me. I don't even have my car."

Joel smiled and for the first time in weeks his wife returned affection to him when he gently hugged her. "It's okay. She left you in good hands. Here're the keys to my car. Pick me up at six o'clock and bring the children. We'll all go out to celebrate our new beginning tonight."

Andrea took the keys and kissed his cheek lightly. "Thanks, Joel, I don't know how I got so lucky but I'm glad you're my husband."

Joel stood a little taller when he went back to his office that afternoon. He felt like a heavy burden had miraculously rolled off his shoulder. And he couldn't help hoping this was a sign that their lives would go back to at least a semblance of normality.

Andrea called Alex from her cell phone. Surprisingly his secretary put her right through. "Andrea, thank God! I've left you a ton of messages and you never returned my calls. I was about to call Joel at work to find out what the hell was going on with you. How are you anyway?"

"I feel like I'm just starting to walk out of a deep fog. I've had a rough few weeks but I'm doing a little better today. Luella came over and apologized. We had tea and then she insisted I take a long bath, get dressed. Somehow I'd really slipped into a funk. I was a mess and so was the house. She even cleaned while I was bathing and then she took me out to lunch."

"My God, Andrea that doesn't sound like you. I've never known you to let anything go. Least of all yourself or your home. So... that's why you didn't call me back."

"Don't take it personally Alex, I didn't return calls to anyone. It was like my life was on hold. Anyway, Luella just pushed her way into my home; and I'm glad she did. It feels good to be back among the living. I definitely needed a shove in the right direction."

A stunned Alexander sat at his desk with his head in his hands, the very thought of losing his only sister was more than he could bear. In an uncharacteristically soft voice he said, "I had no idea. Is there anything I can do to help?"

"Well, actually there is one little favor I'd like to ask. Joel joined us for lunch and Luella informed us we need to go away for a week together, just the two of us. Can you imagine? We've never vacationed without Thomas and Tiffany. She insisted we do it. And she suggested we ask you to move into our home and bond with the children as their favorite uncle while we're gone. Would you do that for us Alex?"

Silence.

Finally Alex answered hesitantly and then spoke slowly and carefully. "Whew, I don't know if I could handle the pressures of a whole week. Favorite uncle, huh? I just don't know."

"Luella said she'd help out one or two evenings if you needed her. Please, Alex."

He felt he couldn't refuse her, she'd never ask him to do anything for her and it was obvious she and Joel needed a break. He thought, well they'd be in school during the week and I can easily handle one week.

"Okay, I'll do it; it might even be fun. Everyone needs a change of scene from time to time. Do you know which week you'll be gone?"

Andrea's heart soared with anticipation. "You'll really do it? Oh thank you, Alex, I'm so excited I can hardly stand it. And to think only yesterday I was still slouching around in my pajamas. What a difference a day has made. No, I haven't made reservations yet. I had to find out if you'd be willing to help us with the children first. I'll get back to you with the dates as soon as I have the info. Thanks."

"Hey, Andrea, before you go we've got to talk about Mother's house. The realtor has an interested buyer. This isn't the best time to talk about it, but we've got to do it sometime. I was pretty ticked off at you when you didn't show up that Sunday; I worked sorting through piles of papers for hours and then again the next weekend, but I've barely made a dent. They have outfits that just buy estate households. Is that what you want to do? Maybe you should think about it and talk with Joel. But please get back to me as soon as possible."

"Okay, I'll talk to Joel about it tonight and get back to you tomorrow, Alex."

The travel agent was very helpful. Andrea narrowed the search down to a condo in the Florida Keys and all inclusive resorts in the Bahamas and Hawaii. All three had last minute bargain prices for a departure date only ten days away. Unable to wait till evening she rushed back to Joel's office to share the news with him.

His secretary, Karen, said he was alone but on the phone. Andrea barged in and dropped the brochures and price lists on his desk. Joel quickly ended the phone call as he studied the choices of exotic destinations in front of him. He compared the three brochures and their varying prices. Then he smiled at Andrea, "Which one do you like the best, honey?"

Andrea smiled, "I like the looks of every one of them. You decide. I talked to Alex and he agreed to stay at the house and look after the children."

Alex grinned, "I thought it would be more expensive. These prices are reasonable."

"Did you notice the dates? These are last minute special prices. If we book one of these, we have to leave in ten days. Can we do that?"

Joel nodded and walked to his office door. "I think so. Karen, would you come here for a minute? And please bring my schedule for the next few weeks."

Karen walked in. "Should I close the door?"

"No need for that. Just please check and see how complicated it would be to reschedule all appointments starting on the twentieth through the thirtieth. I'm going to take my wife on a vacation. You'll have a bonus paid vacation that week too."

Karen studied the office planner and sighed. Then, she smiled at Andrea and Joel. "A bonus vacation week is an enticement that makes it all very doable. Enjoy your vacation. You've earned it. Are you taking the children out of school?"

Andrea answered with a relaxed smile. "Can you believe it's our first vacation without children? My brother's going to stay with them."

Andrea and Joel stood gazing at each other across the room like star crossed lovers.

"Well, if that's all then I think I'll get started on this right away. See you later." Karen smiled as she walked out and quietly closed the door behind her.

Karen thought it'd be nice to jump start her fall house cleaning, read a couple books and maybe take a long weekend trip to visit the grandchildren.

Alexander stared out his office window, a few remnant leaves gently tossed about the town square as a reminder that summer and fall were gone and winter would soon be here, the long cold months of winter. He often wished he was a skier but he hated the cold, had always hated winter. He often wondered why he lived here. A good question and the answer was embarrassingly simple, he'd simply never got around to leaving.

Jackie buzzed his intercom, "Your three o'clock is here."

Alexander sighed, "Send him in."

And so the afternoon went on.

Jackie popped into his office at five. "I'm heading out now. See you tomorrow. Good night, Alex...you've been awfully quiet this afternoon. Are you okay?"

"Jackie, I have one question. How do you manage to get your work done and leave on time every day? I mean I'm barely out of here by seven. How do you do it? See, I've promised Andrea I'd stay with her children for a week while she and her husband go on a vacation. I'll need to get out by five, too. I don't know how I'll manage."

"I'll tell you what, starting tomorrow; I'll help you develop more efficient time management. We'll have you out by five any day you want to be. Alex, I huh...well, I always thought you hung around because you didn't have any reason to hurry home. And don't worry; you'll have a ball with your niece and nephew. They must be nearly teenagers by now? Have a nice evening."

Alex waved her off and quietly laughed. "Not quite teens yet, thank

God! Okay, tomorrow you start training me to manage my time. Good night, Jackie."

He realized that girl always knew how to make him feel better. She's a real trooper and he was damn lucky to have managed to keep her with all the departmental changes. Working with her had made him a better person.

He closed his office door, returned to his desk and sat down. Unable to concentrate he turned his chair to the window and watched the first snowflakes of the season bounce gently against the glass.

Alex mulled over his relationship with his mother and wished that she could've seen he was a better person than she ever thought he was. She never actually said so, but he always knew she'd been disappointed in him. He'd never meant for her investments to go bad. Sometimes that's just the way it goes in this business. Maybe he'd never left this town because I hadn't wanted to be away from her... maybe, he really didn't know.

He muttered to himself, "Maybe I should've followed Lori to California. No. We were doomed, it wouldn't have mattered. But maybe I'd have had a better relationship with Cassie if I had. And maybe not. She was always her mother's child more than mine. I just pay their bills."

Several minutes later Alexander turned his chair back to his desk and proceeded to finish some of the accumulated paperwork that his brooding certainly hadn't expedited. Two hours later, forced concentration resulted in a huge stack of filing for Jackie in the morning, a clean desk top and a man ready to learn better time management starting the next morning.

Alex answered his cell phone on the way home. It was Sam Marconi, the realtor. "Hey, Alex, I have a check for one thousand dollars to hold the house. These kids are serious. They'll make your mother's house into a great little home for themselves. They've got a two-year-old and she's expecting another next spring. They're good people."

Alex asked, "Are they offering our asking price?"

Sam howled, "They're moving here from Washington D.C. and they didn't even blink. They think they've found a real bargain."

"Amazing! Do they need any of the furniture?"

Sam answered, "I'll check with them and get back to you tomorrow on that. Will you be talking to your sister? If not, I can give her a call."

"Yes, I'll tell Andrea the good news. Thanks for calling, Sam." But somehow it didn't feel like such good news. When Mother's house is sold, that'll be the end of an era. Now we've really got to move on it. Maybe the new family will want some of the furniture. At least Mother left her car and house for us.

Andrea agreed to meet at their mother's house at five p.m. the next day. Joel would pick the children up and arrive later. They'd each choose something of their grandmother's as a keepsake. Alex would choose something for Cassie.

True to her word, Jackie showed Alexander a few time management tricks that saved him at least ten minutes every hour and he was able to leave his office at ten after five.

He mumbled as he walked to his car. "I think Jackie enjoyed telling me what to do all day. I know I asked for it, but she'd best not forget who's the boss."

As always ambivalent feelings washed over him the minute he pulled into his mother's driveway. Andrea was already waiting in the kitchen with two large steaming boxes of pizza on the table. He embraced his sister.

"It's good to see you. How are you, Andie? Hey, that pizza smells great."

"I'm doing okay, I've been better, but thanks for asking. How're you doing?"

He gave her an affectionate hug. "To borrow your phrase, I've been better."

"Go ahead and have a slice. I put a few bottles of water in the frig too. Joel and the children will be here any minute. So what have you done so far?"

Andrea slumped into a maple kitchen chair and leaned forward, elbows on the table and her head in her hands. She murmured, "I feel overwhelmed and I have no idea where to start."

Alexander patted her shoulders gently. "I could finish clearing out the paperwork in her office, since I've already created havoc during my last two visits in there. You could join me or start in another room. It's up to you, Andie. It's all gotta be done. What did Joel think about selling the contents to an estate agent?"

She answered quietly, "He thinks we should think it over carefully before we sign a sales contract because once we do there'll be no turning back. It just doesn't feel right being here...without Mother."

Alex put his arm around his sister. Somehow she reminded him of a wounded bird. "Don't worry, Andie, together we'll get through this. You'll see."

Joel and the children arrived a few minutes later and attacked the pizzas like a pack of starving wolves. Conversation was subdued as they shared a sense of intrusion even though it was the house Andrea and Alex had grown up in and was legally theirs; every room oozed with the spirit of Olivia.

The adults were surprised by Thomas and Tiffany's serious demeanor as they walked through the rooms of their grandmother's home.

Tiffany said, "It's too hard to decide on just one thing."

Andrea asked, "What are you trying to decide between?"

Tiffany looked at her mother with watery eyes, her voice quivered, "I can't decide, Mommy. I don't understand why Grandma's gone."

Joel and Alex exchanged glances. Alex said, "Hey, Thomas would you help me choose something special for Cassie?"

Thomas and the men headed back downstairs. Andrea put her arm around Tiffany's shoulder, "Let's look in Grandma's bedroom. I bet you'll find something special in there."

Andrea set the jewelry box on the bed and together they carefully looked at the sentimental and costume pieces. Tiffany opened a drawer and found a smaller white bundle with her name on it, "Mommy look! Grandma wrote my name on this." She ripped the tissue paper and found a beautiful string of pearls with a note attached...

"*A string of lovely pearls for my beautiful granddaughter. Love, Grandma*"

Andrea hugged her daughter as their tears flowed freely. They opened the other drawer in the jewelry box and found another small white bundle with Cassie's name on it.

She said, "Tiffany, I'll keep these for you until we go home and I'll give Cassie's package to Alex. You go ahead and look around. You can pick out two or three more things. Take your time, and Honey, you're not limited to just the bedroom."

Awhile later Thomas stood in the living room slowly twirling the globe. "I think I'd like to take this." He picked it up and a piece of paper fell from beneath it. He leaned over to pick it up and shouted, "Mom, Dad, Uncle Alex...Grandma left me a note too...

"I leave my *world* in the very capable hands of my one and only grandson. Love, Grandma"

Even Thomas was moved to tears. Andrea embraced her usually untouchable son.

Alex looked at her and muttered, "This is almost too weird. What next?"

Thomas and Andrea sat on the sofa. He whispered, "How did she know that's the one thing I'd want? I don't understand."

"I guess she knew you better than you realized. Don't forget she taught school for many years and she was good at understanding young people. She loved you, Thomas."

Thomas sighed, "I wish she wasn't gone."

Andrea squeezed his hand, "Me too, if you want, you can pick out a few more of Grandma's things to take home. I better get busy or Alex will be after me with a stick!"

Andrea decided to start with the framed photos in the living room. Joel walked in, "Want some help? Tiffany and Thomas don't want to leave yet."

"I'd appreciate it. Let's start by removing these photos from the frames. We can stack the frames in the corner and decide what to do with them later."

Joel appreciated having something to do, "Your wish is my command. Did you have a chance to book our vacation today?"

Andrea looked at him and smiled, "You bet I did! I pick up the tickets tomorrow. We leave a week from Saturday. Ernest Hemmingway's Florida Keys, here we come!"

As she refocused on the task at hand, she noticed that some of the old photos weren't...old. "Joel, look at these pictures. When they were in the frames they all looked the same. But these glossy ones have to be recent copies."

Andrea felt faint as she looked at Joel. Totally unaware tears were streaming down her cheeks, again. "This puts a whole new spin on Mother's disappearance, I, ah...I want to know what happened to her and why. I just don't get it."

Joel called up the stairs. "Alex, would you come here for a minute please?"

Alex came down the stairs grumbling. "I was in the middle of..." One look at Andrea and Joel and he stopped complaining. "What's going on?"

Andrea was unable to speak, Joel said, "Look carefully at these pictures and tell me what you see Alex."

Alex glanced briefly at the photos. "It's obvious some are new copies. Where did you find these?"

Joel explained, "We were removing the photos from the frames. In the frame they all looked like originals..."

Alex paled as he looked at his despondent sister and her husband. "Are you thinking what I'm thinking?"

Joel slowly spoke. "Maybe it's time we hired a private investigator to make some sense of all this. There are just too many questions without plausible answers...I'll make a few phone calls tomorrow morning."

Alex nodded and asked, "Do you really think a private investigator could find more clues than the police, even after all this time?"

Joel replied. "I do. Maybe the police were a bit hasty when they bought into the suicide set up so readily."

Andrea smiled feebly. "Well, better late than never. Let's hope we can get some answers that make sense. My mind is so convoluted, part of me wants to believe she's gone, but there are just too many unconnected lose ends."

CHAPTER EIGHT

Life Goes On

ANDREA AND ALEXANDER

JOEL CONTRACTED THE HIGHLY recommended private investigation services of J.C. Konwinsky. Every Friday J.C. filed a report with him; so far he'd gathered no more information than the state police. And for this they paid five hundred dollars a week! They knew now that Olivia had bought a car under the name of Alice Smith and driven east. But there'd been no further trace of her since the third day after her disappearance. How does someone just disappear!?

And how long could they continue to pay J.C. the money if he kept running into brickwalls? Joel decided to put it out of his mind till they returned from Florida. After the last couple months, he couldn't think of anything they needed more than a vacation…

Andrea and Joel felt rested and relaxed as they walked, holding hands, on the nearly deserted beach near their hotel in Key West.

As they soaked up the gorgeous red sunset and the gentle ocean breeze, Joel said, "I feel like we've had a taste of heaven this past week, I can't believe this is our last night."

Andrea sighed. "I know what you mean, feels like we just got here…I wish we could stay another week, but reality calls us home. I'm sure Alexander is near his wits end with the children by now."

Joel suddenly stopped and pulled Andrea to him, wrapped his arms around her and spoke in a husky whisper. "Andie, this week has been wonderful. Let's promise to do this again next year and the year after that and every year. I think we owe it to each other and the children. If Alex can't handle the childcare, we'll hire someone to live in for a week."

Andrea looked up at Joel and saw the man she fell in love with and married, not the preoccupied, dutiful, and sometimes boring man she lived with. "Joel, did you ever feel the spark had gone out of our marriage?"

He cupped her face in his hands and gazed into her eyes with an intensity that turned her knees to jelly. "Well, it's a little hard to feel romantic when the kids are fighting, the phone's ringing and I'm in the middle of an important case...there're just too many distractions in everyday life to keep the fire going all the time. Here it's easy, but I've never once doubted my love for you and you know you can always count on me."

Andrea circled his neck with her arms and they kissed with a passion that could've started a wildfire if it hadn't been for the surf splashing around their feet. "Joel, I love you forever."

Meanwhile Alexander was immersed in the role of his life as caregiver uncle. He found himself in awe of his sister's stamina to keep up with this all these years. While he'd always thought she'd been living the easy life. Then there was Mother, she'd done all this and worked full-time as a teacher! He felt drained with the responsibility of two children. But there was an upside: they loved him and they helped fill a void in his life. Their high energy often left him feeling rejuvenated and ready to take on the world.

True to her word, Luella called Monday evening to see if Alex needed help. She agreed to be at the house everyday after school until he arrived home from work. "You're a life saver, thanks, Luella."

"How are they doing? I think this is Andrea and Joel's first vacation without them."

Alex answered slowly. "Well, I don't quite know what to say. I'm most comfortable with Thomas; he's a bright and determined boy. Sometimes Tiffany seems like a creature from outer space. I never know what to expect from her. Her moods seem to fluctuate from one minute to the next."

Luella reassured him. "It's her age. Nothing against you personally, Alexander, her hormones are a bit out of whack. She can't help it and don't forget how close she is to her mother. They've really never been separated before."

Late Monday night, unable to fall asleep, he reasoned. "If Lori hadn't taken off for California like she did and I'd had regular contact with Cassie, well, I might've been better prepared for this. But all and all, I think I'm doing a little better than fair."

Tuesday night after a door slamming tantrum from Tiffany, he'd felt so overwhelmed he'd been attempted to call Andrea and tell her, "Cut your vacation short and get back here to take care of your own kids!"

But he bit the bullet and refused to give into the urge to call his sister.

Alexander enjoyed leaving work on time. As he left the office last Friday with his secretary, he said, "Thanks for showing me how to get out of work on time. It's amazing what a person can accomplish in an evening with an extra couple hours away from work everyday."

"Alex, I'd always figured you stayed late because you didn't have anything better to do with your time. And I'm pretty sure I was right. You're looking younger and more relaxed this week. Taking care of your niece and nephew has been good for you. And I'll bet they've had fun with you too. What you need is a good woman and a family of your own."

He felt his face blush. "What makes you so sure I'm having fun?"

"Good grief Alex, it doesn't take a rocket scientist to read your face! Once I got to know you a bit, your facial expressions were as easy to read as the newspaper."

"Maybe I should just look for a secretary who's not so damn smart!"

She retorted, "Nothing like shooting yourself in the foot!"

"Jackie, you're a wicked woman! Have yourself a good weekend, I'll see you Monday."

She flashed him a smug smile. "You, too, Uncle Alex."

He stopped on the way home to buy a few groceries for the week end and picked up a video to watch with the children. A frantic Luella met him in the driveway. "I've gotta go. Hank's had a heart attack.

He's in the ER."

She practically jumped into her car.

"Luella, let me drive you to the hospital."

She shook her head. "I'm okay, the E.R. called no more than ten minutes ago. I'll let you know if I need you."

Alex couldn't help noticing her quivering hands and the tears welling up in her eyes. As she drove off, he reflected on how Luella and Hank have been like an aunt and uncle to Andrea and him as long as he could remember. She and Mother were always a team and old Hank just kind of waited on the outside for a chance to be included. Always reminded me of a stray dog who was happy to get whatever table scraps Luella would throw his way. He'd never understood their relationship, but the look on her face today, you never really know. And Mother; now there's a perfect example of not knowing.

Suddenly Thomas came running out the back door grinning like a cheshire cat. "Uncle Alex, you're home! Where's Luella? Tiffany said she's gonna kill me!"

Alex grabbed the boy's shirt as he tried to run by. "Why would your sister want to kill you? What did…"

Just then Tiffany all but flew through the back door carrying a baseball bat, her face red and wet from angry tears. "Uncle Alex! Please let me have him alone for just five minutes. I hate him! I really hate that moron."

Alex stifled a smile as he remembered Jackie's comments only one hour earlier. He silently wondered how in God's name could this mediation/childcare make anyone look younger and more relaxed.

Tiffany came charging toward Alex and Thomas, ready to swing the bat. Alex shouted, "Tiffany, drop the bat. Drop it now!"

She allowed the bat to slip slowly thorough her fingers and it bounced off his foot. "My God! Tiffany, what's come over you?"

Sobbing, she looked at Thomas and then Alex. "Ask Thomas, just ask him!" She turned and ran back inside the house.

Alex put his hands on Thomas's shoulders and turned him to face him. "Okay, young man, what did you do to your sister this time?"

Thomas smirked, while trying to look serious. "Aw come on, Uncle Alex, you know how she is."

Alex said, "Help me carry these groceries inside and then do not leave the kitchen. You and I are going to have a talk."

The phone was ringing as they walked into the kitchen. Alex was pleasantly surprised to hear Andrea's voice, though the connection was very scratchy. "Hello Alex, how's it going?"

"Hey, how's it going yourself? We're okay here, having a good week. Everyone's doing okay. Nothing to worry about. So, when will you be home?"

"That's why I called. A tropical storm hit this morning and all flights are cancelled for at least two days, till they can clear the airport and repair power lines."

Alex sighed, "Andrea, this connection stinks…did I hear you say you're delayed for at least two more days?"

She shouted, "Yes, that's right, sorry!"

"Be safe, we'll see you when you get home."

"May I say hello to the children?"

"Sorry, but it's not a good time, I'll tell them you called." He hung up the phone and mumbled, "Two more days!"

"Uncle Alex, why wouldn't you let me talk to Mom?"

"Because you and I are going to have a man-to-man talk and it wasn't the right time to talk to your mother. You haven't earned the right. She's on a badly needed vacation and she doesn't need to hear about your nastiness when she's too far away to do anything about it. Hell, if she and your Dad heard about you and Tiffany's latest fiasco, they might decide to not even bother coming home."

That comment caught Thomas's attention and the smirk vanished.

"Now I want to hear what happened before I arrived today. Only the truth. No excuses."

Thomas bit his lip. He looked at the floor and then at his uncle. "I sent an email to Sean Mathews from Tiffany's computer. She thinks he's a hottie. So I just told him what I've heard her telling her girlfriends on the phone."

Alex remembered doing something very much the same to Andrea when they were in their early teens. Only Andrea hadn't taken after him with a baseball bat!

Alex maintained a somber air. "Thomas, I'm very disappointed in you. Do you realize statistically the person you will have the longest relationship with in life is your sister? The odds are you'll both outlive your parents, and marriages often don't last a lifetime. Just look at me! Besides, you've already got at least a twenty year jump on sibling relationships before marriage. What I'm trying to say is you're old enough to try a little kindness with your sister. And, you owe her a sincere apology."

Thomas sat stone-faced, "I really didn't mean to hurt her. I was only teasing and having a little fun."

Alex looked at his nephew sternly and tossed him a small tablet. "I want you to put these groceries away and set the table for dinner. I'm going upstairs to talk to Tiffany. After you've finished your chores, use this paper to write why you pulled that stunt on our sister and an apology. No television, no phone calls and no computer. Got it?"

He muttered, "Yes, sir."

Alex quickly set the oven and put in three Stouffers' frozen dinners.

Then he hurried up the stairs and knocked on his niece's bedroom door. "Tiffany, I want to talk to you. Please open the door."

Through muffled sobs he heard, "Go away."

"Please, unlock the door. Tiffany, your brother played an atrocious trick on you and you have every right to be upset. I want to talk to you before dinner."

He waited patiently for a minute. No response. Then he knocked on the door again. In a loud and stern voice he repeated, "Tiffany, open the door now!"

A minute later a red-faced Tiffany, with puffy eyes, opened the bedroom door.

Alex walked in. "Thank you for opening the door, Tiff." He moved a few books and stuffed animals before sitting on the window seat.

He handed his niece a box of tissues. "Here, use this to wipe your eyes and blow your nose. You've cried enough."

She glared at her uncle, wiped her eyes and took a few deep breaths, and folded her arms. "So what do you want to talk about?"

"Why don't we start with what's got you so angry?"

"It's not fair! You don't know what it's like to have to live with such a moron. How am I ever going to face the kids at school when Sean tells all the other kids that I sent him an email like that? Thomas has ruined my life!"

Alex reasoned, "I'll bet your life won't be completely ruined by this. Besides if this Sean is such a great guy, why would he even mention your email to the other kids?"

"Uncle Alex, I didn't send the email! You don't understand."

"I understand more than you realize. Sit down, Tiffany. Now tell me what you were planning to do with the baseball bat once you caught up with your brother. You were carrying it like a weapon. Using it as a club could be a very dangerous habit to get into. Have you ever done anything like that before?"

She slumped down on the edge of her bed, facing her uncle. "It's not a big deal. I didn't hit him, did I?"

"Good grief, Tiffany. And what if I hadn't been there, what would you have done? When would you have stopped?"

She stared at the floor and mumbled. "I don't know. He's pretty fast; he would've probably got away."

"Tiffany, probably got away? My God what kind of answer is that?" Then he explained the responsibility of lifetime sibling relationships...

He added, "Now I want you to splash some cold water on your face, comb your hair and come down for dinner. Okay?"

She muttered, "Okay, Uncle Alex."

Dinner was subdued, but civil. After dessert Alex asked Thomas to read his apology and rationale.

Thomas glared at him.

Alex held his ground. "Read."

Thomas read. "To Whom it May Concern: This is my official apology to my sister, Tiffany Marie O'Donnell. I didn't know you'd get so mad. I only emailed Sean because I thought it'd be funny. And it was, until you tried to kill me with the ball bat and then Uncle Alex getting so mad at me. I wish you didn't feel sad so often. I'm sorry, Tiffany. You're my only sister and I'd like us to be friends.

Yours Truly, Thomas J. O'Donnell."

Thomas was teary eyed by the time he finished reading.

Alex looked at Tiffany; she sat staring at the floor. "Well, Tiffany, what do you have to say to your brother?"

She mumbled, "I think you made him write that apology, Uncle

Alex. I don't think he means what he said."

Alex waited a few minutes and finally he broke the silence. "Tiffany, look at your brother. Is he a good actor or does he look like he means what he said?"

Tiffany reluctantly looked at her brother.

"Thomas, did I tell you what to write?"

He spoke hesitantly, "No, sir, you told me to write why, and once I started thinking it over I realized I did a really dumb thing, and I don't want my sister to hate me forever."

After a few minutes of silence, Tiffany said in a taut voice, "I don't hate you, Thomas. You're my brother. And I didn't really want to kill you, I was just so mad and the ball bat was leaning against the corner, I just grabbed it. I'm glad Uncle Alex was here. Mom and Dad would have freaked."

Tiffany stood up and slowly walked to Alex and gave him a peck on the cheek. "Thanks, Uncle Alex."

Alex put his left arm around Tiffany, reached out with his right arm and said, "Come here, Thomas, group hug time." To his pleasant surprise, they each hugged him back. Alex was relieved to feel a sense of harmony slowly replace the escalating tension.

Alex took a deep breath and blinked back his tears as he remembered being a child with Andrea and the group hugs his mother had always insisted on when things had gone sour for them.

They approved of the video he'd brought home and agreed to watch it at eight o'clock. After a very competitive game of 'Sorry', Alex made popcorn and they enjoyed watching the movie.

Luella called Saturday afternoon. "Alex, it looks like Hank's going to make it this time, but we've all been put on alert. It was touch 'n go all night in I.C.U. He's living on borrowed time now."

"Glad to hear Hank's going to make it. You sound exhausted. Are you alone there? Do you need me to give you a ride home?"

"Thanks for offering but Hannah's been with me all night and Larry arrived a couple hours ago. Besides I'm staying right here beside my man."

"If there's anything I can do, please let me know, and keep us posted on how Hank's doing. I really appreciate your help with the kids this week. Thanks for calling Luella."

"They were no trouble at all. They're good kids. Bye now."

Andrea and Joel arrived home tanned and tired late Tuesday evening. After welcome home hugs and greetings, Alex brought his luggage downstairs.

Tiffany and Thomas had grown very comfortable with Uncle Alex.

Tiffany stammered, "Noo, please don't go!"

Thomas chimed in. "Hey, what's your hurry?" He turned to his parents, "Uncle Alex doesn't have to go yet, does he? Dad, tell him we've got room for him, please."

Andrea and Joel flashed questioning glances at each other. Joel spoke first. "Well, it sounds like you three had an excellent week. Of course, we can always make room for Alex, but I'm sure he misses his own place."

Alex smiled. "Okay, you two, how about a goodbye group hug for Uncle Alex? I had a great week and I accept the offer of a home away from home. But now, I must get to my place and get organized for another week of work. We'll see each other more often. I promise."

Thomas hugged him hard. "I'm really going to miss you!"

Tiffany echoed, "Me, too."

Watching the group hug flooded Andrea with childhood memories.

Alex picked up his luggage, turned to his sister. "So Florida was good for you?"

She absently nodded to Alex with a puzzled expression. "Definitely."

"If you ever want to get away again, I'd be happy to stay with my niece and nephew. I'll talk to you tomorrow. Get some rest."

"Thanks for everything, Alex. Good night."

Alex turned to face his sister and Joel as he was about to walk out the door, and smiled. "It was my pleasure. Good night."

Joel closed the door.

Thomas stood with his arms folded leaning against the foyer wall. "So you liked the Florida Keys? Did you feel like you were on your honeymoon again?"

Tiffany perched herself on the stairs about five steps from the bottom. "What did you do? Did you ever think of us? Did you miss us?"

Andrea smiled and sat down beside Tiffany and put her arm around her daughter's shoulder. "Yes, we loved Key West and sometimes it did feel like we were on our honeymoon again, except that we kept missing you both so much. Why don't we tell you about the trip tomorrow? It's late now and we all need our sleep."

Thomas and Tiffany hugged their parents. "Welcome home and good night."

Andrea looked at Joel and whispered. "Well, what do you think of that?"

He pulled her closed to him and smiled. "It's like a miracle! We've been home thirty minutes and they didn't argue once. Remarkable!"

Andrea whispered back. "There's always tomorrow. Come on, let's go to bed. I'm not unpacking tonight."

Tiffany and Thomas were up and ready for school the next day without being awakened by Andrea. They did not bicker, not even once. Andrea cooked eggs and bacon, Joel sat down at the table with his family. "I don't know when we've all sat down to breakfast together on a school morning. But I like it. I want you both to have great days in school today, you hear me?"

Tiffany nodded and Thomas answered in unison, "Yes, Sir!"

Later that morning, Alex called his sister. "How's it feel to be back home?"

"Great, we had a wonderful time. Its paradise when the sun shines, but the last two days of tropical storms made it easier to leave. Now pray tell, what kind of a magical spell did you weave on our children? They've not bickered once since we've been home!"

"No magic. I just told them about you and me. That's all."

Andrea asked out of curiosity. "What about you and me?"

"You know the lifetime relationship thing and…friendship. Maybe they're starting to see the light. I don't know."

Stunned, Andrea was without words.

"Andrea, are you still there?"

"Yes, I, huh…I just don't know what to say."

"I know you're probably thinking this just seems a little out of character for me. I'm glad Tiffany and Thomas learned from me, because I learned a lot from them too. They reminded me of us in many of their interactions and some of what I saw, I didn't like being reminded of. We had a couple heart-to-hearts. They're good kids. I really like them."

"Well, whatever happened, thanks. Why don't you come over for dinner tomorrow night? You need to make yourself more of a regular fixture around here.

"Joel will be able to give us the most recent update from J.C., let's hope he's found a solid lead about mother by now."

"Sounds good to me. What time?"

"How about six o'clock?"

"See you then…oh, I almost forgot to tell you about Luella. Hank had a heart attack Friday afternoon and he's still in the hospital. Hannah and Larry are helping her. It looks like he's going to make it for now anyway.

"Well, I must get back to work. See you tomorrow evening."

CHAPTER NINE

Billy the Kid

OLIVIA

CHRISTMAS WAS FAST APPROACHING, my first Christmas away from my family. I couldn't help feeling like a fish out of water. I decorated the apartment with a four-foot fiber-optic tree, a Holy Crèche and two cheerful wreaths, one on the inside and one on the outside of my door. Compared to how I had exhausted myself decorating my home every other Christmas, it was like I didn't even decorate.

Ray's son Billy hadn't shown up yet, though every couple weeks Ray received another message from him saying, 'I'll be home soon.' Ray's not been the same since Billy's been promising, or should I say threatening to come home.

Despite Ray's recent gloomy mood, he smiled. "Dorothy, looks and feels like Christmas in here. I always used to like Christmas. Sophie did, too. But, I ain't liked Christmas since she's been gone. I have a feelin' this year's gonna' be different."

Irene invited me to lunch and then to be her guest at the Ladies of the Library Holiday Tea. It was only one week till Christmas; a sunny, brisk winter day and the town was decked out in all its holiday splendor. I met her at a charming café on a side street that I'd never even noticed before.

As soon as I walked in, she waved and motioned me to her table. "Thanks for meeting me for lunch and the tea this afternoon. It'll put us in the spirit of the season. I've had such good intentions of calling you...but, on that accord, I guess you can call me a procrastination queen! Are you ready for your first Christmas in Harmonyville?"

I answered, "No need to apologize, I understand how quickly the days can fly by. I was happy you invited me today. I guess I'm about as ready for Christmas as I'm going to be. It will be a simple, quiet one this year. Are you ready, Irene?"

She grinned smugly. "I just go to the bank and get a stack of their gift envelopes and put money in them. We put up a small tree and hang a wreath on the door and we're ready for Christmas. Our children host the holiday parties now. There are certain advantages to growing older!"

Irene waved the waitress away, her elbows on the table and her chin rested on her hands, she asked me in her usual forthright manner. "Dorothy, I hope you don't mind my asking, but will this be much different from your last Christmas?"

I could feel my stress level rise as I tried to sound nonchalant. "Well, in some ways, yes, and in others not really. I've been a widow for eighteen years. Ray is the first male friend I've had in all this time, so that's quite a change. My Christmases have been quiet for a long time."

Irene said with more compassion than I'd have thought possible, "Well...I see. I had no idea. I'm glad you and Ray have found each other. After all, life is for the living. How is our good friend Ray doing? Walter said he's been keeping himself pretty scarce lately."

"I don't know how to answer that. He remains very friendly and pleasant with me, but he's been so preoccupied. He's says he has to do all these busy tasks getting everything ready for winter."

Irene interrupted me, "Wait a minute, has Billy been calling or sending letters? This is exactly what Ray's done for more than twenty years, every time Billy says he's coming home."

I was impressed. Irene really did know Ray. I nodded, "Yes, he has. For the past several weeks, Billy's been leaving messages or sending letters saying he'll be home in a couple days. Now it looks like he must be planning on coming home for Christmas. Ray refuses to talk about it."

Irene said with an uncharacteristic harshness, "That's how Billy affects his father. Used to break poor Sophie's heart. Bad enough that

Billy is what he is, but when Ray puts up all those walls round him, I think the poison of their bad feelings slowly killed our Sophie."

I couldn't help asking. "Just what is the problem with Billy? All Ray will say is 'don't hold anything against me for the way my son may talk or behave'."

Irene sighed. "Maybe we should order our lunch first."

We hastily ordered two turkey club sandwiches with two hot herbal teas.

Irene looked at me intensely. "I feel like I know you, but of course I don't. I've lived here all my life and everyone in town knows me like an open book, as I do them. You, Dorothy, you're a mystery to me. How did you end up in Harmonyville and involved with our Ray?"

I gave her my calmest friendly smile, trying desperately to cover my resentment for the inquisition. "Irene, there's nothing to tell. I haven't exactly had an exciting life. I taught school for forty-five years. I've been a widow for eighteen years. I wanted to find a peaceful place to live out the rest of my days. Anything else is just unnecessary details." I maintained eye contact and tried to show her I was confident and calm.

Irene almost huffed as she smiled, though her eyes indicated a simmering anger. "Well, I guess Ray won the jackpot. Can't say he didn't deserve a turn of good luck. To understand about Billy we've got to go back about fifteen years before he was born. Sophie and Ray married young. They decided not to have children for a few years. They both worked and saved money to buy their first home. Then seven years later they had beautiful little Sarah. She was an enchanting child. Everyone loved her. She came down with leukemia when she was four and died a year later. It nearly destroyed Sophie and Ray. I wondered at the time if they'd ever get over it. Then Sophie went through three midterm miscarriages over the next six years. Finally ten years after Sarah died, they had Billy. They were so thrilled." Irene dabbed her eyes as they filled with tears.

The waitress served our lunches.

"That's terrible…I…I feel like crying, too. Thank you for telling me. Ray has never mentioned any of this to me."

Irene said, "I'm not surprised."

I tried to lighten up the conversation. "This is a delicious sandwich and such a charming little café. I'd never even noticed it before."

"Yes, I like to lunch here occasionally and you can always count on the food being exceptionally good. The owner is a high school friend of our daughter and she's a grandmother now. It's enough to make me feel like I might be getting old!"

"I was surprised by the sign on the door. They close at three p.m."

"Yes, Julie doesn't like to work evenings. This is strictly a breakfast and lunch café. And it's worked well for her for nearly twenty years now."

Irene looked at her watch. "I think I have just about enough time to tell you about Billy before we leave for the Holiday Tea."

I said, "They must've been very happy when they finally had another baby."

"Oh, indeed they were. By then Ray was thirty-nine and Sophie was thirty-seven. In those days anything over thirty five was considered high risk for having children. But, they had a bouncing, healthy baby boy. You never saw two people happier than they were when Billy was born. He was a restless cranky baby and near exhausted his mother. In retrospect, it was obvious even then that he and his Daddy mixed like oil and water. The closer Ray came to him, the harder he'd cry."

"Then as he grew it was one problem after another. He fought with other children in school; he lied, he cheated and he'd been accused of stealing ever since he started first grade. By the time he started junior high school, he smoked and even went home drunk a few times. He consistently mixed with the wrong crowd."

"Sophie and Ray tried everything in their power to get him on the right track. Yet they covered and paid restitution without consequence for Billy. They took him to church every week and sent him to church camp every summer until he was expelled with a detailed letter explaining why under no circumstance would he be permitted to return to camp, ever!"

I stared into my cup of tea. I wasn't sure if I wanted to hear anymore of this, but I knew there was no easy escape. Besides, part of me really did want to hear the rest of the story. I couldn't help remembering a few students I'd had during my teaching career whose profile she could've been describing. I searched my heart and silently prayed that

I had been kind to their parents.

Irene continued, "Poor Sophie and Ray. Billy made their lives a living hell while he was in high school. He barely graduated but decided he wanted to go to college anyway. So, of course he did. They found a small junior college in Ohio that accepted him on a probationary status. That lasted one semester. By then he was into drugs too. He drifted through the southern states for a couple years, picked up construction work when he needed money, worked in sales; he had a way with words and charm that few have. Billy enlisted in the army but that didn't last even a year till they booted him out. Even worked a season at Disney in Orlando."

The waitress brought the check to the table and asked if we needed anything else. We answered in unison, "No, thank you."

Engrossed, I leaned forward, "Please, tell me the rest of the story."

"He'd pop into visit his folks from time to time. He brought home a couple different girls to meet his parents. But I never heard that he married. Billy stayed once for about a year; got a job and Sophie was thrilled. Ray built the apartment onto the garage and for awhile it seemed like Billy was done sowing his wild oats. Then Sophie got sick. Billy's drinking escalated and he started dealing drugs from the apartment. Ray tried to talk to him."

Irene took a sip of her tea and shook her head. "Finally, the state police surrounded the garage and he was arrested, but not without a loud belligerent scene with Billy resisting arrest. The police had to rough him up. Ray didn't want Sophie to know about it. But all those sirens and bright lights... even with the draperies closed and the music blaring, she knew something was going on. She managed to get out of bed and hobble to the window to watch in horror as her only child was taken into custody. Ray found her on the floor by the window; the top of her nightgown was soaked by her tears before she'd collapsed."

Irene's eyes were teary as she continued. "Billy was sent to the State Penitentiary for six years. Sophie suffered a severe stoke three months later. It seemed she lost the will to live the day they took her boy away. She existed in the nursing home until she mercifully died five years ago. Ray spent every afternoon with her in the home. Billy was released two years early for good behavior. Ray never mentions any of this to his old friends. I think parenthood has puzzled him ever since that boy was born. His little Sarah had been the complete opposite of Billy in every way. Ray's a good man. But beware of his son. He has all the charm of a snake oil salesman."

"Thanks for telling me about Ray's family. It's a sad story. I really don't know what else to say."

Irene stood. "Nothing else needs to be said. Just remember, you've been warned."

The Holiday Tea was delightful. Joyce came in and rescued me from Irene, which I think was a relief for both of us. Joyce's natural enthusiasm for life oozed from her soul as she hugged me. "Merry Christmas, Dorothy, come let me introduce you to a few old friends. Everyone's dying to meet Ray's mystery lady!"

I couldn't help smiling as I protested. "I'm hardly a mystery lady and Merry Christmas to you!"

Joyce put her arm around my shoulder. "Before I forget, I have to ask you to talk to Ray for us. We want you both to come to our house Christmas Eve for dinner at six and then go to special service at church at eleven. Be sure to take a nap that afternoon because it becomes a very late night. But it's such a beautiful way to celebrate our Savior's birthday. Ray's always refused to join us, but I think he might come this year because of you. We celebrate with a few friends on the twenty-fourth and family on the twenty-fifth. We consider you and Ray to be friends *and* family."

Joyce was a naturally gregarious person, she loved people and everyone seemed to brighten up in her presence. During the Christmas caroling segment of the Tea, she sang off key with such gusto that I couldn't help feeling light-hearted and full of the holiday spirit.

I picked up a few groceries before driving back to the apartment. Ray was tinkering in the garage; I invited him for hot chocolate. He started the fire while I made the hot drinks.

"How was your day, Ray?"

"Not bad at all. Got lots o' my winterin' work done up an' I'd say I'm jes in the nick o' time with this weather. So how was your tea party, Miss Dorothy?"

"I had an interesting lunch with Irene at the cafe and a delightful

time at the Holiday Tea with Joyce. She is like a breath of fresh air.
Harry is a lucky man. She invited us to a Christmas Eve Dinner at
their home and then later in the evening to attend the Christmas Eve
service at their church. I think it sounds like a nice idea. Will you go
with me, Ray?"

"I don' know about Christmas Eve. Glad ya had yourself a good
time today. Well, I got ya a good fire goin'." He started toward the
door.

"Ray, where are you going? Your hot chocolate's ready."

He pulled out a chair and sat down at the table, staring at the floor.
"Mercy, I forgot ya were fixin' me somthin'."

I turned on the tree lights and the lamp by the sofa. The room
looked especially nice with the inviting glow from the fireplace. I
carried a tray with our cups of hot chocolate to the coffee table.
"Come on over here and enjoy the warmth of the fire as we drink."

I patted the sofa for him to have a seat beside me.

He reluctantly shuffled over.

I noticed his eyes were teary. "Ray, please tell me what's hanging
so heavy on your mind."

He stared at the fire. I sipped my hot chocolate. "Okay, you sit there
and think about talking to me and I'll put our dinner in the oven. I'll
be back in a few minutes. Remember, I'm living here because we're
friends. And friends share each others concerns."

I turned on the radio and listened to NPR news as I fixed our
dinner. Ray continued to stare at the fire, but he also sipped his hot
chocolate. I reasoned that at least it was a sign of life.

I put a scalloped ham and potato casserole in the oven, set the
timer and put the plates and silverware on the table for dinner. I
glanced out the window, noticed it was still snowing and put another
log on the fire.

I sat down beside him and decided to enjoy the fire and wait until
he was ready to talk. I must've dozed off. The next thing I knew Ray
was patting my arm. "Sophie, the oven timer's ringin'."

"Thanks, Ray. Sorry, I didn't mean to fall asleep."

He stood up and looked at the kitchen table, "That's okay. Sophie,
by the look o' your table, ya mus' be spectin' someone for dinner."

I removed the casserole from the oven and opened a can of corn for our dinner. "Of course, I'm expecting you to stay and eat with me, Ray. Do you realize you just called me Sophie...twice?"

"I'm sorry, Miss Dorothy. I ain' been any decent company for weeks now. I'm real sorry about that."

I walked over and put my arms around him and laid my head against his chest. "That's quite all right, Ray. I've heard so many wonderful things about Sophie that I'll take it as a compliment. Though I'd prefer it if you'd call *me* Dorothy."

He embraced me tenderly and it made me hope that the man I'd met a few short months ago would be back in time for dinner. I'd been missing the Ray I met in the diner. And I had to give him credit for trying during that dinner.

While I loaded the dishwasher he added another log to the fire. We sat down on the sofa and he held my hand. It was a sweet comfortable time together. I said, "Do you believe destiny brought us together, Ray?"

He sighed and turned to look at me and brought my hand to his lips and kissed it. "My dear Dorothy, if it wasn't destiny then what could it be? I'm sorry I've been so moody lately."

I was still swooning from his kiss on my hand that I almost didn't notice his apology. But I didn't want to lose the chance for a truly open talk about his life.

"Ray, I wish you'd tell me what's been bothering you. It's Billy, isn't it? Irene told me about him and little Sarah over lunch today. I'm so sorry you lost your daughter and that you've had such difficulties with Billy over the years. Will he be home for Christmas?"

Ray let go of my hand as if it were a hot coal; leaned forward with his elbows on his knees and his fists under his chin starring into the fire.

I thought way to go, Juliet! I seemed to have a knack for pouring cold water on what was developing into cozy moments with my Romeo.

After several minutes of silence, it felt like an hour to me...Ray muttered. "My Sarah was an angel; we never really got over losin' that little girl. Billy called today. He cried. A grown man an' he cried to his father. Says he's been delayed cause he had some trouble an' wound up in some small town jail out in Michigan. He thinks they'll release him tomorrow or the next day an' buy him a one-way bus ticket to Pittsburgh. I tol' him I'd pick him up at the bus station. It is Christmas an' I'm the boy's father."

"That must've been a heart wrenching conversation for both of you. Has he ever cried before when he's called?"

Ray shook his head and whispered, "Never."

"Maybe it's an indication that he's ready to turn over a new leaf."

"Maybe. But I learned a long time ago not to get my hopes up when it comes to my boy."

"No wonder you've been so preoccupied. If there's anything I can do? Remember I'm here for you, Ray."

He sighed and leaned back, resting his head on the back of the sofa with his eyes closed. He reached for my hand and gently squeezed it. "Thank you, Miss Dorothy. An' in my heart I do hope you're right... maybe this time things will be different."

Two days later Ray had another call from Billy. He said he was due at the Pittsburgh Bus Terminal in four hours. Ray stopped in to tell me he was leaving and it'd likely be late when they returned. I was glad the weather forecast was clear.

The following morning Ray came over for a cup of coffee. "Billy's sleepin' late. I left him a note on the kitchen table. Tol' him I'd be over here."

I put a fresh pot of coffee on. "So how is he, Ray? Did you have a chance to talk driving home?"

"Nothin' special. He was tired an' nervous. I told him I'd rented out the garage apartment an' he wasn't too keen on that. I says to him, 'how do ya expect to run my life when you're never aroun', an' besides you're not doin' so hot runnin' your own from the looks o' things.'"

I shook my head, "Oh...Ray, couldn't that have waited? How long has it been since he's been home?"

He answered quietly. "This is the first time since his Mama's funeral five years ago. And that was a real bad visit."

"Well, funerals are stressful times for everyone. This visit will be better."

It was nine a.m. and we were startled by the abrupt knock on my door. I opened it and stood facing a younger version of Ray, but far more haggard and hardened. I smiled, "You must be Billy. Please come in. Welcome home! I'm Dorothy. May I fix you some breakfast? You're so thin; it looks like you could use some good home-cooked food."

I poured coffee for them and made a large egg omelet and a big stack of buttered toast with a bowl of fresh fruit.

Billy had a good appetite and thanked me for breakfast. He kept glancing around the apartment that he'd lived in so many years ago. "It looks nice. It feels comfy like someone really lives here."

I motioned to the living room,."Thanks, Billy, that's kind of you. Come, let's sit on the sofa. On a cold winter day, it's always coziest by the fire."

Ray interjected, "I'll bring in some more firewood and stoke it up a bit."

"Thanks, Ray. So Billy, please tell me about yourself."

"Not much to tell, Mam."

"I'm a retired school teacher; what kind of work do you prefer?"

Billy turned to look at me; his eyes revealed his inner turmoil and pain. "Whatever's available is what I do. I move around a lot. I figured you for a school teacher."

"Well, thank you, I think. Did you ever want to settle down? I know your father would be very happy to have you stay on. Do you realize how much he misses you and worries about you?"

He gave me a puzzled look and muttered. "I doubt that."

Ray came in, set the firewood on the ledge by the hearth and shivered. "I think we're gonna' have a white Christmas this year for sure. It's freezin' cold out there. This afternoon I'm gonna' bring a stack o' firewood into the garage. It'll be a lot easier to get to when ya wanna build a fire."

"Thanks, that'll be very helpful. I have to go in town for a few errands this afternoon; would you like to ride in with me, Billy?"

He answered, "Maybe. If we get the wood stacked before you leave, I'd like that."

Ray looked at his son. "Ya don't have to help me with that…"

"I know I don't have to, but I want to and I will."

Ray kept his back to us as he started the fire. Once he had it going Ray leaned back on the recliner chair; we all sat quietly and contentedly watched the fire. The majestic beauty of Handel's Messiah floated across the room from the kitchen radio. It was one of those rare moments of peace when all seems to be right in the world.

About a half hour later I broke the silence. "Christmas Eve is only three days away and Joyce wants all three of us to come for dinner at their home and then attend the midnight service at their church with them. I think it sounds lovely. How about you two? They wouldn't have invited us if they didn't want us to be there. What do you say, Ray? Billy? I promised Joyce I'd let her know by tomorrow morning."

Ray and Billy threw a few darting glances at each other as if they were afraid of what the other might think. Finally, Billy asked, "Who's this Joyce anyway?"

"Ya remember Harry Ryan? She's his second wife. Nice lady. A retired nurse. Everybody likes her an' she likes everybody. Never heard her say a bad word about anyone. She's not known for bein' much o' a housekeeper or cook. But she sure makes people feel good. Joyce is a lady who seems to truly enjoy life. What do ya say, Billy?"

"I don't know, Dad. I think I'd rather hibernate at home for the whole season. Why don't you an' Miss Dorothy go? I'd rather stay home an' watch TV."

I said, "Nonsense! You can't be serious about spending Christmas Eve watching TV alone!"

Ray added, "That's right, Billy. But jes maybe it's time ya come outa your cocoon. Hold your head high and have some pride in who ya are, son. Whatever mistakes ya made, Billy, you paid your debt to society. And that's jes the way it is."

"And I'd like to invite you both here for Christmas Day dinner and an afternoon card marathon. Billy, won't you please come with us on Christmas Eve?"

Billy stared at the fire.

Ray and I glanced at each other and silently agreed to let it rest at that.

Billy finally spoke. "I don't know about all this Christmas stuff. When I was a kid I liked it, but I haven't celebrated Christmas for so long now, I just don't know. Seems like any other day o' the year to me now, just a hell of a lot o' commercialization an' fussin' around for nothing. I'll think about it." Then he looked at me. "But thanks for askin' me, Miss Dorothy."

The wind whipped the snow against the kitchen window and we sat quietly till the fire burned low. Then Ray announced, "I guess I'll carry that firewood into the garage for ya now."

Billy stood up. "I'll help, Dad."

I closed the fireplace doors and tidied up the apartment. As I was about to walk out of the bedroom I stopped by the dresser, my eyes resting on the photo of my own children when they were so young and we'd all been full of hope. I couldn't help wondering how their holiday plans were playing out this year. At that moment I couldn't help feeling melancholy when I thought about the life I'd left behind.

Disgusted by my own sentimentality, I decided to do something to prevent myself from giving into a moment of weakness. I emptied my purse on the bed and found a neatly folded photo I'd hastily ripped out of a magazine the last time I'd been at the library. I went to the kitchen and carefully cut the picture of the prison bars covering the window as an elderly woman gazed out helplessly. Then I placed it on the dresser under the framed photograph of my children's smiling faces to provide an antidote for future attacks of nostalgia. After all photographs can so easily make the past seem so much better than it ever was.

I hurriedly finished reorganizing the contents of my purse. I asked myself; doesn't every stage of life deserve equal respect? I carefully put the saran wrapped letter addressed to Andrea back in.

I lost track of time as I lost myself in a good book and was startled when I heard a knock on the door. When I opened the door, I looked past Billy and was impressed by the large stack of firewood against the garage wall.

He hesitantly said, "Miss Dorothy, if the offer still holds, I'm ready to go in town whenever you are."

"Of course," I glanced at the clock and saw it was half past noon. "Does your father want to go with us? I think we should treat ourselves to lunch out at the diner. How does that sound to you, Billy?"

Billy shuffled from one foot to the other with his hat in his hands. Making eye contact was obviously not easy for him. "Dad went home to take a nap, he's tired from the drive last night and, yea, the diner sounds good. I haven't been there in years. Dad tells me that's where you two met."

I smiled at the recollection. "Yes it is, wait here till I grab my coat, purse and car keys, and we'll be off for lunch."

We had a quiet drive to town. I cautiously maneuvered the snow covered roads; they'd been plowed with cinders on the intersections and curves.

The town was bustling and festive. We each enjoyed a cup of chili and grilled sandwiches for lunch. A few locals recognized Billy and stopped by our table to chat. He seemed to perk up some. I tried not to watch him too closely, but I couldn't help wonder how he became this person he was. I wanted to believe this time he'd really be able to get a grip on his life. Yet I knew the odds were against him turning his life around at the age of forty.

By the time the seventh person had stopped by and said, "Merry Christmas," Billy looked at me with a frown, "Does anyone even know what the hell Merry Christmas means? Why do they all go around just parrotin' empty words? Good God, bein' here I feel like an exhibition at the county fair. I don't know what I was thinkin' comin' here with you. I need a drink."

It wasn't like I hadn't been warned, but I was still startled by his sudden mood change. "I'm sorry you feel upset, Billy. I just have a few errands and then we'll head home."

Then I asked, "Billy, would you like to buy your father a Christmas gift?"

He glared at me. "It's probably no surprise to you but I'm broke. I got no money for fuckin' Christmas presents for anybody."

The intensity of his escalating anger was beginning to make me feel uneasy. "If you'd like to come with me to the men's clothing store down the street, I'll pay for a gift for you to give to your father. I know it'd make him very happy."

He scowled. "I don't want your charity."

I held his gaze evenly. "Let's not look at it as charity; I have a few odd jobs that you could do to pay me back."

Billy sneered. "But you wouldn't give me cash to buy the gift on my own, would ya'?"

I smiled and shook my head. "And if I did, wouldn't you take me as quite the fool?"

We continued to lock eyes as if in a showdown of wills for what seemed like minutes...

Finally I said, "I have to get my errands done. I'll meet you at the car in one hour." And I walked away.

An hour later he was waiting by my car for a ride home.

CHAPTER TEN

It's Always Something

OLIVIA

CHRISTMAS EVE -2000, HARMONYVILLE, PA.

THE LAST FEW DAYS had been very tense. Ray was aging before my eyes and Billy's moods were like Jekyll and Hyde. One thing I knew for sure, he was not to be trusted and I no longer felt secure in my cozy little apartment. I was careful to keep the doors and windows locked, even a chair against the door knobs at night. I hung festive noisy bells on the doors and windows that jingled with any movement. I knew I couldn't live like this indefinitely. I felt guilty wondering how long Billy would stay.

I called Joyce. "I'm planning to come tonight but things are uncertain with Ray and Billy. I'm sorry we can't be more definite than that."

Upbeat as always Joyce said, "I'm so glad you're coming, Dorothy. I hope Ray and Billy will decide to come too but you're a smart woman not to allow yourself to get pulled into their quagmire. Oh well, I'm not going there! It's Christmas, one of my favorite times of the year. Come over any time, dear. Dinner's at seven."

I wrapped two boxes of Christmas chocolates; one for the Hewitt's and the other for Joyce and Harry. I'd wrapped two packages for Billy, a flannel lined denim shirt and a pair of jeans with four pairs of heavy socks. I had a flannel lined denim shirt for Ray and new leather gloves, as well as heavy socks. The apartment looked bright and festive with the packages arranged by the tree. I even had an extra gift for Ray in my bedroom in case Billy decided he wanted to give his father a gift.

My shopping had been minimal this year. I'd had to force myself to bypass the children's departments. I couldn't look at things there without thinking of Tiffany and Thomas, although they were too old for most of the toys on display. It hadn't been that long ago at all, maybe I'd been more of a factor in their being spoiled than I'd realized. But I couldn't allow myself to think about my old life in Nebraska; I was barely able to suppress nostalgic memories of Christmases past as well as lingering doubts about my decision to start over at the age of seventy.

Ray still came over everyday, but not as early and he didn't stay as long. Billy sometimes came. He rode back from town the day he'd gone with me, but he refused to eat dinner at my apartment that evening. Ray did, but he was clearly uncomfortable leaving his son alone. I sent him home early with a plate of hot food for Billy.

The next night he conned his father into dropping him off at a tavern on the other side of town with a loan of fifty dollars. Ray had adamantly refused to loan his son his truck for a night of carousing. He'd picked up the tab for those nights once too often.

He told his father, "I just wanna' see if any o' my old buddies are home for the holidays. Don't worry, I'll find a ride home. Don't wait up! Thanks Dad."

Billy was dropped off in front of Ray's house at ten the next morning. He reeked of stale alcohol, had blood shot eyes and was effusively apologetic.

Ray looked at him sadly. "Go take a shower and clean yourself up boy."

Ray busied himself tidying up his already tidy home. Then he went for a walk through the woods behind his home, warm salty tears nearly froze to his cheeks as the wind whipped through the wide valley. He finally sought refuge in his garage to escape the cold. He sat on an old chair in the far corner of the garage.

He held his face in his trembling hands and prayed softly. "Lord, ya know I ain't been a prayin' man since ya took our Sarah. Yeah, I bin pissed off at ya for a good long time. Now I'm at my wits end with my boy, Billy. Lord, he's forty years old. He's done nothin' with his life. Nothin.' How can a man jes do nothin' but drink and only you know what else. I don't know what to do with him or for him. When is enough enough? Please show me the way Lord. He's all the family I got. I'll be waitin' for help with this here problem. That's all for now Lord. Amen."

He sat there contemplating his Christmas plans; he didn't know if he dare go to Joyce an' Harry's... And then he heard the muffled Christmas music from the apartment. A smile sneaked up on him.

He bowed his head, "Lord, I didn't want ya thinkin' I'd only be talkin' to ya when I got a problem. One more thing Sir, I do thank ya for that woman in there, Lord."

A few minutes later he tapped on my door. When I opened it he stood there smiling as if he hadn't seen me for weeks and then out of the blue he hugged me.

We enjoyed a quiet lunch with the radio playing cheerful holiday music and for the first time since Billy's return Ray wasn't worried about what his son would eat for lunch.

Ray said, "I still don't know if I'll be going to the Christmas Eve dinner or not. But I can tell you for sure I'm coming for your Christmas dinner, with or without Billy."

"Well, I decided I'm going to Joyce and Harry's tonight. I hope you can come too, but I understand if you don't."

"I'm glad you're goin.' No sense in ya sittin' here by yourself tonight of all nights. Would you like a fire this afternoon?"

I glanced at the clock and hesitated, "Thanks, but I don't think so. I'll be leaving in a couple hours and the fire would hardly have time to burn down. Let's just save the firewood for tomorrow."

"Your tree looks pretty with all those gifts by it." He slowly scanned the room. "Your place is enough to put even the Grinch in a Christmas spirit."

He sat back on the sofa relaxing with arms folded behind his head and his hands covering the back of his neck. He smiled at me with the sweetest twinkle in his eyes.

I smiled right back and sat down beside him on the sofa. The radio continued to play old-fashioned Christmas music.

Ray said in hushed tones. "It's been a good day despite Billy's drunken binge last night."

Then the obvious dawned on me. I raised my eyebrows and looked at him. "And where in the world did Billy get enough money to go out drinking? I had the distinct impression he was about broke when we went to town a few days ago."

Ray looked at me sheepishly. "I…ah, I gave him some money an' drove him to the bar. He said he wanted to check an' see if any o' his old buddies were home for the holidays. He said he'd find a ride home. He asked to borrow my truck and I refused him on that."

I shrugged and hesitantly said, "Oh …Ray. Maybe this isn't the best time to suggest this, but I was wondering if we aren't enabling Billy's immaturity by calling him 'boy and Billy.' I don't know. It was just a thought. I know in teaching by third grade we'd stopped calling the children Kenny's, Billy's, Debby's etcetera. Thereafter, they were called Ken, Bill or Deborah. Maybe it wouldn't make a difference. *Maybe* it would."

He sat silently for awhile and then in a very quiet voice said, "Why didn't I ever think o' that? It makes sense. No wonder he never grew up. Guess I do still talk to him and treat him as if he were a child. Maybe I been makin' it too easy for him to avoid responsibility."

Ray looked so pathetic, I couldn't help smiling. "Maybe you do and then again…"

He reached over with his calloused hand and gently touched my hand. It felt so good and natural. We sat together comfortably for a long while just listening to the Christmas music.

About an hour later there was a knock on the door. I wasn't surprised to see Billy standing there when I opened the door. He was freshly showered and appeared friendly.

"Please come in Billy." Then I stepped back with my hands on my hips and asked, "Would you mind if I call you Bill? Billy just seems like the name of a youngster to me and here you are, a middle-aged man…?"

Billy walked in and smiled. "It doesn't matter to me. The only place anyone calls me Billy is 'round here anyway." He guiltily looked at his Father on the sofa. "Sorry about last night, Dad. I didn't expect to be out all night."

Ray lied. "I didn't even know you weren't home until you walked through the door this morning. I slept like a log. What have ya decided about the Christmas Eve dinner at Harry's? I've decided I'm goin.' Miss Dorothy's goin.' It's up to you but you're most welcome to join us."

I gave Ray a surprised glance and smiled approvingly. I was impressed. Yet I knew how hard it must've been for him to take such a firm stand with his son.

Billy hesitantly replied. "I, huh, I think I'd like to go with you tonight...if it's still okay."

I couldn't resist giving him a hug. "I'm so happy you decided to come. It will be such fun and you'll get to see your father's old friends. It's going to be a wonderful Christmas, you'll see. Now, how about a cup of coffee and a sandwich, Bill?"

He looked a bit embarrassed by my spontaneity. "Sounds great, I'm starved."

They went home two hours later to dress for the evening and I changed into my good black dress topping it off with a red silk scarf.

Ray and Billy were back at my apartment by six-forty p.m. and looked quite dashing. I offered to drive my SUV since there'd be more room in it for three people than in the pick up. The two handsome Clinger men graciously accepted my offer. We arrived ten minutes after seven. The weather was brisk with a fresh dusting of snow. It looked like a perfect Christmas Eve. I felt contented.

Joyce, the ever affable hostess, made Ray and I feel welcome and relaxed. Even Billy seemed to lighten up. Lovely Christmas music filled their home. It was a delicious sit-down dinner for twenty. Harry helped her with the serving and she seemed to have eyes in the back of her head, flitting from one guest to the next, managing to make each one feel like their presence was the key to making the party a success. The food was extraordinary. And the evening went by like the blink of an eye.

The midnight candlelight church service at the Episcopal Church was the perfect ending for the evening and the perfect beginning for Christmas Day.

By the time the congregation softly sang 'Silent Night,' tears were trickling down my cheeks. Needless to mention, it wasn't the only Christmas Eve gathering on my mind.

I composed myself for the drive home. Surprisingly, Billy was the first to speak. "Now I think I know what people mean when they say Merry Christmas, tonight feels like Christmas."

As we drove home, I glanced at Ray and felt happy to see him smiling. Indeed it was already Christmas Day. The radio softly played Christmas carols and the snow covered countryside sparkled like fields of diamonds in the moonlight.

Billy headed straight to his father's house after he hugged me briefly. "Merry Christmas, I'll see you tomorrow, I mean later today."

"I'll be over in a few minutes, Son."

He hesitated briefly, then wrapped his arms around me. "Thank you, Dorothy, for a wonderful Christmas Eve. I hate to think how empty my life would be without you."

I relaxed in the comfort of his arms, resting my head on his chest. "Likewise I'm sure." Then I yawned, "Goodness, I'm so tired."

He put his hands on my cheeks, gently turned my face to him and kissed me. "Merry Christmas, dear Dorothy, you're the sunshine of my life."

I smiled, "Merry Christmas, Ray. I'm so glad you and Billy went to the party and candlelight service with me, but now I think we need to get some sleep. I'll see you later."

It was one fifteen a.m. I wasn't used to such late night hours. I laid my head on the pillow and went to sleep almost immediately. I didn't notice the blinking red light on the answering machine…

I awoke shortly after ten a.m., turned on the radio and tree lights, prepared the stuffing and put the small turkey in the oven as Christmas Carols floated throughout my cozy apartment. I was still basking in the afterglow of the night before. I dressed in a festive red sweater and black slacks after my shower. I thought as I combed my hair, "Yes, it's going to be a good day."

Snow continued to fall lightly on Christmas Day. Ray and Billy came over around one p.m. They looked happy and practically shouted, "Merry Christmas Dorothy!"

They each carried two packages and carefully arranged them by the tree. Ray immediately busied himself stoking the fire. I went to check on our dinner preparations.

Billy followed me to the kitchen. "May I set the table, Miss Dorothy? It smells so good in here. You've almost made me into a Christmas-in-the-heart kind of guy!"

I looked at him, put my hands on my hips and smiled. "And just exactly what is a Christmas-in-the-heart kind of guy, Bill?"

He grinned sheepishly. "You know, someone who likes Christmas music, comin' home for the holidays an' all that stuff."

I whispered. "Bill, did you get a gift for your father?"

He blushed and sighed. "No Mam, I didn't."

I smiled and handed him the dishes, silverware and napkins. "Here you go, please set the table, I'll be right back."

I brought the extra gift for Ray from my bedroom and handed it to Billy. "All this needs is for you to fill out the name tag, you can work off the forty dollars it costs starting tomorrow. It's the shirt I wanted to show you after we had lunch at the diner the day. I bought it just in case you'd change your mind the last minute."

He carefully finished setting the table and looked at me through misty eyes. "Thanks, Miss Dorothy. You're too much. I never met anyone like you before."

He wrote a brief message to his father on the tag and added the box to the others near the tree.

By then Ray had a toasty fire going.

Billy said, "Just being here makes me feel like I'm in one of those corny Christmas card pictures. Yet there's nowhere else I'd rather be today."

I opened a bottle of nonalcoholic sparkling grape juice and poured three goblets. We sat by the fire and toasted, "Merry Christmas to all!"

Harmony in Harmonyville best describes our Christmas Day. Ray and I both made an effort to call Billy, 'Bill' and he responded favorably to the change in his status. Dinner turned out nearly perfect except for the overdone rolls.

I appreciated their help cleaning up after dinner. Then we exchanged gifts. Ray was pleased with all his gifts and especially that

Billy had managed to give him a nice gift for the first time in years. He didn't come right out and say that, but I knew. Billy liked his gifts and he'd sorely needed the new warm clothes he received from us. I was happy to receive a lovely red snowflake cardigan and even a gift certificate to Lands End catalogue.

We played Chinese checkers and then pinochle on the coffee table until we were hungry for leftovers…they went home about nine p.m. Yes, it was a very nice Christmas indeed.

After my shower I noticed the flashing red light on the answering machine. I pushed the play button, wondering who in the world would leave me a message. A metallic computer generated voice stated, "It took some doing to find you, but I couldn't let the holidays go by without wishing you a Merry Christmas…Is it 'Dorothy' you go by these days?"

A chill went through me like a flash of lightening. My knees became so weak I had to sit down. "My God! Who could've left this? It's not like I've committed any crimes. I knew it wasn't Andrea or Alexander, they'd have left a real message not a masked threat… who then?"

I felt a few stray tears escape as I slowly came to realize, I'd had a nice Christmas here in Harmonyville, but it was on a superficial level. In the back of my mind, I was thinking of Andrea, the children and Alexander. I may have taken myself out of the family but somehow I couldn't take my family out of my mind. Even though we're far apart they're always with me.

I had to pour myself a glass of wine to take the edge off my anxiety, I felt old and tired. And I don't often feel old. That night I did. "Who would go to the trouble to leave me such a taunting message?"

Sleep was not my friend that night. I tossed and turned and fretted. Billy? Would he or could he be so devious and mean? Then guilt would flood my very being. What was wrong with me? After all Billy was Ray's son. He'd had problems, but he was trying to turn his life around, wasn't he? Sure he messed up the night before Christmas Eve, but he'd been remorseful, hadn't he? Yet the taped message did have the tone of an ominous warning of more to come; there was no one I could go to for help. There'd be too many questions that I couldn't answer. I'd never felt more alone. Maybe it was all a mistake. The last time I looked at my clock it was four a.m.

I slept till ten. I woke up under a cloud of doubt. I didn't want to see Billy or Ray. I made a sign and hung it on my door. "Not feeling well, please no visitors today."

I wanted to call Luella. But I dared not take the chance. Not yet and not from here. Tomorrow I'll drive to Pittsburgh for a day or two. I'll check the Scottsbluff web page and call Luella using a phone card at a public phone.

I sipped my hot tea on the sofa and sighed. "Tomorrow."

I'd heard Ray in the garage before lunch and appreciated his respect for my sign on the door. He called around one. "Dorothy, how are ya?"

I purposely made my voice weak. "I'm just a bit under the weather, Ray. I'm sure I'll be fine. Probably one of those twenty-four hour bugs. How are you?"

"No problems here. If there's anything I can do for ya, please call. I've grown pretty darn attached to ya and it's a worry when ya feel under the weather."

I couldn't help smiling. Ray was really such a sweet man. "Thanks, Ray. I'm sure I'll be back to my old self in no time at all."

I turned on the radio and listened to the five day forecast as I packed a few things for my trip to Pittsburgh. Thankfully, there were no anticipated snowstorms. The first thing I did was pull out the two money belts I'd bought, the kind to be worn around my waist and under my clothes.

I opened the photos on the dresser, removed the money. Then I looked at the bed, I hadn't expected to move the mattress and box springs again so soon. I heaved; shoved and slid them until I could reach inside the springs and remove the money poach.

I collapsed on a chair. Taking the bed apart was exhausting and I considered that I might need to come up with an alternative banking system.

I carefully divided the money into two stacks and placed one in each money belt. I put them on and looked in the mirror. I'd definitely have to wear heavy bulky sweaters to avoid looking conspicuous. I put the bed back together and changed the sheets before putting the comforter and pillows back on.

As I packed my bag I felt more in control and less intimidated by yesterday's phone message. I couldn't be sure Billy was behind it, but it didn't seem an unreasonable suspicion. My thoughts were interrupted by the phone.

I felt my heart palpitating as I hesitantly answered, "Hello."

"Thank God I caught you at home, Dorothy! How did you survive your first holiday in Harmonyville?"

"Good morning, Joyce, I had a lovely Christmas and we had such a nice time at your Christmas Eve party. It was absolutely delightful. Thanks for including us."

"I'm glad you enjoyed it. Harry and I had a good time and you know they say that's a good sign. How did you ever pull off getting Ray and Billy here? And Billy on such good behavior? You must be some sort of a wizard!"

She had a knack for making me smile. "Actually I just told them I was going and a couple hours later they decided to come too. They both said they really enjoyed it."

"Well, I'm glad to hear that but...but, well, just be careful with Billy. He's an odd one, very slippery. What you see is not always what you get with him. Never has been reliable."

I answered cautiously. "I think I know what you mean. Believe me, I'm very careful."

Joyce asked, "Would you like to have lunch tomorrow?"

"I'd love to, but I'll have to take a rain check. I'm already locked into another commitment."

"Okay, Dorothy, maybe next week." I heard a noise in the background, like a car horn blowing. "Goodness, I must go. Harry's back from his errands already and I promised I'd come right out. We're driving over to his son's home for dinner this evening. See you soon, Sweetie."

Ray called again around six and wanted to bring me something to eat. "Thanks, Ray, but I've just finished eating. You're always so kind to me and I really do appreciate it."

"Miss Dorothy, if ya only knew...I think about ya all the time. And when ya ain't feeling well, it's like I live under a huge dark cloud."

It did make me feel good to have someone care about me. "Please don't worry about me, I've still got a few good years left in me.

"You know I care about you too...Ray, ah...something's come up and I'll be away for a couple days. I should be back before New Year's Eve."

He didn't say a word for a few seconds and then his voice was laced with bitterness. "I don't s'pose it's anythin' ya wanna talk about…"

After so many years of independence, I resented feeling I needed his permission to go away for a few days. But I simply answered him. "I have some personal business I need to take care of."

The next morning I put my luggage in the car and was glad Ray and Billy were no where to be seen as I drove away. It was a brilliant sunny day and sunglasses were an absolute necessity.

I checked into a nice mid-range hotel near the convention center and proceeded to locate an inconspicuous computer café where I read recent copies of the newspaper from back home. There was no mention of Alexander and Andrea. That's good, maybe things are settling down. Then I found a phone bank in an alcove near the back entrance of the once elegant lobby.

I hesitantly called Luella's number. Hallelujah she answered the phone!

I wanted to shout, but I instead my voice came out in a hoarse whisper, "Luella?"

She hesitated several seconds before responding, "Oh my God! Olivia? How are you!?"

I answered honestly. "I'm okay, except I really miss you and everyone. I'm a bit homesick. How are you? Please tell me about Andrea and Alexander."

Luella replied. "Oh everything's about the same around here, except you're gone. Andrea's had a real rough go of it since you left. Alexander's still scheming, just like he always has. I hear about him through his sister. They've sold your house and car. Where'd you finally settle? Please tell me about your new life."

I answered carefully. "There's nothing much to tell. I live in a small apartment just outside a small town. But I think it's best if I don't tell you where I live. I've met some nice people that I enjoy spending time with. I even have a gentleman friend. Can you imagine that?"

"Well, of course, I can and it's about time. I can't think of anyone who deserves it more than you. What's he like?"

"It's strange after being alone so long to have someone looking out for me….he's even my landlord. He's been a widower for about five years after a long and good marriage. He's eighty and in good health. He has only one son who's home for the holidays on a rare visit. He seems to be a troubled forty year old boy."

I hesitated briefly…and then told her about the intimidating Christmas phone message and feeling I have no recourse because of my false identity.

"Olivia, do you feel threatened, are you in danger?"

"I don't think so. I think it's more of an ongoing intimidation; if it's Billy, I don't think he'll try any thing too obvious. He has a record and I'm sure he wouldn't want to take a chance of blowing his parole."

"How long will he be there Olivia? It sounds like you've traded one set of problems for another. Is your gentleman friend worth it?"

"I've thought about that. You know fighting for my freedom by escaping Alexander's snare and then ending up so far away feeling trapped all over again makes me feel damned no matter what I do. At this point, I'm really not sure what much of anything is worth."

"Olivia, please go to the police if you receive any more threats. You don't know how far he might go. Does anyone there know where you keep your money?"

I answered, "Absolutely not."

"Well, at least that's good. Oh Olivia, I wish you'd have never left."

"Sometimes I wonder if I did the right thing. Was I selfish in running off like I did? It seemed so right at the time. Enough about me please tell me about Andrea, the children and Alexander."

Luella slowly answered. "They really don't get it. One minute Andrea is mourning your death and the next she's sure you're still alive somewhere. In fact, Alexander filed a missing person report on you and even posted a modest reward. They hired a private investigator and they managed to trace you to the first used car you bought and your first alias, Alice Smith. Then the trail went cold. He's convinced you're not dealing with a full deck. Personally, I think you're pretty damn clever to have pulled this off."

Luella sighed, "So much to tell you, what next? Oh yes…Andrea withdrew from most of her daily activities. She was confused and unsure what to believe. She doesn't understand why you would've disappeared like you did from their lives. She pushes herself to interact with her children. She's put Joel through the fires these past few months. She wants you back. I talked her into going to counseling.

"And she and Joel took a nice vacation to the Florida Keys, just the two of them. Alex stayed at their home and bonded with the children while they were away."

Olivia hung carefully to every word.

"Sometimes they insinuate that I may be withholding information from them...Tiffany and Thomas have taken an historical stance in balancing the loss of their grandmother. They love and treasure the things you left for them in your home. I'm sorry you're not here to see what fine young people they're becoming.

"My Hank had a heart attack, he's okay now but we both know he's living on borrowed time."

I took a few deep breaths and held back my tears. "I'm sorry Luella... I miss you all so desperately. Maybe it's the holidays, but this is so much harder than I ever thought it would be." I couldn't believe a tough old bird like me was sniffling like a sentimental fool, but I was.

I whispered hoarsely. "Happy New Year, Luella. I'll call again —soon."

I hung up and hurried to the ladies room just as the dam burst. Later, I was amazed that I hadn't drowned in my own tears.

CHAPTER ELEVEN

Ray and Me

OLIVIA

JANUARY WAS EXCEPTIONALLY COLD even for Harmonyville and a time of soul-searching for me. My holiday siege of homesickness slowly subsided and I grew more comfortable and contented with my new life...and with Ray.

Billy left January tenth. He didn't fall off the wagon again after his bender before Christmas. He was consistently respectful to me and his father. I hadn't received any more phone calls like the one on Christmas Eve. All I had were my nagging suspicions that he'd been behind it. There've been times my instincts have proved to be right and then sometimes I've been way off.

I bought a treadmill and Ray helped me set it up in my bedroom. It was too cold and icy to continue my daily walks. I've always been a believer in physical fitness and I attribute my longevity and good health to my daily exercise program. Of course, I know genetics has a lot to do with it too. But those same genetics hadn't helped Eloise...

Ray and I developed a pleasant routine. He'd bring the newspaper to my apartment by eight every morning and build a fire. I'd fix breakfast for both of us, usually hot oatmeal and fruit. We'd go to town about three days a week and eat lunch at the diner. Then we'd do whatever errands needed to be done and return home to play cards, read or watch a movie. Joyce and Harry met us for lunch several times and then joined us for cards and casual dinners at my apartment. It was a relaxing time. Ray and I grew closer with each passing day.

We'd enjoyed attending church so much on Christmas Eve that we just kept going back almost every Sunday. Life was good. Still not a day went by that I didn't think about Andrea and Alexander, though seldom in that obsessive melancholy way. I continued to visit the public library and use the computers to stay informed with the happenings back home. It seemed that Andrea was again involved with her charity work. One day there was a nice picture of her and her friends at a hospital fund raiser. I was thankful Alexander's name was not listed in the Court Beat. All that meant to me was the authorities hadn't figured him out yet.

Since leaving, Billy had taken up a new habit of calling his father once a week. He'd found a job as a maintenance assistant in a large apartment building in Cleveland and part of his pay was a furnished studio apartment. The conversations were short but cordial. I knew Ray was very happy about their new relationship.

It was a freezing cold Valentine's Day when Ray walked in looking embarrassed and happy. He handed me a small box. "Somethin' for ya, jes to show ya how much ya mean to me. Ya been bringin' somethin' special to every day o' my life since I met ya...Here."

He gently shoved the box into my hand. I was stunned and just stared at the beautifully wrapped box.

He shuffled his feet nervously and then pulled a chair out from the table and sat down. "Well, are ya gonna open it or stand there gawkin' at it all day?"

I smiled and felt my face blush. "Ray, I don't know what to say."

He stammered, "Well, then stop yakkin an' open yur gift."

I pulled off the shiny red bows and opened the lovely foil package. My heart felt like it was beating double time when I opened the box. "Oh my God! Ray, what have you done? This is the most beautiful ring I've ever seen...but why?" I had to wipe tears from my eyes as I stumbled to sit down on a kitchen chair.

He leaned across the kitchen table and handed me his handkerchief. "Do ya like it Dorothy? Will ya wear it for me?"

"Oh Ray, it's too much, I don't know what to say."

"It don't mean we have to git married or anythin' like that. At our ages, what the hell does marriage mean anyway? If ya'd have me, I'd marry ya in a minute, but I know how ya feel about that. This ring is a token of how much I love ya, Dorothy. That's all. I love ya like I never knew a man could love a woman. Here I am a hobblin' ol' man fallin' head over heels in love with a beautiful white-haired lady from 'out west somewhere.' Who'd o' ever believed this coulda happened to an ol' fogey like me?"

I could feel the hot tears as they slowly escaped my eyes. "Ray, I'm-without words….you are the kindest and dearest man I've ever known. You've given new meaning to my very empty life."

I reached across the table and tenderly stroked his hands. "Ray, I'll never forget the day you stopped by my table at the diner." The sweet memories of those very special moments never fail to make me smile. "I appreciate you not pushing me to the altar. As long as we know we love each other, isn't that all that really matters?"

He squeezed my hands softly and tried in vain to hold back his own tears. I stood and walked over to him, sat on his lap and kissed him right on the mouth. And he kissed me back. I could tell we were both feeling a fire that we'd assumed had died out in us a long, long time ago.

He slipped the ring on my finger. It was a perfect fit. "Ya've made me a happy man."

I took his hand in mine and led him to the sofa. The apartment was chilly with no fire yet in the fireplace. But we hardly noticed. He held me in his arms. I rested my head on his chest. I felt like a young woman. We kissed again and again. It felt natural and right as we slowly caressed each other…

An hour later I made us a hot breakfast while Ray built a fire. We couldn't stop smiling and every time we were within a couple feet of each other, one of us would lightly touch the other as we stoked the simmering fires inside us. What a day it was.

And, oh how I cherished that ring! The diamond sparkled from every angle and the sapphire stones set around it added a touch of elegance. I couldn't help extending my hand as I went about my chores to admire my ring from as many positions as possible. Ray watched me with a silly grin on his face. On that Valentine's Day our friendship moved from one of committed friendship to one of mutual commitment. We were both surprised to realize that we were capable of such a depth of ardor.

And it felt so good to be loved again.

Ray insisted we go to The Club for a special Valentine Dinner. It was as beautiful in the winter as in the summer, though driving there was definitely more treacherous. It closed during the winter except for special occasions. And it was the most special Valentine's Day I could remember! Melvin had been a good steady man I could count on, though thrifty almost to a fault. He'd never have bought me such a ring or spend the money to take me to a place as pricey, (and romantic!) as The Club.

'Yes, Virginia', there's still romance after the age of seventy; however, a year ago I'd have never believed it!

We enjoyed The Club's special Sweetheart's Dinner as beautiful instrumental love songs floated softly through the air. Everything was perfect until we were leaving.

Ray unfortunately misjudged the distance between his truck and a black Mercedes as he was driving away from The Club; he banged it fender to fender. I have to admit that incident put a bit of a damper on our Valentine celebration but it didn't put out the fire.

We were happy. The days turned into weeks and then months. I'd been frugal with my money, but the motor in my SUV had to be replaced in July which left me with an expensive car repair bill. I decided to make a quick trip to New York City before another winter set in. It'd be nice to sell a few diamonds and see a couple shows. And maybe even buy myself a new outfit. I wasn't in a hurry and doubted if Ray would be willing to make the trip with me.

One hot, muggy evening in mid August as we sat on the small deck behind my apartment with tumblers of ice tea, I asked, "Have you heard from Bill lately?"

Ray had a far away look in his eyes as he answered. "Jes the usual, he's still workin' an' I don't think he's been back in jail. I don't wanna sound like I'm braggin' or anythin' like that, but I'm hopin' this time he jes might make it. It's good to know where he is an' that he's got a roof over his head."

"That's happy news. Please, next time you talk to him tell him I said 'hello.' Would you like a refill of ice tea?"

He wiped his brow with his handkerchief. "That sounds good, jes 'bout what the doctor ordered. Sure has been a hot one today an' doesn't feel like we'll get much o' a break in the weather tonight either."

I scooped three ice cubes for each of our glasses from the ice bucket and poured fresh tea in both our glasses. I took a drink. "Mmm, there's nothing like a cold drink of ice tea in this summer heat."

Ray took a big swallow and smacked his lips. "Ya sure are right 'bout that, Dorothy."

We sat there enjoying the comfort of each others company on that hot summer evening. I hated to break the spell, but decided I might as well tell him I'd be going away for a few days come next Tuesday. "Ray, I'd be happy to have you come with me if you'd like to make the trip."

He looked at me long and hard. Then he stared straight ahead. "An' jes where might ya be goin' on this trip?"

"I'm driving to New York City for a few days. I'll catch a couple shows, shop a little and take care of my business. Then drive home again."

He abruptly turned to me. "New York City?! That's even farther than Pittsburgh. My God, woman! You are a puzzle to me. At your age, business in New York City! In my whole life I ain't never been to that place an' I don't 'spect to start changin' my personal travel history any time soon! Sometimes it feels like I don't even know ya."

Dusk was setting in. Ray sat there frowning with his arms stubbornly folded across his chest.

"Well, if you change your mind, be sure to let me know. I must make the trip before winter; I've already made my appointment and hotel reservation."

He turned to me with a wounded look in his eyes. "I won't be changin' my mind."

"Ray, for heavens sakes, this isn't about you. It's just something I have to do. Please don't act so...hurt. Life is already complicated enough."

He looked at me as if he was seeing me for the first time. "It is, huh?" And then brooded for a half an hour, before announcing, "I best be gettin' on home. Good night, Miss Dorothy."

He even skipped breakfast with me the next morning. Later he came into the garage as I was returning from my morning walk.

"You missed breakfast this morning."

"I stayed up watchin' a movie on television last night an' when I finally got up this mornin' decided to eat in my own kitchen for a change. Figured ya'd need some time to pack an' all for that trip o' yours next week."

"Would you like to talk about what's bothering you, Ray?"

He glared at me. "Ain't nothin' botherin' me. Is somethin' botherin' ya, Miss Dorothy?"

I felt my dentures grinding as my jaw clenched in an automatic response. "Right now I think it's safe to say you're bothering me, I have to get some groceries. Do you need anything?"

"No thanks, I'm all set."

"Okay. I'll see you later." I had to blink back tears as I drove into town. I was angry and hurt but I was sure we'd get over the tiff.

I kept thinking about what an obstinate old goat he was as I completed my shopping.

Late that afternoon he knocked on my door and handed me a bouquet of fresh flowers. "Wanna' go in town to eat tonight, Dorothy?"

"Are these for me? They're beautiful!"

He scowled, "O' course they're for ya. Who else do ya think I'd be givin' flowers to?"

I smiled as I put the flowers in a vase. "What a lovely idea, I haven't even thought about dinner yet. What time?"

"Six oughta' be 'bout right. How about a movie after dinner? It looks like a pretty good one playin' at the Movie House. It starts at seven-thirty and there's always a bunch o' previews so we'll have plenty o' time for eatin'."

I walked over and put my arms around him, and smiled up at his frowning face. "Well, aren't you just a regular Mr. Romance! Flowers, dinner out and a movie! That's just about as good as it gets."

I could feel his tense body relax and when I stood back from him, that smile I'd grown to love was right back where it belonged.

When we walked into the diner, Darlene came over and hugged us both. "I never see you two anymore! Where you been hidin'?"

Ray answered, "Better question is where've ya been? We keep comin' in here lookin' for ya an' ya ain't been here once. We figured ya must a' left town."

She led us to our table. "Yeah, right, like I'm gonna' skip town with them babies o' mine. I'm just not workin' as many hours, cause I've got me a pretty heavy load o' classes this semester."

I asked, "How are you doing? That sounds like a lot of pressure. And how are the twins?"

"We're hopin' to have them both potty trained by Christmas. I'll save a darn fortune when I don't have to buy disposable diapers anymore. Me, I'm holdin' up okay. Can't complain, never a day goes by that my babies don't make me laugh. My Mom an' Dad love bein' grandparents an' are makin' monkeys outa' them."

She beamed, "My classes are real interestin'. It's gettin' harder but as long as I do the readin' and study for the exams, I do pretty good. Thanks for askin.' So do ya want a menu or the daily special o' chicken n' biscuits as long as it lasts, served with a side salad or cole slaw?"

Ray and I looked at each other and nodded, I said, "Make that two chicken n' biscuits with two slaws."

We both left generous tips for Darlene. And we enjoyed the movie. The evening was a pleasant change in routine and put us back on solid ground.

My trip to the city was uneventful. It might've been more fun if Ray had been with me, but then again he'd likely have been so overwhelmed with the entire city experience that he'd have been a royal hemorrhoid. I enjoyed two Broadway matinees; "The Producers" and "The Full Monty". I stayed at The Marriot in Times Square so I could easily walk back to my room after the shows.

Wednesday morning I called Luella from the phone bank in the hotel lobby. No answer. I was disappointed. But, I tried again at noon and it was a joy to hear her say, "Hello."

"Luella, it's me, how are you dear? My God, I've missed you!"

Just hearing her voice brought tears to my eyes. My vocal chords strained as I attempted to mask my sadness. "So what's new? How are Andrea, the children and Alexander?"

"Things have been quiet around here. Alexander continues on

as always. I don't see him, but Andrea stays in touch and keeps me informed. Tiffany and Thomas are honor roll students and are very involved in sports and their music lessons. Andrea has scaled down her volunteer involvement, and seems to be slowly getting her stride back."

I had to swallow hard and take a deep breath before I could speak. "I'm so glad to hear they're doing alright. I really miss them. Sometimes it's very hard. But I'm okay."

"Are you and your fella still so cozy with the each other? Is that messed up of son of his still giving you trouble? Tell me your news."

I sniffled. "Sorry, I have a cold and it makes my voice sound strange. My life has been going well; my man is a real gem. His son left in early January and hasn't been back since. It's a small, friendly town and feels almost like home. I drove to New York City for a few days taking care of business. You know how I've always liked to visit the city. How's Hank and the family?"

"Everyone's okay, some better than others, but isn't that the way it always is? You can come home to us if you want to, there's nothing they can do to you. Maybe indict you with a couple charges, but at your age, they won't prosecute you. I checked with the police chief as a hypothetical situation to yours."

I felt like I was about to fall down a huge dark crevice. "I'm not coming back Luella. Please don't use me in anymore hypothetical questions with the police! I've made my bed and I must sleep in it. Maybe next year you can meet me in New York City for a few days. You take care. I love you...Good bye."

"You take care of yourself and never forget how much you're missed back home. Good bye, love."

I shopped the boutiques as well as the big department stores. I bought myself two pair of twill slacks, a pair of shoes and a new dress and jacket for next summer from the summer clearance sale. Thursday morning I was waiting for the doors to open at the Metropolitan Museum and stayed till late afternoon.

I took a cab to the diamond district Friday morning for my appointment with Isaac Mayer. I felt comfortable completing my transactions with the same dealer each time. As he welcomed me into his tiny office, I wanted to ask him, "Does it ever bother you to have those long braids hanging by your face? It certainly makes all the men of your sect stand out in a crowd."

But I knew I'd never talk to him about that. He provides me with a valuable service; few of the shops in the diamond district would even bother with a small potato like me. But Isaac accepted my business with a rare professional kindness. Mission accomplished in thirty minutes and I hoped I wouldn't need to come back to see him for at least two years. Isaac called a cab for me and I hurried back to check out of my room.

As I drove back to my new life in Pennsylvania and Ray, I glanced at the beautiful New York City skyline through my rear view window. The Twin Towers soared above the host of other skyscrapers like the proud parents of a very large family and created an unrivaled view of modern civilization. It was August twenty-fourth, a sunny hazy day with rain predicted by early evening. It was a good time to leave the city to avoid the late afternoon rush hour traffic. I stopped for lunch at a fast food restaurant about two hours later in Pennsylvania and arrived home before nine. Ray saw my headlights and came rushing right over. He hugged me with the grip of a mountain lion.

"Ah, Dorothy it's good to have ya home agin'. I've missed ya."

"And I missed you, Ray; it's so good to be home. It was a long drive today."

Ray's voice had an edge to it. "Let me carry your bag in for ya. Did ya git your secret business done in the big city?"

I felt a flash of anger and avoided his eyes. "Of course, but it would've been nice to have had someone to go to the shows and eat dinner with." We talked awhile and then he went back to his house.

And so our lives went on as before. Ray got over the negative feelings he'd had about my trip to New York City. That's one of the things I hold so dear about him. He has a kindness that doesn't leave room for hostile grudges.

Billy even came home for Labor Day week end. He looked like he was still trying hard to stay clean and sober. He spoke about his job with pride and was hopeful that it might lead to better positions in the maintenance field someday.

His visit left us both feeling more optimistic about his future.

Mary called a few days later. "Dorothy, where have you been hiding?

I haven't seen you in weeks!"

"Bob and I are planning a little dinner party for our most favorite guest at the Bed and Breakfast, to celebrate the anniversary of you and Ray's first date."

I was stunned. "Are you sure you really want to do that? Goodness I think we're a bit old for first date celebrations."

"Nonsense, your age only makes it more special!"

As we talked, I marked the date on my calendar, October twelfth.

Then September eleventh came; it started out as a beautiful sunny day and ended with everyone in America feeling singed by the tragedy and uncertainty due to the terrorists' vengeful suicide acts.

A month later, Mary hosted the dinner party; Joyce and Harry were there as well as Irene and Walter.

Bob stood and toasted us. "May your young love live longer than you do!"

Mary wagged her finger at him. "Bob, for heaven's sakes! Is that the best you can do?"

Everyone laughed. Harry beamed. "Joyce, darlin' is there anything sweeter in this world than old young love?"

Joyce gave a good natured huff. "Harry, dear, how would a young thing like me know a thing about being old?"

Walter and Irene were more quiet than usual. But then, small talk was not one of her strengths. Walter was talkative and even jovial when she wasn't with him. But when they were together, he was like an obedient pet, just wanting to keep his mistress happy. Her domain seemed to be gossiping or as she so aptly puts it, "There're certain things you might never understand about Harmonyville, so I just wanted to enlighten you."

Joyce, Harry, Ray, Mary and Bob and I kept light-hearted barbs bouncing around the dining room for more than two hours after dinner. Their consensus was, "Lucky day for all of us when Dorothy first knocked on the door of Hewitt's Bed & Breakfast!"

Despite Irene's cloud it was a delightful relaxing evening. I felt like I was just exactly where I should be. I loved my freedom. Yet I loved feeling like I truly belonged somewhere, that someone would miss me if I didn't get out of bed some morning.

Ray kissed me good night at the door and I was heading straight to bed, when I noticed the red light beeping on the answering machine. Since I rarely received phone calls I listened to the message immediately. It was the same eerie metallic voice as the call I received Christmas Eve. *"How long is this Dorothy game going to last? Aren't you afraid you'll miss the wizard?"*

It stopped me cold. "My God…who was doing this to me? Why?" I had been so busy enjoying my new life that I'd almost forgotten about the mysterious Christmas Eve message and now another one.

I made sure I was alone in my apartment and then double checked all my locks. The white hairs I kept in the picture frames were untouched and the clear tape I kept on my mattress and box springs was exactly as I'd left it. My private security system was intact. There was only the menacing message on the answering machine and there was no one, absolutely no one, I could talk to about my uneasiness. I didn't want to jeopardize my relationship with Ray; so I certainly didn't want to tell him about it. An hour later, I forced myself to go to bed, but sleep was elusive.

Ray came bright and early the next morning and noticed the change in my mood immediately. He kissed my forehead.

"Not feelin' well today, Dorothy?"

"Morning. I had a bad night, didn't get much sleep."

"I'm sorry, can I do anything for ya?"

"Well, if I could just go back to bed and maybe get a couple hours of sleep, I might feel a bit better."

Ray looked at me intently and the volume of his voice rose with each word, "Dorothy, did somethin' happen? Ya seem so different all o' sudden. Did somebody say somethin' insultin' to ya? Are ya scared o' somethin'?"

He was so sweet I couldn't help smiling.

"Ray Clinger, where were you all my life? No one's insulted me and nothing's happened. It was just one of those nights, maybe I was keyed up from our anniversary party; I don't know. It left me feeling like a tired old woman today. But, please don't worry, I'll be okay."

"Guess I'll head on into the diner for breakfast. Do ya need anythin' from town?"

I managed another smile and kissed his cheek. "I can't think of anything. Enjoy your breakfast. I'll see you later."

I leaned against the door after I'd locked it and the tears came flooding down my face again. I thought, "I truly wish I could tell him everything, but of course I can't. I must leave my past where it's at. But who's behind these menacing messages?"

I went back to bed and my tears evolved into sobs. I told myself, "Good grief Olivia, get a hold of yourself!"

My pillow was still damp when I woke three hours later, but my thoughts were more rational. I listened to the tinny message two more times.

"How long is this Dorothy game going to last? Aren't you afraid you'll miss the wizard?"

Somehow in the light of day it didn't seem quite so ominous as when I'd heard it last night.

CHAPTER TWELVE

Calamity Strikes!

OLIVIA

THREE YEARS LATER EVERYTHING suddenly changed. Harmonyville was in a state of shock. Four people had died: an elderly woman and a handicapped middle aged man, as well as two toddlers. Darlene's twins were hit hard. Her small son, Andy, had been the first death and his sister, Annie, was critically ill. Darlene walked around like a shadow of her old self. The spark was gone. The diner clientele mourned with her…and for themselves.

The locals had little else on their minds besides the water sickness. People were panicking. The stores could barely keep up with the demand for bottled water. Two dozen more were critically ill in the local hospital. Walter was one of the sick with an uncertain prognosis.

Irene was despondent and angry. She seethed, "Why Walter!? Why Harmonyville? Nothing like this is supposed to happen here!"

Rumors flew and grew. Had the water supply been intentionally poisoned? The remote isolated safety of the small town was suddenly and …forever shattered. The F.B.I. sent in special investigators.

And of course the media descended on Harmonyville with a vengeance.

I knew this was not a good situation and decided another trip to the city might be necessary very soon. I didn't want to end up on the evening news…no way, no matter what.

Nerves were frayed. Investigators and reporters were questioning everyone. Within a few days, paranoid theories were free-floating all over the close knit community. Formerly trusting neighbors were suddenly suspicious of each other.

And then out of the blue Billy showed up at his father's door. "I couldn't stay away when my home town was the lead story on the national news every night."

"Billy! I can't believe you're here." And without thinking he hugged his son like there was no tomorrow.

"Geez Dad, are you okay? How's Miss Dorothy holding up?" He awkwardly returned his father's embrace.

Ray released his son and patted his shoulder affectionately. He stared off as if in a trance in the direction of the town. "I'm jes glad I live outside the borough. Good God! It's a crazy damn circus in Harmonyville. I stay outa town as much as I can. An' I only drink bottled water now, don't even trust water from my own well. Bin drivin' clear over to Spencerville an' buyin' bottled water by the cases. They're always runnin' outa bottled water in town. Miss Dorothy's doin' good; plannin' on gittin' away for a few days with all this uproar."

Then Ray turned to his son and squinted in the intense afternoon sunlight. "Ya ain't had that job but a few months, how'd you manage to git time off?"

"I told my boss I was worried about my dad. He watches the news, too. He's coverin' for me. Pops, I've been so worried about you that I was near outa my mind. Sometimes I think it was easier when I was drunk or high most of the time."

"Your boss must be a decent sort to help ya out like this. An' I'm glad you're on the wagon. Bin a damn scary time 'round here for everyone. Worst of it is, nobody knows what or who to believe and it seems there're more nosey strangers than local folk 'round town anymore. Ya want a cup o' coffee or somthin'?"

"No, thanks. I'll just take my stuff up to my room."

As Billy started up the stairs, Ray said, "It's good to have you home."

"I'm glad to be here for ya Pops." He grimaced as he trudged up the stairs and mused, if he knew why I was *really* here, he wouldn't be so glad to see me.

"I was just headin' over to Miss Dorothy's; come on over when you're done an' be sure an' lock the house when you leave. Too many strangers around these days to leave anythin' unlocked."

Ray knocked on my door as he always did. The idea of just walking in never occurred to him; after all I was still technically his tenant. He heard the locks turning. When I opened the door, he said, "You're always a healin' sight for my tired sore eyes, Miss Dorothy."

I automatically relocked the door.

He touched my left forearm. "Do ya have an extra hug in your pocket for a tired ol' man?"

"What do you think?" I smiled and fell naturally into his arms. "Ray, is something else wrong? You seem tense."

He hesitated, and then muttered. "Billy's home, got here about a half hour ago."

I know he felt my apprehension as I broke away and quietly busied myself in the kitchen. "I was just about to start dinner. Hope you're hungry for steak. I've had two marinating all afternoon. I'll slice them and serve with light gravy over rice."

"Billy and I can eat at home; ya don't have to feed us, my dear."

"Of course, you'll eat here, what else would I do with all this food? Have you heard how Walter's doing?"

Ray answered slowly. "He ain't outa' the woods yet, that's fer shur. Irene's near beside herself. I hate to think how she'd get on without ol' Walter. I don't know if ya ever noticed, but Irene could be on the judgmental side and was a little tough on folks that didn't live up to her standards. I jes don't know if the ol' girl's up to walkin' in widow's shoes…"

"Ahh…yes I, ah…I've picked up on Irene's attitude when I've visited with her. Walter is such a fine gentle man. I hope he starts responding to treatment soon."

"From what I've heard he's barely conscious. Almost delirious with fever."

There was a noise at he door and then a loud knock. Ray opened it. "Come on in, Billy. Dorothy's fixin' another feast for us, even in these troubled times; I know I'm a lucky man."

I managed to smile and took his hands in mine as a gesture of hospitality. "Bill, what a nice surprise, welcome home! I just wish the circumstances were a bit better. Can you even imagine such things going on? Please, have a seat and relax. Dinner will be ready in about an hour."

"Good to see you again, Miss Dorothy; you're looking well. I couldn't stay away when this was all I heard about on the news. Worried about my Dad and folks I grew up with."

I set the timer and carried a tray with three large glasses of ice tea to the living room. Tears welled up in my eyes as I sat down in my favorite chair and sighed. "I'm sorry, but sometimes I can't help...it's all so unfair. When I think of all the innocent decent people who are suffering so, poor Darlene...Joyce called this afternoon. They don't think her surviving baby's going to make it either."

Ray's eyes filled with tears at the thought of Darlene and the twins.

Billy asked, "Who's Darlene?"

"A nice young girl, about twenty-two, works as a waitress part time while she's goin' to school to learn nursin'. She's lived with her folks since her no good husban' took off with a barmaid. Left her with two beautiful babies, twins. Darlene always calls me Uncle Ray." He reached for the box of tissues as the tears streamed down the leathery valleys of his cheeks. "Her boy, Andy, died this week. A tragedy."

We sat in silence, each lost in our own thoughts. When the buzzer went off, I gladly escaped to my little kitchen for the last minute dinner preparations.

No one felt like socializing after dinner and it turned out to be an early evening. Ray still felt a bit unsettled about his son's sudden appearance. Billy was cordial, but then sincerity had never been part of his character. I had a sense of overwhelming sadness.

Billy borrowed his dad's truck and drove around town that evening and again the next day. Even he was astounded with the bumper to bumper television vans and crews and the blatant obviousness of the special government agents.

Late the next afternoon Billy asked, "Hey, Pops, can I borrow your truck again this evening? I'll pick you up a few cases of bottled water over in Spencerville. I won't be late. I talked to my boss today and he wants me back before the weekend. Has some sort of family emergency he has to tend to."

"Shur', Billy, jes be careful with the ol' girl. I expect her to las' me to the end o' my days."

"I will, Pops. Thanks."

I was still unsure when I'd be leaving, but packed a bag for a few days in New York City. I could hardy wait to get away.

Billy drove ten miles to Spencerville, loaded ten cases of water in the back and then stopped for a sandwich and drink. And as so often happens to Billy...one drink lead to another.

He was Mr. Personality and no one in the Dew Drop Inn would forget he was there that night. "Give me one more for the road!" Somehow he managed to spill it all over himself.

He grinned, "Shit, that's a waste of a good beer! Gimme another one..." It was ten p.m. when he finally staggered out of the tavern.

The patrons shook their heads and grinned. One man said, "Now there goes a fella who can hold his drink."

A woman glared from across the bar and slowly exhaled her cigarette. "Yeah, right, an' I'm Miss America."

Billy drove with cautious determination, he felt confident he'd managed to impress the patrons of the tavern that he'd been there and he was drunk. But he knew he'd had no where near enough to reach his limit of alcohol tolerance. Instead of going directly back to his father's home; he cruised Harmonyville's Main St., and took a right onto North Bennett St. The man walking the dog went down quickly when the truck hit him. Billy stopped, hesitated, then put the truck in reverse and ran over the man again.

"Oh, my God. Now I've really done it. Oh, my God!" He drove directly home, barely able to see the road through his tears and parked the truck in the garage. He sat there several minutes with his face buried in his hands as he leaned forward against the steering wheel.

Finally he mustered the strength to check for any damage to his father's pickup. He found an old bottle of Windex, sprayed the lights and front bumper, used his shirt and wiped off tell tale signs of blood before walking into his father's home.

The next morning news of the hit and run was on the radio with an eye witness description of the dark pickup that hit him. "Surprisingly, the victim was not who his neighbors of the last five years thought he was. Joe Moore was really an alias for Stan Trovosky, famed informant on the Russian Mob, living quietly in Harmonyville under the federal Witness Protection Program. Therefore the F.B.I. promised to work closely with the sheriff's office in the investigation of the hit and run ..."

I served Ray his eggs sunny side up just the way he liked them. Ray shook his head as he listened to the news. "What next?"

I turned the radio off, sighed and sat down to eat my egg and muffin. "I don't know what to think, it's so bizarre. Of all the people to be killed by a hit and run, someone under witness protection?"

Ray answered despite his mouth being full of food. "I talked with Joe a few times at the diner. Nice enough sort, quiet and kept to himself. Now I know why."

"Did he have a family?"

Ray answered grimly, "Yep, a wife and three children. Mostly grown up. I think the youngest may still be in high school. Damn shame."

I shook my head. "Seems to be no end to trouble in this town. Billy sleeping in this morning?"

Ray nodded, "He got home later than I expected an' I'm afraid he fell off the wagon agin'; don't know for sure but his bedroom smelled like a brewery when I walked past it this mornin'."

I reached across the table and caressed his hand. "I'm sorry, Ray. As if you didn't have enough worries already."

The telephone ringing interrupted us. I answered, an unfamiliar male voice asked for Ray, and I handed him the phone.

"Uncle Ray, this is Wally Harnet. I wanted you to know that my father passed away late last night. They couldn't get his fever down and then he slipped into a coma yesterday...he never came back to us after that."

"I'm so sorry, Wally. How's your mother?"

"I can't tell. I think she's on automatic. You know how she is."

After dinner that evening Ray, Billy and I paid respects to Walter's family at the Good Shepherd Funeral Home. Irene was serene; those who knew her realized she was obviously tranquilized.

Another elderly woman had died that day and the other side of the Good Shepherd was being readied for her family to say their last good byes.

We were in a genuine state of shock and grief. After several minutes of silence on the drive home I reported, "Joyce told me Darlene's little girl has stabilized and is out of danger."

Ray replied softly, "That's the best news I've heard since this whole mess started."

Billy asked, "When will they know what's caused the water poisoning?"

Ray's voice was sad and flat. "I heard they're pretty sure it's E. Coli bacteria. But they can't figure out why now and how it's causing all this damage to our water reservoir. Don't make a lick o' sense."

A short time later, we said good night and went to bed with our private thoughts on the unfolding tragedy.

Sheriff Mac arrived as I was returning from my daily walk late the next morning. "Hello Sheriff, how are you? I'm Dorothy Myers, Ray's tenant; I live in the apartment behind the garage."

"Nice to meet you, Mam."

"I'm getting a bit of a chill. Would you like to come inside to talk?"

"No, thank you, Mam, I just have to talk to Ray for a few minutes."

Ray walked over from his house. "Good mornin' Mac, what can I do for ya? A damn shame what's been happening in Harmonyville the last week."

"Tough times we're livin' in. Ray, I, ah, I ah...gotta take a look at your truck. Cause o' that hit-an'-run the other night. I gotta' check every black pick-up truck in the whole damn county! Do ya' know how many there are? Well, I'll tell ya' this much, I'm already sick o' takin' orders from those FBI punks in their look-alike suits."

A chill raced down my spine as I thought of Billy's use of Ray's truck.

Ray opened the side door, we walked into the garage and he turned on the overhead lights. "Sure, Mac, come on in. There it is, check it out for yourself."

Mac slowly walked around the truck and carefully looked it over, then walked back to the front of the dusty pickup. He stood there with his arms folded and stroked his left cheek with his right hand. "There's jes this one thing worrisome to me about your truck, Ray."

"An' jes what might be worryin' ya' about my ol' pickup, Mac?"

Mac answered Ray's question with another question. "Did anyone other 'an you drive your truck night before last?"

Ray answered, "I'm old, but I'm not stupid… For God's sake Mac, what're ya' really tryin' to do here?"

"Goddam it, calm down, Ray, I'm jes tryin' to do my job. Lookie here, your whole truck is dusty an' dirty. Hell, everybody's in the same boat with all the water restrictions and dry weather. But then, look here at your front bumper, it's shiny as a show room car. It makes me wonder, how'd that one part o' your truck get so damn clean?"

Ray quietly frowned as he stared at his truck, then at the sheriff. "Mac, I ain't got nothin' else to say to ya' right now."

"So be it, Ray. I'm gonna' have to cordon off your truck till we get some people out here to take a closer look at that front bumper."

Mac meandered back to his patrol car, brought a large spool of yellow crime scene tape back to the garage and wrapped it around the old black truck, twice.

"Ray, ya' better be ready to talk by tomorrow. I'll try to keep a lid on this for a little while but you know I gotta' report this."

"Report what? A man havin' a clean bumper's a crime now?"

Mac shook his head sadly and shuffled back to his car. "See ya' later, Ray."

I slipped my arm around his waist as we watched the sheriff's car drive away. Ray broke the silence…"I gotta' have a talk with my boy."

He silently walked back across the lawn to his home and stomped up the stairs. Ray burst into Billy's bedroom and pulled the blankets off his bed.

He bellowed. "Rise and shine Billy boy, we gotta' talk and we gotta' do it right now! I'll be waitin' in the kitchen."

A scruffy Billy stumbled into the kitchen a few minutes later. "What's goin' on Pops?"

Ray poured them each a glass of red wine. "Sit down, son, an' tell me how the hell the front bumper on my truck got so damn clean."

Billy stared at the wine. His father had never before offered him any thing stronger than coffee…and first thing in the morning? He bit his lip.

"Pops, I don't know what to say."

Ray glared at his son. In a strange muted voice, "Look at me, when I'm talkin' to ya, boy. Ya' could try the truth on for size. Once ya git used to tellin' the truth, ya might even like it. Ya'll never know till ya give it a try."

"I went for the water and stopped for a few drinks. Then I came home and cleaned the headlights so you'd see better; they were so dirty I could hardly see a damn thing."

"Okay, Billy… And is it possible maybe part o' the problem may o' been that dead man's blood? Billy, answer me honest now."

Billy sat sullenly, his wine untouched.

"I'm stayin' right here till I git' me some answers." Ray took a sip of his wine, but his eyes never left his son's face.

Billy didn't touch his wine. He continued to fidget and finally said, "Pops, I gotta take a leak."

"If ya'gotta go, ya'gotta go."

Billy walked to the bathroom and when his father walked in with him, he turned abruptly and shouted. "What the hell are you trying to prove?"

"Only thing I'm trying to prove is that ya don't do any sneakin' out. This is one conversation we're gonna' finish come hell or high water."

Billy's neck flushed and he realized his upbringing wasn't a total waste because he'd have slugged anyone else. He thought there're a few boundaries, not many, but a few I won't cross. But don't push me, ol' man.

They returned to the kitchen table. Ray sat down, quietly remembering all the years he'd helped his son with his math homework right here at this very table. Even back then, Billy was lookin' for an angle…an easy way out. This table's held up better n' either one o' us. I'm nothin' but a broken ol' man and Billy's a loser or I never saw one.

Billy sighed and squirmed. Ray continued to glare at his son in silence. Minutes turned into hours as storm clouds gathered on the horizon.

They sat silently watching each other like a couple of crafty wolves sizing each other up for the kill.

Ray asked again, "Billy, are ya gonna' tell me 'bout my truck?"

Billy stared at his father defiantly and lifted his glass of wine, swallowing it in one quick gulp. "I already told ya, what else do ya want from me?"

Ray took a slow sip of his wine, set the glass down, leaned forward and slammed the table with his fist. He growled through clenched teeth, "I wan' the truth, boy, an' I wan' it now."

Billy flinched and tensed up. He escaped behind an invisible wall, his armor of insolence, and refused to respond to his father.

Ray said, "Okay, if that's the way it's gonna be, I got all day, all night and all day tomorrow. I'll jes wait till the spirit moves ya to give me an honest answer."

Silence.

Finally Billy sneered at his father. "Aren't you gonna call your girlfriend and tell her you're not comin' to see her?"

Ray held steady. "Reckon Dorothy'll know I'm not comin' if I don't show up. Too bad ya don't have a decent woman o' yur own, ya mighta' had a better life, but who knows, ya may have jes drank yourself to an early death anyway."

Billy's dander got fired up with that comment. "Who the hell do ya think ya are anyway? What makes ya so sure I don't have a good woman? And so what if I've screwed up a few times in my life, besides you, who hasn't?"

Wearily Ray leaned forward, focused on his wayward son, and shouted. "How could I know anything about ya life? Hell ya'd disappear for years at a time without nary a letter or phone call home. We didn't know if ya were dead or alive. **Now ya tell me, jes what kinda son would do that to his parents?**"

Billy leaned in close to his father, and shouted. "**What do ya want from me, ol' man?**"

Lightening flashed across the kitchen followed by a thunderous boom that shattered their protracted silence. They stared at each other as sheets of rain pelted the windows creating an eerie sense of edgy gloom. Ray paced around the shadowy kitchen. Finally he switched on the light above the sink and turned to face his son.

"I want the truth, boy, only the truth. What really happened that night with my truck? I can buy my own water. I'm ol, but I'm not blind, an' I'm not as dumb as ya seem to think I am."

"Look Pops, I'm sorry the sheriff was out here snoopin' around an' gettin' ya all riled up."

"**Enough** with the bullshit! An' stop callin' me Pops, like I'm some kinda throw- away can o' drink."

Billy glared at his father, in a deep passionate voice he menacingly stated. "Okay, Dad, yeah I run over that old codger; I didn't see him until it was too late. What was he thinkin' walkin' his dog down the street in the dark like that?"

Ray's shoulders slumped. "Have you no remorse, son? A man is dead."

Billy stared at his father, his voice quivered in controlled anger. "It was an accident. Would my remorse bring him back from the dead?"

"Ya shoulda'reported the accident. Ya shouldn't took off like ya did. Now it looks like ya was tryin' to hide somethin'."

"Maybe I was...You seem to be forgettin', I'm an ex-con Dad, and I'm on parole right now. I can't even legally leave the state o' Ohio. Hell, I don't even have a driver's license. Do ya really think I wanna share those details with a fuckin' sheriff? Get real, ol' man!"

Ray asked incredulously, "So why the hell did ya come home when ya knew damn well you'd be breakin' laws an' jeopardizin' your parole?"

"I was worried, I did grow up here ya know. Whatever roots I got have come from here. I couldn't concentrate on nothin', every time I turned on the TV; all I ever heard was disaster reports from Harmonyville. I couldn't keep myself from coming."

Ray watched his son; carefully contemplating Billy's story. He scratched his chin and nodded slowly, "Ya know, son, I'd really like to believe ya. But it's damn hard to believe ya feel strong about anything 'round here. I'd think a man who felt so strongly about his roots woulda' showed a damn sight more interest in his folks an' ol' friends than ya ever showed."

Billy stared defiantly at his father and sneered. Between clenched teeth he whispered, "Is that right?"

Ray sat down across the table from his son. He held Billy's stare without blinking and didn't say a word. He slowly began to tap his fingers on the table....over and over again.

Billy finally shoved his chair back from the table and shouted. "Would ya cut that fuckin' tappin'? You're really getting on my nerves. I need another drink."

He stomped across the kitchen to the refrigerator.

Ray leaned back in his chair with his arms folded across his chest as he continued to observe his son in silence.

Billy frantically searched the refrigerator before he slammed the door shut. "Where the hell did ya put the wine?! I wanna drink! Now!"

Ray slowly walked over to block the kitchen door. "There'll be no more alcohol served to ya in this house. Have yourself a glass o' water if you're so damnable thirsty."

Billy glared at his father as venom seethed through his veins. "You're always so high and mighty. You can't stop me from havin' another drink if I decide I'm gonna."

"Ya may be right. But we ain't done talkin' yet. Ya got yourself in a real pickle this time, boy. I don't see how there's anything ya can do but face the music."

Billy pounded the kitchen table with his fist. Tears stung his eyes as he whispered in a guttural tone. "Ya never could understand what it was like for me. Mama knew. I thought she'd always be there for me, but then she left. No one else has ever understood me. No one."

Ray's eyes filled with tears at the mention of Sophie and the unconditional love she held for their only son. "Billy, I always tried to be there for ya, boy. But somehow I always felt like an outsider around ya an' Sophie. But, she wasn't the only one who loved ya."

"Billy, tell me how ya ended up on North Bennett St. drivin' home from Spencerville? That's the part that puzzles me the most, ya grew up here. Even after a few beers, ya'd know that wasn't the way home. Was it really an... accident, son?"

Billy sat strangely silent staring at the floor. A stray tear found its way down his cheek occasionally.

Ray sat silently watching his son while a few tears managed to escape his own eyes.

Billy finally broke the silence and whispered in a shaky voice, "Of course it was an accident, what kind of a question is that! Does it really matter? Would the whys and what ifs bring that man back? I hit him.

He's dead, and I ran off scared...like I always do."

Ray watched him carefully, trying to determine if he finally had the truth. "It matters. It matters a great deal, to me."

Billy began to shake and sob; his tears flowed like Niagara Falls.

Ray set a box of tissues on the table for his son and fixed him a cup of hot decaffeinated tea. And then he waited for the flow to subside.

Finally, Billy said in a tremulous voice. "I been nothin' but a screw-up all my life. Mama refused to believe it. But I know you knew it long before even I realized it. I could tell by that way you always looked at me..."

Ray sighed, "We're gettin' nowhere real fast. We'll finish talking 'bout this tomorrow. I'm goin' to bed. See if ya can get some rest."

He turned his back on his son and trudged up the stairs; the marathon session between father and son had lasted ten hours and the depth of his exhaustion made him feel older than Methuselah.

CHAPTER THIRTEEN

From Calamity to Tragedy

OLIVIA

THE NEXT MORNING RAY awakened to rays of sunshine beaming through the cracks of the closed draperies into his bedroom. He forced himself to get out of bed; with a heavy heart he walked to the window and opened the curtains. The beautiful sunny day portrayed a cunning depiction of life as it ought to be. As usual, his gaze came to rest on the garage apartment. Most days he'd dress with anticipation of an early coffee with Dorothy. But it seemed to Ray those days would soon be over. He slumped back down on the side of the bed and covered his face with his hands.

And he prayed. "Jesus, I know ya an' your Father gotta lota' stuff goin' on an' it seems I never bother talkin' to ya 'ceptin' when I got troubles. But here I am agin. I hate bothern' ya. An' I need your help. My boy's in trouble agin, this time it's big trouble. Another man's a layin' dead. My boy don't know it but he needs your help too. Ya know what I'm talkin' about. Dear Lord, please show me the way"."

A few minutes later Ray stood up and forced himself to shave, dress, and tidy his bedroom. He made a pot of coffee and left a note to Billy on the kitchen table.

He was thankful they still had a certain amount of anonymity and there were no reporters hovering about as he walked to Dorothy's apartment. An overwhelming sense of foreboding hung over him with the realization that Billy would likely be the next big story out of Harmonyville.

I opened the door as soon as I heard a sound in the garage. I was still in my housecoat; I hurried out and wrapped my arms around him. "I'm glad to see you, Ray. I've been worried about you ever since the sheriff's visit yesterday. Then your lights were on till late and ah, you and Billy's muffled angry voices. Did you manage to get any sleep?"

Ray held onto me like a drowning man to a life preserver. "Ah, Miss Dorothy, what a mess, yeah I managed to git some sleep. Don't ya worry none 'bout me."

I stepped back and carefully looked at him. "Let's eat; then we'll talk."

After breakfast, we sat over our second cups of coffee. "Ray, are you ready to tell me what's happened? I've never seen you so distraught."

After several moments' hesitation he answered. "Ya know how Mac's gotta check every black pickup in the county; on orders of the FBI 'cause o' the hit-and-run, an' none too happy 'bout it. I knew I had to talk to Billy 'cause the hit an' run happened the night he'd borrowed my truck."

"Well, at least you don't have anything to worry about, you were here that evening, we played cards and listened to music."

Ray cleared his throat; his voice was soft and hesitant. "Ya know we're all in the same boat with this drought, no one's been washin' their cars, we all have dirty cars. Then Mac found clean front lights an' bumper on my truck…"

Ray's hands trembled as he held his mug and stared into his tea.

I said softly with only a trace of hope. "Well, there must be another explanation."

Ray hesitated and then spoke slowly. "Dorothy, you're a good woman an' I'm sorry ya got stuck in a town with a mess like this goin' on an' now this situation with my boy an' me. I know it ain't the way ya figured your retirement would be."

I gave him a weak smile. "Life is full of surprises. You know all this will pass."

We sat there in an uncomfortable silence. I reached over and covered his hand with mine. After awhile, Ray stood up. "I best be goin', don't plan on me for lunch today."

He leaned over and kissed the top of my head. "Thanks for a delicious breakfast. I'll see ya later."

After he left, I double-locked the door again.

I cleaned up the breakfast dishes and dressed for the day. The weather was clear and sunny, though cooler than usual for Indian summer. A strange surge of panic swept over me when I saw Ray's truck wrapped in yellow crime scene tape as I was leaving the garage for my morning walk.

I chose to walk on the wooded trails rather than the roads to avoid the prying eyes of strangers; still I found the walk did not appease my feelings of trepidation.

As I approached my apartment, the sheriff's car and a black SUV were parked in the driveway. I nodded to the sheriff and ignored the others. I worried the media would be next if my fears for Ray and Billy came true... I knew I needed to leave as soon as possible.

Yet I wanted to stay near in case Ray needed me. I was preparing a light lunch for myself when I heard a knock on my door; I opened it to find Sheriff Mac and three grim looking men in dark suits with him.

"Yes? May I help you?"

"Morning, Miss Dorothy. Mind if we ask you a few questions?"

I invited them in, as if I had nothing in the world to hide. "Certainly, come in. I've just returned from my daily walk."

The man whose nondescript short dark hair revealed a touch of gray just above his ears introduced himself as he flicked an FBI identity card in front of me. "Agent Landers. I have a few questions, shouldn't take more than a few minutes."

The other two agents flashed their IDs in front of me and introduced themselves as Agent Johnson, a tall thin young man, and Agent Diver, a tall black man with the build of an NFL linebacker.

I gestured toward the fireplace area. "Please have a seat. May I offer you a cup of tea?"

The younger agents watched Agent Landers for a cue. He responded, "Very kind of you to offer, but no thank you."

They echoed his words almost in unison. Predictably, Mac, the sheriff accepted my offer. "I'd love a cup of tea right about now. Yes indeed, mighty kind of you to offer."

Agent Landers tried to ask me a question while I was in the kitchen, but I couldn't hear him as I prepared the tea.

Mac smacked his lips and commented after each swallow, "Mm-mm, that's definitely the real thing." It was intentionally disruptive. The two younger agents almost salivated, but steadfastly held court to their leader.

Finally Agent Landers started. "Ms. Myers, what is your relationship to Mr. Ray Clinger?"

I pulled a kitchen chair to the living room and sat across from him; I looked him in the eye and answered. "He's my landlord, and we're friends."

"How long have you known him?"

I tried to calculate quickly. "… I think about four years now."

"Are you acquainted with his son, William?"

I was beginning to wonder where he was headed with this line of questioning. "Yes sir, I've met him."

"Did you see either Ray or William drive the pickup on Tuesday evening of this week?"

I answered honestly. "No sir, I did not see anyone drive the pickup that night. I was right here in my apartment the entire evening."

Agent Landers labored on. "Did you hear anyone in the garage Tuesday night?"

I answered honestly. "My apartment is very well insulated. Evenings I usually listen to my music and read; it would have to be very noisy for me to hear anything in the garage. I don't recall anything exceptional, Ray and I played a few hands of cards after dinner that night."

Landers stood up, followed immediately by the two younger agents, while Sheriff Mac took another long slow sip of his tea.

Agent Landers pulled a business card from his pocket and handed it to me. "If you remember *anything* at all out of the ordinary about Tuesday night, please call me at one of these numbers, even if it seems unimportant and trivial."

Mac stood up as the others were leaving. "Thank you for the drink and your hospitality, Miss Dorothy."

He started to walk out the door and then turned around slowly. He handed me a small beige card; he held onto it just a couple seconds too long, enough to lock eye contact with me in a strange sort of way. "Please feel free to call me anytime."

Then he added with a grim quiet voice. "Hang onto this. Just in case, you never know when something might come up."

I leaned against the door after closing and locking it securely, greatly relieved they were gone. My mind raced with fears that they'd routinely investigate my past and find out I have none. Did Mac somehow already know I was a fake? Or perhaps he was suspicious I was another resident under the witness protection program since no one seemed to know anything about me prior to my arrival in Harmonyville...I felt anxious and tense.

The cars remained parked in the driveway. They'd gone over to Ray's house immediately after leaving my apartment.

I decided it was time for me to make another trip to New York City. I made sure all my curtains were closed tightly and took a shower. It was time for a reprieve from all the craziness Harmonyville had become during the last two weeks.

An hour later the two official cars left the driveway.

I packed my children's photographs inside the box of photos and pulled the extra cash from inside the mattress...just in case. I loaded everything on the back seat and locked my car. Then I carefully tidied the apartment.

Ray didn't come for dinner that night. I somehow knew he wouldn't. He did stop by about seven. My purse and jacket were on the chair by the door.

I greeted him with a tender embrace. "How was your day?"

"I've sure as hell had better." He noticed my things on the chair and gave me a questioning look.

"I'll be leaving for a few days."

"When?"

"Tonight, within the hour."

"My day's goin' from bad to worse in a hand basket. How long ya goin' for this time?"

"I'm not sure, a few days, a week. I don't exactly know."

"It must be nice, bein' footloose and fancy-free. Jes takin' off cause it gets a little too hot by the fire." Ray sounded angry and hurt that I was leaving.

"You knew I was planning another trip to the city. And furthermore, I am a free woman."

"Have yourself a safe trip Miss Dorothy." He abruptly turned to leave and just like that he was gone.

I locked the door to my apartment and carefully backed the car out of the garage and driveway.

I found myself heading for good old I-80, age seventy four and on the road again. I wanted as much distance between me and the fracas of Harmonyville as I could get. And the sooner the better.

By one a.m. I was becoming a dangerous driver; I could hardly keep my eyes open and stopped at the first motel off the highway. I was so tired I just collapsed on the bed. I awoke at ten a.m., refreshed and fully dressed since I'd fallen asleep with my clothes on. I studied my atlas and knew exactly where I was going. I pulled into a McDonalds drive thru and then drove on toward New York City munching on an Egg McMuffin.

Three hours later, N.Y.C. loomed in the near distance. There was something about that city that always brought a smile to my face, but whereas I used to fly in and stay at the New Yorker Hotel in Manhattan... I'd graduated to the less expensive N.J side of the Hudson River and used the ferry to get to the city. My theater attendance would be strictly matinees. Of course, I visited a few of my favorite book stores and the museums were breathtaking as always. The days flew by as they did each time I've been to the city.

One day I bought a specialty sandwich at a deli not far from Central Park, and had a picnic in the park in the company of a wonderful Maeve Binchy novel. The weather was glorious and it seemed to be an absolutely perfect day as I made my way amidst the throngs of New Yorkers heading home after a day of work.

As I hurried to board the subway, I heard a familiar voice and there in the same crowded subway car...were Andrea and Joel. I slumped into a far corner of the car in shock. I was close enough to hear Joel's soft voice over the subway's din and no one could avoid Andrea's agitated responses. I found a discarded newspaper and quickly picked it up to hide behind. I was completely unnerved.

Andrea's voice escalated. "I'll be damned if you're going to make me ride the fricking subway the whole time we're here. I came to see the city again, not scoot around underground like a god damn rat!"

A few people nearby rolled their eyes and shook their heads with disgust. While a well-dressed tired looking gentleman glared at her. "Keep it down."

As the subway rolled to a stop, Andrea turned around and barked at him. "Mind you own business!"

I tried to hustle by her when the subway door opened. It wasn't my planned stop but I needed some fresh air and some space. I tried not to look at her as I left the car but I couldn't help one brief furtive look as I walked by her in the crowded car.

Our eyes locked for a fraction of a second...with an urgent huskiness in her voice, she whispered, *"M-o-t-h-e-r?!"*

I turned and hurried away into the crowd.

I heard her shrieking. **"Mother, Mother please come back!"**

Then I heard Joel shout to a police officer. "No please, I'll take care of her; she'll be okay. She lost her mother recently and saw someone who looked like her get off the subway."

I dashed up the stairs and quickly hailed a cab, gave him the address of my motel in New Jersey. Out of breath, I settled back in the cab, and sobbed quietly with my hands over my face.

My perfect day had turned upside down. My soul was in turmoil.

CHAPTER FOURTEEN

Martyrs Reign

ANDREA

JOEL CONTINUED TO HOLD Andrea as she sobbed. "Its okay, Andie, this happens to lots of people when they lose someone. Remember the doctor told us it's normal to see people who remind you of the one who's passed on while we work our way through the grieving process."

Through ragged breaths, Andrea struggled to regain her composure. What there was left to claim. She whispered in the jerky pattern of the forsaken. "You don't understand, Joel, I'm not crazy. It was her. I saw Mother and I know she saw me, too, *but she ran away from me.*"

Then she began to tremble and sob uncontrollably.

Joel hailed a cab; the driver took one look at Andrea. "Where to, Mister, do ya need a hospital?"

"No, please just take us back to the New Yorker. My wife has suffered a shock. A good night's rest and some quiet time will help her immensely."

"Yea, I know how women are. I gotta wife and five daughters. Let me tell ya, I'm the one who needs peace at my house; my time drivin' this here cab is my quiet time!"

Andrea was finally above ground in a moving cab. She was so preoccupied with having seen her mother she *almost* didn't hear the cabby's comments. Something inside her snapped, she pushed Joel away, took a few deep breaths and leaned forward. "Stop this cab.

And stop it right now."

She saw the cabby look at Joel in the mirror and Joel shake his head slightly indicating the cab driver should ignore her request.

Joel reached for her again. "Andrea, honey, you're under too much stress to think clearly right now. Please just come back to the hotel with me, we'll order room service and maybe watch a movie… if you feel up to it."

Her speech was still raspy. "How dare you assume you always know what's best for me, and all these clubby conversations you find with the poor, oppressed men of the world."

"Andrea, don't make it into something it's not. Just relax, honey. Remember, we came to New York for a getaway."

She leaned forward and saw the cabby's name badge, "Roberto, stop this damn cab or I'll report you for unlawful abduction! *I want out and I want out right now!*"

Joel used his attorney air of authority tone. "How much do we owe you, Roberto? I guess this is the end of our ride."

Roberto thought he'd seen it all, but every so often something would happen to prove him wrong. This was one of those times. That guy oughta' tell that broad where to go.

He raised his eyebrows, pushed the meter tab. "Eight dollars'll do it."

Joel gave him a ten as they left the car.

He ran to catch up with Andrea who was nearly half way down the block by the time he caught up with her, and silently kept pace.

He gritted his teeth as he counted to ten before speaking. "Andrea, what exactly happened back there?"

Andrea refused to acknowledge him for several steps and then spoke in a soft determined manner. "*It was Mother, I saw her and she saw me.* You didn't see her, but I'd bet she saw you too. We never did find a body and remember the newly copied framed photos? The dead end trail the police and J.C. found? I don't know what's going on with her but I know my own mother and I just saw her on that subway car!"

Joel used his soothing lawyer voice. "Ah Andie, baby, you've gotta' let go of this and move on with your life. I know it's been hard and seeing your mother's look alike didn't help."

Andrea stopped suddenly and turned to her husband. The

sidewalk was only slightly less crowded than the subway station. Her eyes blazed with anger. "I am not a psycho and you can stop your pompous bullshit right now, Joel!"

Joel was stunned. "Andie, I never thought you were!"

People kept shoving by them. One man snarled. "For God sakes, take yourselves outa' the way, can't ya' see there are people who aren't on vacation an' we gotta' work for a livin'!"

Another woman didn't even excuse herself as she elbowed Joel as she jostled by, and snidely cursed. "Frickin' tourists! There oughta be an open season on the dumb ones that stop right in the middle of busy sidewalks!"

Joel gently put his hand on Andrea's arm. "Come on; let's find a better place to talk."

She followed his lead without resistance as had been her pattern throughout their marriage, though with each step her resentment toward Joel's official supremacy grew.

He found a small coffee shop and ordered two herbal teas with a pastry to share.

Andrea sat down compliantly, staring at the table.

Joel sipped his tea and took a couple bites of the pastry and waited for Andrea to calm down.

Finally she took a sip of her tea, looked at him squarely. "Do you have any idea how it feels to know something to be true and have the person who is supposed to be your best friend act like you're some kind of nut just because he didn't see what you saw?"

He listened to her and contemplated her words and demeanor before responding. "You're absolutely sure the woman you saw was your mother?"

She sighed deeply. "Of course I am! Otherwise I wouldn't have become so frustrated with you when you assured me, "It's normal to see people who reminded us of our beloved departed"!"

He sipped his tea and sighed. "Well, I don't want to add fuel to the embers, but I seem to recall you were quite agitated about riding the subway. You wanted a cab Andie; I was only trying to stretch our travel dollars a bit farther."

Andrea glared at him again. "Are you insinuating that I wasn't seeing clearly because I was pissed off? Well, if that's the case then I could be declared legally blind, because I find myself seething more often than I'd like to admit!"

Joel was startled by her admission, his mouth opened, but no words came out.

She frowned. "Come on Joel, you know me too well to have not noticed the frequent swells of my anger! I've tried for years to suppress it, but I don't think I can live like that any more."

Joel looked stricken as he stared at her. "What are you saying?"

Andrea sighed once more. "Joel, I want some respect."

"Andrea, you're my wife. I've always respected you. I do my best to take care of you and the children. What more do you want?"

She watched him as if from afar and slowly remembered why she'd fallen in love with him. Back then it was his strength, confidence and straight-forward manner, the very things that lately had annoyed her so intensely. "Trust, Joel. And to be taken seriously when I express myself. I don't need to be taken care of. I'm not a child. So stop patronizing me as if I were some sort of idiot!"

An unfamiliar mask of weariness covered his once handsome face. "I don't know how to reach you anymore, Andrea. No matter what I do, I can't seem to please you. Tell me what it is you want from me."

Warm tears sneaked down her cheeks and Andrea felt her anger begin to dissipate. She reached across the table and touched his hand, instinctively stroking his wedding ring as she murmured. "Joel, I guess I just want you to listen to me. Everything has seemed so, so... weird since Mother's been gone. I saw her on the subway and you trivialized my claim with no consideration that perhaps I was right. I feel so very sad and then angry when you routinely write me off like that.

"You've said ever since she disappeared that there was something very strange about the whole thing. You'll never convince me that I not only saw her, but I made eye contact with my mother today in that subway car."

Joel lowered his head into his hands and rubbed his eyes. He thought how this woman was wearing him down, and how he felt like an old man living his life on eggshells.

Nonetheless, he slowly responded to his wife's assertion. "Andrea, let's presume the woman you saw was your mother. She apparently didn't want to talk to you, did she? Do you have any idea where to find this woman?"

"Of course not." She frowned as if in deep thought and then wistfully stated. "Maybe she has amnesia and didn't recognize me."

"Andrea, you've already said you believed the woman recognized you too. But she ran away.

"Also, please remember how your mother transferred ownership of her house and car to you and Alexander. Amnesia sufferers don't make those kind of preparations."

Andrea resolutely sighed. "As long as I live, I will never understand."

OLIVIA

My heart feels pulled apart! My daughter was always demanding and dissatisfied. Her glass was never half full. Not once. I know she saw me. I don't know what I'd have done if there hadn't been a cab available. What could I possibly say to her at this point? I can't go back. Everything would be just as before, except they'd forever hold it over my head that I ran away and that proves I'm not competent when I'm perfectly capable of making my own decisions and what's done is done. No, I can't go back.

Yet that was my daughter and son-in-law, part of me wishes I could have a relationship with them. I know Joel will spend the better part of the day trying to convince Andrea she didn't see her mother, only someone who looked like me.

And what are the odds of us being here on the same weekend and then running into each other by chance in a place like New York City? Life is sometimes stranger than fiction.

I'll have to find another place to stay for a couple days…just in case they try to find me. I've come too far to go back now. They'd never understand.

An hour later I'd checked out of the motel and was on the move again. Twenty miles down Interstate 95, I found a Hampton Inn that looked very inviting. I was lucky to be able to check in with cash and my Dorothy Myers driver's license as identification. I wanted to use the pool, but decided to stay in my room out of sight for the rest of the evening. I always carry a few granola bars with me and bottled water.

I made myself a cup of tea with the complimentary electric water/coffee maker available in the room and finished my Binchy novel. It was a very relaxing evening and the novel helped distract me from the anxiety I'd felt from the subway brush with my past.

Before sleeping, I checked CNN and found no mention of the Harmonyville catastrophe on the national news. That was a relief in itself.

The next morning I brought my breakfast to my room from the hotel lobby. I carefully planned my day. I'd wear a scarf, sunglasses and take the bus in from Hoboken and get off on 47th Street.

I was glad Isaac had been able to accommodate me on short notice. What would I ever do without him? He offered me a cup of tea and we conducted our business. I appreciated his unobtrusive efficiency. Thirty minutes later he called a cab, walked out with me and gallantly opened the cab door.

I boldly covered his hand with mine and said, "Your mother must be very proud to have such a kind son as you. Bless you, dear Isaac."

His face turned scarlet and he whispered, "Godspeed to you, Olivia Hampton."

I took the cab to the bus terminal and caught a return bus to Hoboken where my car was parked. I'd decided to drive north of the city and stay a couple days in Mystic, Connecticut. I was glad I'd already seen two new Broadway plays since I knew I must avoid Manhattan the rest of this trip.

I'd been to Mystic only once before when Melvin and I celebrated our seventh anniversary…before the children were born. We'd wanted to start a family for years, but my periods had been so irregular, I'd almost given up hope. And unbeknownst to us, there I was already expecting Alex.

We'd stayed at the New Yorker for three nights, went to three Broadway shows, shopped, visited the Metropolitan Museum, the Museum of Natural History and ate at the nicest restaurants. New York City had been a whirlwind, so he decided we should spend the rest of our week at a more relaxing pace and it was wonderful. I think it was the happiest, most carefree time of our lives; there I was returning forty years later and I didn't know why.

It's a question I can't answer because I don't understand what's drawn me back. The cozy hotel we'd stayed in was gone and in its place stood a small tourist shopping plaza. It almost looks like any other ocean-side town except for the unique seaside and walkways; those were virtually unchanged. And that's where Melvin and I had spent so many hours all those years ago, walking hand in hand, watching the beautiful sunsets over the Atlantic and listening to the rhythm of the ocean's surf. On that vacation, our innocent dreams would never have allowed us to believe what our future held for us.

Luckily, I found a small out-of-the-way Bed and Breakfast, very reasonable and happy to accept cash payment. I stayed three days and enjoyed the peace and solitude. I called Ray the next morning and was not surprised to get an icy reception.

"Hello, Ray, how are you? I just wanted to call and tell you I missed you."

"Could this be that elusive Dorothy Myers? I think I used ta have a tenant by that name. Nope, can't tell ya for sure where she is. She's a slippery one, she is. Well I'm doin' all right."

"Ah Ray, I'm sorry I had to leave so quickly. You haven't rented out my apartment to someone else have you?" I joked.

"Dorothy, what do ya think? Course not. Ya got your rent all paid up till the first o' next month."

"So, what's new? Have things calmed down? How's Billy?"

"Things been pretty well quiet roun' here the last few days. But I know the sheriff's cookin' up somethin'. He tol' Billy he's not to leave the county till he cleared him for travel. Did ya ever hear o' such a thing?"

"That does sound menacing. What does Billy say about it?"

"He don't say much a'tall. Never saw him quiet like this before."

"I'm sorry you have to deal with all this. Sometimes life seems so unfair.

"I went to see two Broadway shows and visited the museums. I just need to do this for myself sometimes. I realize my trips must surely look suspicious to you, but I've been independent for a long time. I enjoy our special friendship, but I still consider myself to be a free spirit."

"Ya won't get no arguments from me about that, Miss Dorothy; ya just about as free as a spirit can be! So where the hell are ya callin' me from anyway?"

"Oh, I'm relaxing for a few days at a nondescript little Bed and Breakfast in a small coastal village. I'm planning to drive home Sunday afternoon. I'll see you then, Ray."

"Travelin'mercies to ya, Miss Dorothy."

I enjoyed my time in Mystic. I bought a couple large print novels, went to a matinee movie and enjoyed watching the ocean surf. It was a lovely peaceful respite from the tangled web my life had become back in Harmonyville.

Sunday morning after I'd checked out, I stopped at a pay phone and called Luella. I knew she'd be up preparing her Sunday dinner. She always put it in the oven just before she left for church. She had her children and grandchildren for dinner almost every Sunday at one.

"Oh my God! Olivia! Are you alright? Haven't heard from you in months! I can't believe it's you and on a Sunday mornin'!"

"Yes, dear I'm okay. I've been resting in a small town on the coast of New England for a few days."

Luella spoke slowly in a hushed tone, "Honestly, I can't keep track of you; how on earth? Wait a minute; don't tell me you're in… Mystic!"

"You know me too well, my friend. I stopped to call you on my way out of town; I stayed in New York City, but only a few days."

Luella sighed, "How was your trip to the city?"

I hesitated before answering, somehow I knew she knew why I'd come to Mystic. It's like that with a true heart friend. "It started out like all my trips to the city, I saw a couple nice shows, enjoyed the museums and then I ended up in the same subway car as Andrea and Joel! I left at the next stop, luckily found a cab and got away. But she made eye contact with me briefly as I went out the door.

"I thought my legs would give out from under me, it was such a shock, I wanted so much to reach out to her and be part of her life again but I knew I couldn't. It's too late for that now. She'd been angry with Joel and complaining loudly about riding the subway, same old Andrea."

Luella added softly, "So you lit outa' town and just happened to end up back in Mystic. Did it help going back?"

"Yes, I think it has helped, I've regained my equilibrium."

Luella sighed again. "That must've been some vacation you and Melvin had there all those years ago. Has it changed much?"

"Yes and no, the ocean and walkways are much the same but it's become a major tourist destination and there are so many big resorts and casinos. It was what I needed for a few days though. I'm heading back to my new life now; I just wanted to hear your voice. Have you been well?"

"I can't complain, as well as could be expected at my age. My God, what are the odds of running into your daughter and her husband in that huge city? It must've been part of your destiny, unbelievable!"

"I'm glad to hear you've been okay. I miss you so very much, my dear."

"I miss you - more than you'll ever know. Do take care, my friend."

After our lingering good byes, I hung up the phone, got in my car and drove southwest towards Pennsylvania.

CHAPTER FIFTEEN

Reality Blues

OLIVIA

I ARRIVED BACK IN HARMONYVILLE at half-past-eight on Sunday evening. I'd been gone ten days. The town looked almost normal; most of the outsiders seemed to have moved on.

Ray saw my lights and came right over. I was happy to see him again and it gave me a warm fuzzy feeling to know he was so pleased to see me. It's safe to say it was a blissful reunion. Despite the long drive, I was too excited to feel tired. We agreed not to talk about the situation that had prompted my hasty departure. There'd be plenty of time for that later.

Ray turned on the radio and we slow danced to a couple songs on the Golden Oldies station. It felt so good to have his arms around me and to feel his closeness. I knew I was one lucky old lady.

He went home by eleven thirty. I locked up extra tight, unpacked and showered. I was sound sleep within five minutes of laying my head on the pillow.

The next day I had toast and tea for breakfast; then started my laundry and bought groceries. The hours passed by quickly and by five p.m. I realized that I hadn't seen Ray all day...

He didn't come over till late Monday evening and one look at him told me something was wrong, very wrong. His face was tense and haggard and his eyes were puffy and red as if he'd been crying.

"My God, Ray, you look terrible! What's happened? Sit down and tell me. I know something's dreadfully wrong." I fixed him a cup of

Irish coffee. He looked like he needed one if ever anyone did.

Then he told me of his marathon night and day.

"Last night after I went home, Billy was waitin' for me in the kitchen an' he finally wanted to talk an' I said to him, son, jes tell me what the hell is really goin' on 'round here.

"Billy crumbled in the kitchen chair; he looked like an ol' broken man with tremblin' hands he picked up his cup of coffee, his voice quiverin' as he told me the ugly truth.

"When Billy was serving time he met some bad people. An' he made some shameful compromises. Then when he got out, he took some short cuts; said he was always tryin' to get ahead...so we could be proud of him. Nothin' ever worked out like it shoulda.

"Anyway he tol' me, "When this whole mess happened here in Harmonyville, I'd talked too much about this bein' my home town an' Boris was watchin' the news one night an' saw Trovosky plain as day standin' there in a crowd in front of the court house. They never forget or forgive an enemy...an' they'd been lookin' for him for years.

"So, Boris sends two of his boys down to my apartment. I was scared, Dad."

I just sat there numbed with dread and quietly waited for him to tell me the rest of his story.

"Then Billy continued, "I knew it was no social visit. I owed him an' I figured he was callin' my debt early. I didn't have the money. They drove me to Boris' office an' nothing really bad happened except they showed me Trovosky's photo over an' over so I'd remember his face. Then they gave me three days to give him a fatal accident. They'd a killed me if I didn't."

"It nearly broke my heart to see him sit there and cry like that. Then suddenly my sympathy vanished an' I felt nothin' but contempt and disgust for my boy.

"I tol' him, everyone always has a choice an' ya made yurs. Now ya'll have to live with the consequences, whatever they may be.

"Billy paled as he whispered hoarsely. "Ya mean your gonna' turn me in?"

"I said to him, 'doubt I'll have to. They've already put ya' on travelin' restrictions an' they got my truck cordoned off. Ya' might wanna' think 'bout turnin' yourself in, they may go a little easier on ya. I don't know what to tell ya son.

"Billy's face was puffy and red from all the cryin'. His breathin' was shallow and raspy; still he couldn't hold back on his anger. He raged at me, "That's it!? Your gonna throw me out to the wolves? I'm your only son! You got no one else. When it comes down to it; it's just you and me, Dad"

"I tol' him, 'I don't see it that way. I got good friends. True friends."

He looked me cold in the eye and said, "Say what you want about your friends, Dad, but you an' me, we're family.'"

"I jes sat there thinkin', I'd lost count years ago of the number of times Sophie an' me had sat around that very table worryin' over Billy. My God, I felt old an' tired.

"I finally broke the silence, "Billy, if you get outa' this mess, tell me what you'd do with the rest of your life."

"He looked at me skeptically and slowly avowed, "I'd start fresh in a new city; I'd go to a technical school and get certified in welding, electronics or maybe computers. I'd make you proud of me, Dad."

I walked around the table slowly, stood behind him and put my hands on his shoulders, "Billy, when ya came straight home that night, I drove back to town and accidentally run over Joe or Trovosky as ya call him. I was so befuddled I didn't stop to get help for him...that'll be our story...and may God have mercy on our souls'.

"Billy stood up an' hugged me like he'd jes won the lottery or somethin', "Pops, thank you... you're the best! I'll make you proud, jes wait and see."

"Miss Dorothy, ya're lookin' at a man who's out on bail with charges o' manslaughter hangin' over his head for that hit-n'-run." His hand trembled as he lifted his cup.

I sat in a shocked silence for what felt like a piece of eternity.

"But Ray, the night of the hit and run, Billy had your truck...I don't understand."

"The law seems mighty sure it was my truck, an' Mac's deputies treat me okay. But they don't give my boy no respect. They'd jes as soon lock him up an' throw away the damn key. I saw with my own eyes how they worked him over. It was disgustin'. I'm an ol' man; I've lived a good life. My boy deserves a chance, I can't help thinkin'o' his dear mother an' how she'd prayed for him all those years. I couldn't let my Sophie down."

I struggled to find my voice; finally I managed a guttural whisper. "So you're taking the rap, to give Billy yet another chance?"

He stared into his coffee cup. "Yes'm, I'd say that's what I'm doin' all right."

I thought I might faint and then I heard myself implore indignantly. "But Ray, that's a travesty of justice!"

"Miss Dorothy, please don't take no offense, but ya can't understand what it is to be a parent if ya ain't never had no youngin's of yur own. Teachin' other peoples youngins' jes ain't the same thing."

I was stunned and angry, if only he knew…yet I felt absolute sorrow for Ray. This would be slow suicide, the final chapter in the life of a wonderful man whom I'd grown to love as a dear friend and yes, more than just a friend, during the last four and a half years.

"An' I have to ask ya to keep this conversation 'tween us. Outa respect for me an'…us, I expect ya to honor my request."

I felt warm tears on my cheeks. I nearly choked as I whispered in a hoarse voice that I barely recognized as my own. "Oh Ray, what've you gone and done?"

"I'm sorry, Miss Dorothy, it seemed like the only thing I could do to help my boy outa this pickle he got himself in."

"Ray, this isn't a pickle, a man is dead and you know Billy did it. When will enough ever be enough for Billy?"

He looked at me pleadingly. "He's my son. I gotta help him."

I built a fire in the fireplace and we sat on the sofa, watched the fire and held hands in silence. The only sound was an occasional crackle from the hearth.

Awhile later he got up to add another log to the fire.

"How long do you have?"

He answered in a flat voice devoid of emotion. "I was formally charged this morning and I posted my bail this afternoon, only one hundred dollars cause they trust me. If ya' coulda' seen the way they treated me an' the way they were treatin' Billy, it was like night an' day. I wouldn't o' believed it if I hadn't saw it myself. Mac said I could remain out on my own recognizance till the trial an' they're pushin' for that in about two months."

"It might be more complicated and nasty since the FBI'll be involved because Joe was in Witness Protection."

Ray was suddenly flooded with emotion as he sobbed into his hands. I put my arm around him and tried to offer solace to my dear friend…but there was nothing I could say or do. The tragedy seemed to have mushroomed out of our control.

I put another log on the fire and sat down beside Ray again, his breathing became calmer as a steadfast serenity settled over him. "I'm so sorry, Miss Dorothy. Sorry about breakin down like this…an about everythin'."

I took his hands in mine and kissed them gently. "Ray, what are friends for? Don't worry; you just keep proving to me what an extraordinarily kind person you are. You did what you thought was right. I admire you for that even though I deem it a colossal mistake. Your secret will be safe with me."

He kissed my hands and whispered. "I'm mighty proud to o' been your friend, Miss Dorothy; I never been sorry I talked to ya in the diner that day."

We sat there quietly watching the fire until he fell sound asleep. I waited until the fire burned down to embers and then helped my sleeping friend stretch out on the sofa and carefully covered him with blankets. I locked up and turned off the lights. Ray stayed all night; he was totally exhausted after the previous night's marathon session with Billy and his day of confession and legalities.

The next morning I sat in the kitchen reading a book with a cup of tea, Ray stretched and looked around as his face slowly turned scarlet. "Oh my God, Miss Dorothy, I didn't mean to sleep here, I'm so sorry. Ya pay me good money to have a place o' your own an' then I barge in on ya an' stay all night long. It ain't right."

I handed him a cup of hot tea. "You talk nonsense, Ray Clinger. Here, drink this and see if it puts a bit of sense into your thick head!"

He took it meekly, though his eyes twinkled beneath his thick white eyebrows. "I do wonder what you're talkin' about, Miss Dorothy."

"I think you know very well what I'm talking about. Ray, do you even have a lawyer?"

"Don't see why I need a lawyer since I already 'fessed up to the crime."

"Surely you're not serious, this is a federal case."

He patted my hand gently. "Mac'll take care o' everythin'. Don't ya' go worryin'. I know what I'm doin' here."

I fixed scrambled eggs and toast with fresh fruit for our breakfast. I enjoyed having him there in the mornings, but I knew all too well leisurely breakfasts with him would soon be just another memory.

"Miss Dorothy, that was another fine breakfast an' I thank ya kindly for it."

"Ray, it was nice to have your company this morning."

He leaned back on his chair, the way he does when he had something important to say and spoke slowly. "I believe you're a lady who's always deserved a damn sight better than life's dealt ya. Anyway that's what I think."

I gave him my stern school teacher expression and a half smile, leaned forward, elbows on the table with my chin on my hands. And waited to see where he was going with this topic.

"I got one big favor to ask o' ya, Miss Dorothy. I know I got my nerve even thinkin' I could ask ya for such a thing…but I was hopin' I could count on ya for keepin' an eye on Billy when I'm not aroun'. He's not like other men his age; he can't seem to help himself."

I was stunned to several minutes of silence before finally answering. "I'm sorry, Ray but that's not a promise I can make in good faith. And I assure you, Billy wouldn't want me to keep track of his activities for you or anyone else. He's over forty and it's my opinion if anyone should keep an eye on him…it should be a prison warden!"

Ray's face reflected disappointment, but not surprise. "Well, I was afraid you might feel that way, but it did no harm to ask. I best be headin' home, only God knows what today holds."

CHAPTER SIXTEEN

Reality Bites

OLIVIA

R AY AND I TRIED to live each day as if were our last day together. And we had some great times those next few weeks. But there was always the cloud of prison hovering just beyond the horizon.

Then Mac came by one afternoon and acted real friendly. I fixed us a pot of hot tea and then out of the blue he asked me, "Miss Dorothy, you must have some concerns about this whole deal with Ray and Billy. Anything you'd like to talk to me about?"

I looked him squarely in the eye and answered in my calculating stern teacher voice. "No, sir, that's something I try not to get involved in. If you have questions about Ray and Billy, you should ask them, not me. I will not come between a man and his children. Never have and don't plan to start at this point in my life."

He seemed to squirm as he took another sip. "Well, I thank you kindly for the hot drink; it's been gettin' right cold out there, I appreciate it." He stood and started for the door, then turned and gave me a strange look, pausing just long enough for an awkward silence. "If you think of anything you might want to talk to me about, whether it's your mysterious past or more recent events, don't hesitate to call. Here's my card."

I was speechless as I closed the door. I wondered if he'd intended to intimidate me. If so, he'd been a colossal success.

After locking my door behind him, I laid his card on the counter and shivered. I poured myself another cup of tea and sat down on the sofa.

I asked myself. "My God, how did my life get so complicated? Do I want to stay in Harmonyville after Ray's sent to prison? What's the right thing for me to do now?" I didn't know the answers and tears sneaked out of the corners of my eyes; damn, I hated it when I got so emotional!

After lunch I decided to go to the library and on my way home buy a few groceries. I felt the need for some real old-fashioned comfort foods. What was happening to me? And did Mac speak for most of the town when he referred to my past? Was I still a mystery woman? Why did they even care? I felt like I was becoming a bit unglued. And I didn't like that feeling at all.

At the library I claimed a computer as soon as it became available and immediately searched out the local news back home. There was no mention of Andrea or Alexander, which should mean they were settling down and their lives had taken on a semblance of normality. The club news was identical to the pieces I used to write except for a few name and date changes. I wondered if they'd made a standard form based on my club reports and had the club reporters submit their updates by filling in the blanks. Ah, but what did it matter?

I searched the internet and discovered new information about the Federal Prison System. Two hours slipped by and no one seemed to notice how long I'd been on the computer. The library was busy but there were still two empty computer stations on either side of me. Much later I stopped for groceries and on my way home, decided to treat myself to a fresh sub at the Sandwich Shop.

I noticed the air was distinctly colder and decided to get my winter coat out of storage as soon as I put the groceries away.

I started to unlock my door… but it wasn't locked. I remember thinking, that's strange, I was sure I locked it. I began to doubt myself until I walked in and found my apartment literally almost ripped inside out. I stood there in shock. And then I heard sounds of movement in my bedroom. Somewhere in my frozen brain, I heard a voice deep in my subconscious whisper, "Get the hell out of here, *now!*"

But I couldn't move and as if in slow motion, the bag of groceries slipped out of my hands and fell to the floor with a thud.

The bedroom suddenly became quiet. Then I heard an unfamiliar sound, sort of like a metal click, followed by someone's movement and then Billy walked around the corner, a small black revolver pointed right at me.

I whispered in a hoarse voice, "Billy!"

He sneered. "I didn't expect you back so soon, Miss Dorothy."

I stumbled to the kitchen chair, sat down and took a deep breath. I was able to think a bit clearer as more oxygen got to my brain. I quickly looked at the mess created by Ray's son. I sighed and asked with my stern school teacher's voice, "Billy, what are you looking for?"

"Money. You must have some around here somewhere."

"I'm a retired widow of modest means, I live very frugally. You won't find money here because I don't have any."

"No money, huh? So, how much do you have in your purse?"

I opened my purse and tossed him my wallet.

He rummaged through it, papers and cards fell to the floor. "Three thousand bucks, not bad for a start."

He grinned menacingly and glanced around at the mess he'd created, I glared at him. "That's all I have. I sold some jewelry in the city when I was away. I have no money. My checks are automatically deposited and I use the phone and internet when I need to contact my bank."

I reasoned a thief didn't deserve the truth. And there was no way I'd divulge where my money really was. If he hadn't found any yet, there was a good chance it wouldn't happen.

He thrust the phone at me and demanded, "Call your bank, I want ten thousand dollars and I want it today."

"Billy, you never cease to amaze me. You've been around long enough to know it doesn't work that way."

He stuffed my money into his pockets and tossed my wallet into the strewn rubble in the far corner of the room. "Don't start your teachin' preachin' on me! It might work on my ol' man, but it sure as hell won't never work on me."

Then he stomped over to me, menacingly pushed the barrel of his revolver against my head and thrust my phone into my hand. "Call your bank, Bitch!"

I pretended I'd make the call and then faster than I've moved in years, I stood and knocked that gun out of his hand and kneed him in the crotch. He screamed obscenities as I bolted for the door. He must've grabbed his gun and clubbed me across the back of my head. I guess I'm lucky he didn't shoot me.

The next thing I knew, Mac was quietly talking to his deputy at my kitchen table, a young police photographer was snapping photos from different angles of the crime scene, my apartment.

I had one hellish headache when I came to. Once I got my wits about me, I knew I'd be okay. I refused to go to the hospital, of course.

Ray's crestfallen face was ashen, like his heart had been cut right out of him. He sat on the sofa and sullenly stared at the floor.

Mac reached over and checked Ray's pulse. "What do you say we take you to the hospital for observation tonight? You're not lookin' too good, Ray."

The medic took Ray's blood pressure. "I think that'd be a good idea Mr. Clinger. Your blood pressure's high enough to put you in the danger zone."

Ray answered softly. "Hell no, I'm not goin' to the damn hospital. I'd have to be a dead man walking if I didn't have some kinda' reaction to the mess I walked into. I'll be okay, jes' let me be."

I slowly walked over to him. I felt a bit dizzy, but there was no way I'd mention that to the boy medic. I reached Ray and stood behind him with my hands on his shoulders, and asked him in a soft voice that I didn't recognize as my own, "Ray, are you sure about not going to the hospital?"

He reached up and patted my hand with his clammy hand.

Lonesome tears trickled down the well worn lines of his cheeks, tears that had stolen the sparkle right out of his eyes.

"Miss Dorothy, I just need to sit a spell and chew all this over in my mind."

I nodded, "In the meantime, I think we could all use a good cup of tea."

We sat in a suspended space of silence until the kettle whistled; then the medic took Ray's pulse and blood pressure again.

He looked at Mac and shrugged. "His blood pressure and pulse have both dropped to high normal ranges."

Mac said, "You might as well go on back to the station. Thanks for all your help, Kevin."

I poured their tea and added a bit of honey to each mug without even asking if they wanted the sweetener.

Mac pulled out his notebook, looked at us and sighed.

"I think you both realize this could have gone a lot worse than it did today. I guess your allotted time in this world just isn't up yet. Miss Dorothy, do you want to tell me what happened here today?"

I described the scene I walked into when I returned from shopping…

They both looked at me like I was a freak.

Sheriff Mac shook his head in disbelief. "You mean to say, you knocked his gun out of his hand while he had it pointed at your head? And then you kneed him? My God!"

"Well, I've taken self-defense classes; besides no one ever expects anything from old ladies. Perhaps it was foolish of me, but I refuse to be taken advantage of."

Mac raised his eyebrows and kept writing. "And about what time did you arrive home?"

I answered, "Probably around two."

Mac sighed, "Miss Dorothy, I don't think I'd have taken a chance like that with a gun to my head, but there's not much sense in tellin' you what to do. Seems like you're a stubborn woman who makes her own decisions. And a damn lucky one at that."

Then he turned to Ray, "Are you up to tellin' me what you saw when you walked in here?"

Ray took a slow sip of his tea. "I like the tea with honey added, it's right good. Thank ya', Miss Dorothy."

Mac waited.

"Well, I came out to my garage to repair a part on my ol' vacuum cleaner an' I saw Miss Dorothy's apartment door open. She never left it open, so I walked in to see if she was okay. The first thing I noticed was her layin' on the floor face down. I knelt down to see if she still had a pulse, an' called her name. It wasn't till after I realized she was alive that I even noticed groceries scattered on the floor beside her an' then looked around and saw the apartment turned upside down. About then I heard footsteps behind me, an' I looked up, an' Billy was standin' there pointin' a gun at me, his own father. I ain't never seen such an empty coldness in anyone's eyes before."

Ray took another sip of his tea. Mac took a large swig of his.

Ray continued, "I said to him, Billy, what the hell do ya think your doin'? He snickered, 'Ol' man, it don't take no genius to figure out ya' caught me red-handed robbin' the ol' bag.'"

Ray stopped, choked by his tears. After a few minutes he took a deep breath and wiped his face dry with the sleeve of his plaid flannel shirt. "I said to him, 'Billy, why in God's name would you go and do somethin' as dumb as this? If ya was in need of money, all ya had to do was ask me.'

"He says to me, 'Yea, if I wanna have twenty bucks at a time like some friggin' allowance for a kid or else wait around for ya to croak. I've had it with this town. I wanted some seed money to get the hell outa here an' your Miss Dorothy kindly contributed to my most worthy cause.'

"I told him to put down the gun an' call an ambulance; he looked at me like I was a stranger an' a crazy one at that. I turned back to check on Miss Dorothy and then I remember reachin' for the phone. Next thing I knew I looked up an' ya was starin' right at me, Mac."

Mac kept writing; then he looked up and asked, "What time do you think you came out to the garage?"

"Must o' been about two-thirty."

"I got here about three-fifteen. Nobody came to the door of the house or the garage, all the doors were wide open, so I came on in. I figure Billy took the SUV and hightailed it outa here soon after he whacked you across the head. Ray, he'll probably ditch it and steal another car before long. He knows we'll put out an APB for yours, Miss Dorothy."

He called the station and gave them a description of my SUV and told them to use the file photo of Billy to notify all law enforcement authorities in Pennsylvania, New York, New Jersey, Maryland, West Virginia and Ohio to arrest him on sight and to be aware that he was armed and dangerous.

Ray looked at me with concern. "Are ya okay, Miss Dorothy? I'm mighty sorry about all this. My God! For the first time in my life I looked at that boy and wondered if maybe we brought the wrong baby home from the hospital."

"Yes, I'll be fine, Ray, other than my head's going to be sore for awhile."

Mac was checking the damage to my home. "Is there anything missing?"

I walked slowly to the pile of rubble in the corner and reclaimed my wallet, though I knew full well what was not there. I nodded, "My cash is gone."

"About how much did you have?"

I avoided looking at either of them and answered quietly, "Three thousand and ten dollars."

Mac shook his head and asked, "Why would you have that much cash on you, Miss Dorothy?"

I lied, "I sold some jewelry when I was away and hadn't taken the time to make a deposit at the bank yet."

And then I added some truth. "I wasn't planning on being robbed, you know."

Mac nodded.

Ray said quietly, "I'm real sorry about that. I'll pay ya back, Miss Dorothy."

"Ray, you will not pay me back! You didn't steal my money. If Billy ever wants to make restitution, that would be quite a different story. But I most certainly do not want your money!"

Mac said, "Miss Dorothy's right. If ever there was a father who needed to stop cleaning up messes after his son, it's you, Ray."

Ray glanced at us, an aura of deep sadness radiated from him. "But ya gotta give Billy some credit. He's not all bad, he coulda shot and killed us both; he didn't. He's just a mixed up kid."

Mac sighed. "Ray, he's forty-four years old. It's been a long time since Billy was a kid.

"I think you've both had enough excitement today. I'll let you know of any new developments in the search for Billy. Try to get some rest. And of course, call if you need anything or think of something you may have overlooked telling me this afternoon." He left another card on the kitchen table.

I locked the door behind him and then sat down beside Ray on the sofa again. He put his arm around me and I held his hand. We sat together silently, each of us lost in our own thoughts. It had been a day of infamy for both of us.

Ray leaned his head on mine and softly said, "I'd never o' been able to forgive myself if ya couldn't o' got back up. I love ya Dorothy. I don't know what I'd do without ya. Somehow ya became my everything."

"You know I feel the same way about you. I can't imagine my life without you and I shudder to think what I'll do when they lock you away. I'm almost angry with myself for falling for you; except, it's been grand and I've felt more alive than I had in years since I came to Harmonyville."

We just set there amidst the mess and held onto each other like our lives depended on it; perhaps that day they did.

About an hour later there was a loud knock on the door. I answered cautiously, Joyce and Harry walked in. They set a large picnic basket on the kitchen table, walked through the muddle and hugged us.

"We heard you might need a couple of friends tonight and that's why we're here. And we brought vegetable lasagna for dinner."

I smiled. "Thanks for coming. You'll be good medicine for us and the lasagna smells delightful. I haven't even thought about dinner."

Ray nodded to his old friends. "It's been a hell of a day. Good of ya to come."

Joyce did simple neurological exams and checked our vision. "There, that's all they'd have done in the E.R. except for pricey MRIs and such. You both should take it easy and keep a close eye on each other for a few days."

She gathered up the groceries from the kitchen floor and started to quietly put the kitchen area back together before setting the table and pouring a small glass of wine for each of us.

Harry toasted us. "To my favorite survivors, Dorothy and Ray."

Dinner was excellent. They're wonderful friends who didn't pry and it was good to know anything we said to them would go no farther.

After dinner Harry said, "Why don't you girls go on in the bedroom and tidy up a bit, I'll clear the table and Ray can keep me company."

"Harry, would you be a doll and make us each a cup of decaf tea? Thanks, darling. I'll be in the bedroom with Dorothy."

Joyce and I stopped at the bedroom door and were appalled at the jumbled mess. We could hear Harry and Ray's voices in the kitchen, they sounded serious but upbeat.

Joyce said, "Let's push the mattress back onto the bed and then you sit there and tell me where everything goes and I'll put things away."

All my dresser drawers had been emptied. It repulsed me that he'd handled my clothing, especially my underwear.

I sighed, "Joyce, you may think I'm a real fuss but would you mind just putting all the clothes strewn about right into the laundry basket? I don't want to wear any of it again until I know it's been freshly laundered. Guess it's just one of my residual hang-ups from my years of teaching."

"Not at all. I'm sure I'd feel the same way if I were in your shoes."

Joyce was a cheerful and fast worker. She uncovered the photo I kept on the dresser; it had been under the last of the clothing she'd gathered up. I was relieved the back had not been tampered with though the glass was broken.

Joyce whispered softly, "We'll have to get you some new glass for the photograph. Who are these beautiful children?"

I answered semi-honestly. "They're children I used to know. I was very fond of them when they were young, though I've lost touch with them the last few years."

Joyce set the photo carefully back on the dresser and glanced at me curiously, though she didn't say anything else about it.

"Okay, Dorothy. Could you move over to the chair and I'll straighten the bed for you."

I shuffled to the chair. Then I asked her, "Would you mind putting clean sheets on the bed for me? I feel so violated I couldn't bear to sleep in sheets he touched. How can I loathe Billy so much while at the same time love his father so completely?"

She sat down on the edge of the bed and took my hands in hers. "Honey, listen to me. Under the circumstances, if you didn't feel that way about Billy right now, you'd be a candidate for sainthood!"

I wiped a stray tear from my eye and whispered, "Thank you."

She took the sheets off the bed with great efficiency. I told her where to find a clean set. In no time at all she had the bed looking warm and inviting in fresh clean sheets. My bedroom looked almost normal again.

Then she carried the heaping basket of laundry to the kitchen door, "I'm taking this home with me tonight. I'll bring your laundry back tomorrow and help you tidy the living room then."

"I can work on the laundry tomorrow; you don't need to take it home."

"I know you could, but I've overruled you. Now take it easy and get some rest. Retired nurse's orders."

We hugged them both good night, thanked them for dinner and all their help.

Then I whispered to Harry, "Would you make sure Ray's house is locked up tight before you leave?"

He nodded, "Sure thing, Dorothy. You guys get some rest now, we'll see you tomorrow."

He carried the laundry basket to the car for Joyce. It was a good feeling to have such kind friends.

I turned and found Ray staring out the kitchen window into the darkness; I walked over and wrapped my arms around him with my right cheek resting against his back.

He covered my hands with his. I felt a badly needed sense of security with my arms around him.

I said, "I'm so glad Joyce and Harry came tonight. It was just what we needed."

"Yes, they're fine people."

He turned and held my face gently with his big calloused hands, "Miss Dorothy, how can ya even think of stayin' friends with an ol' coot like me...after what happened today?"

I gave him a rueful smile. "What happened today wasn't your fault. Anyway you're much more than just a friend to me. I can't stop loving you because we've had a bad experience with your son. And like you said, he could've shot us but he didn't."

"You're a good woman, Dorothy."

"And you're a good man. I've a favor to ask you...would you stay the night with me?"

"If it'll make ya' feel better, I can sleep on the sofa agin."

"Not the sofa, I want to feel close to you all night…in my bed."

Ray looked stunned, then blushed and asked me hesitantly, "Are ya sure about this, Miss Dorothy?"

"Absolutely. And would you please just call me Dorothy? Considering that we're about to sleep together in the same bed, doesn't it seem a bit formal for you to call me Miss?"

"Yes'm, I'd say your 'bout right…well, I best go lock my house up then."

"No need. I asked Harry and he said he'd do it as he was leaving."

Despite the horror of the day, it felt like heaven to nestle up against Ray. I hadn't shared a bed with a man for more than twenty years. Yet sexual exploration was not on either of our minds. I didn't know what the future would hold, but that night felt so right. We fit together like two peas in a pod and we both had a deep contented sleep and woke the next morning feeling refreshed except for the pain radiating from our head contusions.

CHAPTER SEVENTEEN

Rest for the Weary

OLIVIA

THE NEXT FEW WEEKS flew by. Billy was arrested four days after the robbery and attack on Ray and me in, of all places, Trenton, New Jersey. He still had fifty dollars in his pocket. They brought him back to Harmonyville for his trial.

Ray recanted his guilty plea to the hit-and-run.

Mac said, "I oughta throw the book at you for a false confession, but I have a son and I understand your misguided attempts to help Billy. Just glad ya finally came to your senses."

Billy was charged with one count of first degree murder, two counts of assault and one count of armed robbery. He refused to see his father when he tried to visit him at the county jail. While waiting for his trial date, he spent a fair amount of time in solitary confinement due to his explosive anger and belligerent attitude. Never once did it occur to Billy that maybe it was his own fault he was in jail.

Billy seemed to be suffering from anxiety attacks and a hyper restless condition; the social worker requested a psychiatric evaluation. Billy refused to talk to the psychiatrist when he arrived for an interview. His court appointed attorney was negotiating for a plea bargain. Billy's only responses to his attorney's questions were guttural grunts.

Ray's friends rallied around him, but the ordeal took its toll on him. He seemed to age ten years in the months that followed.

One night as we were playing a game of pinochle, (it was the week after Billy had been sent to the state penitentiary), Ray looked up from his cards and out of the blue, said, "Dorothy, you're my connection and my life line. I don't know how I'd have ever managed to hold on these last few months without ya."

Then he lifted my hand to his lips and gently kissed it. I think it was the single most romantic moment I've had in the last forty years.

I gently squeezed his hand and stammered. "Ray, you're my best friend...of course, I was there for you."

Since the night of the robbery, we'd developed a bit of a pattern, once or twice a week I'd invite Ray to sleep over. We maintained our separate homes and independence, yet we'd grown closer than most married couples. It wasn't like I wanted to live an immoral life, but considering our ages and circumstances, it made sense and worked for us.

Somehow we cherished each new day even more since we'd all but given up on any future together only a few months earlier.

We participated in Harmonyville fund raisers for the victims and survivors of the E-Coli water poisoning. Mayor Brown had already requested grants from the state and federal governments for a new water purification system. It was one grant request that had been flagged for rapid processing.

Bottled water remained a fast seller in all the stores.

We stopped at the diner one evening about a month later for any early dinner. A gaunt Darlene was our waitress. At first it was almost hard to believe she was the same bubbly girl whom I'd met when I first arrived in Harmonyville, though after a few minutes I realized beneath her muted spirit, her fierce determination was still there, a paradigm of courage.

She greeted us in a flat voice. "Uncle Ray, Dorothy, good to see you again. What're ya' hungry for tonight?"

Without thinking, I stood up immediately and gave her a hug. "How are you, dear girl? How's little Annie?"

She gave me an unenthusiastic hug back. Ray stood and pulled a chair out for her. "Sit down a few minutes, Darlene. It's not busy yet. Would you like a drink?"

She looked at him through baffled teary eyes. "That's what I'm supposed to ask you!" She looked around quickly, sighed and softly answered. "Yes, I'd like a glass of ice tea."

Ray went back to the kitchen and quickly returned with three glasses of frosty tea. "Sal said to take a break. She'll cover your section for the next fifteen minutes or so."

I reached across the table and covered her thin hand with mine.

She sat there quietly for a minute or so and then began, "Annie misses Andy as much as I do, maybe even more…they'd been together since the day they were born. She cries more now than she ever did. It's hard for a five-year-old to understand why her favorite playmate isn't here anymore." She paused and took a deep breath. "My parents are trying their best to keep us going. It's hard. A whole lot worse than when their dad took off, that's for sure. I feel like there's a forever hole in my heart."

Ray slowly replied, "I wish I could tell ya it'll get easier. But I can't 'cause we all know it's an open wound that'll jes never heal. It's been near fifty years since my little Sarah passed on, but not a day goes by I don't think 'bout what kinda life she might o' had. Time may take away some o' the sting, but it never stops hurtin'. Jes ain't a natural thing for a parent to bury a child."

We sat in a comfortable reflective silence for a while. Then Darlene reached over and squeezed both our hands. "Thanks, you two; this is exactly what I needed tonight." She dabbed the corner of her eyes with a paper napkin.

I asked, "How's nursing school going?"

She sighed, "They were very supportive when I had all my troubles. But I did get behind. They've given me a special tutor to catch up with the rest of my class and actually waived a few of the required clinical rotations for me. In another two weeks I'll be back in line with my class. We registered last week for the state board examination next summer. It won't be much longer till I'll be working full time as an RN. I'll miss seeing you here at the diner."

Ray whispered in a hoarse voice, "Don't ya worry, little girl, we'll make a point to get together from time to time. Ya can't git away from us!"

She stood up, gave us each a peck on the cheek. "My breaks over, I best get back to work." She pulled out her order book. "What are ya hungry for tonight?"

"I'll have the chicken and biscuits with coleslaw."

Ray added, "The same for me."

She turned to walk away, then glanced back and smiled. "Thanks, Uncle Ray and Miss Dorothy."

Our dinner at the diner was delicious as always and we felt good about having had the chance to touch base with Darlene. She was so young to have had to learn such harsh lessons about the unfairness of life.

The headline in the next morning's Harmonyville Daily News turned the town upside down and inside out.

Crazed Environmentalist Poisoned Harmonyville Water!

The FBI had arrested reclusive Leonard Oakes who lived in a primitive cabin high in the hills, miles from his closest neighbor. He seemed to be recognizable only to the post office and the small grocery store where he'd picked up his mail and basic supplies once a month for the last twenty years. He had a shaggy unkempt beard and wore his long straggly gray-streaked hair in a ponytail. The newspaper photo caught him scowling at the camera. No one wanted to believe one of their own could've intentionally done such a thing.

He refused a lawyer, wanted to defend himself against the imperialistic legal system. He made bizarre statements, like, "The time has come to show the world there's no place to hide."

When confronted by angry policemen about the victims of his venomous deed, he sneered at them through clenched teeth. "Innocents have suffered in every war throughout history; at least the Harmonyville heroes gave their lives for a worthy cause."

The FBI found Leonard after extensive testing of the reservoir revealed constant acute amounts of coli form bacteria in the water supply.

Even after massive disinfectant treatments the bacteria count continued to spiral. A twenty-four-hour surveillance team was set up around the reservoir. The second week they observed Leonard backing his old Ford pickup to a craggy section of the water's edge as he shoveled dark clumps into the water.

One team followed Leonard home and brought him in for questioning. Another immediately went into the reservoir at the sight and withdrew samples from the water. Human and animal feces.

Leonard was completely unremorseful. The media started to

return to Harmonyville before the day was out. They scoured the town trying to find someone who knew Leonard and would make a few comments about him.

I asked, "Ray, did you know this Leonard Oakes?"

"Long time ago, he was a few years ahead o' Billy in school. Real brainy kid, always a loner. I forgot all about him even livin' out in them hills till I read about him in today's paper." Ray shook his head slowly and stared out the window.

"I've never understood what makes people do such things, so senseless. What kind of family did he come from?"

"Both o' his parents were killed in a car wreck right after he finished high school. He sailed right through college, was workin' on bein' some kind o' agriculture doctor when he jes dropped out. Bought a section o' land up on that mountain an' built himself a cabin, I ain't seen him in years."

"I can just imagine how the media will play this one up. I do wonder what ever happened to make him just drop out like that and finally do this atrocious act of vengeance."

The press had a difficult time finding anyone who wanted to talk about Leonard. It was as if Harmonyville was in a state of shock.

As the trial concluded and Leonard was given five consecutive life sentences, Ray couldn't help but think of Billy.

"Ya know, Dorothy, I bin thinkin'. Maybe it's 'bout time for me to take a trip out to that prison where they got Billy locked up an' pay my boy a visit."

I answered, "If that's what you want to do, then I guess you should do it."

"Would ya wanna come along? We could make a little vacation outa the trip?"

"Ah, Ray I don't think that's a good idea. If you want us to take a vacation, then we'll have to plan a real one. Visiting a prison is not my idea of a vacation. Besides, I'm sure Billy wouldn't want to see me. Maybe you should call the prison before making the trip, to find out if he's even willing to see you. After all he's refused all your letters."

A month later, a hopeful Ray boarded a coach bus for the seventeen hour trip to the prison in Minnesota. I wished him well. Then I made plans for lunches, movies and shopping with Joyce and Mary.

Five days later, Ray returned. Billy had agreed to see him twice, but the visits hadn't gone well at all. Billy remained angry, defiant and belligerent.

Ray was discouraged. "I ain't never again gonna' make a trip to that prison to see my boy. But o' course, if Billy ever 'fesses up an' says he's sorry, I might have ta change my mind. I'm jes thankful his dear momma's not here to see what he's come to."

CHAPTER EIGHTEEN

Back in Nebraska

ANDREA AND ALEXANDER

ANDREA HAD JUST RETURNED from another meeting with the Hospital Auxiliary when the phone rang.

"Hello Luella. How are you? Hearing your voice always reminds me of Mother."

"I've been well, dear. And how are you and the family?"

"We're all doing okay. Tiffany had her senior photos taken already. It's hard to believe she'll start her last year of high school in a few more weeks."

"How time flies! Little Tiffany…amazing. Hannah's son will be a senior this year, too. How's Alex doing these days?"

"He and Jackie are expecting again, we just celebrated Alex Jr.s' second birthday last week end. He's such a doll and Alex is like a different person. Jackie's the best thing that ever happened to him."

Luella laughed. "That's wonderful news; maybe a good woman was what Alex needed all along."

Andrea smiled. "Luella, you're beginning to sound like a romantic! I think maturity and timing are as important in the Alex equation as a good woman!"

"You're probably right about that. Do you realize its six years today since your mother passed away?"

"Went away is more accurate, but yes, of course I know it's been six years. I miss her everyday."

"And she's missed so much of your lives. It's a tragedy."

"You know I don't believe she's dead? I know I saw her on that subway when Joel and I went to NYC five years ago. But she ran away from me and she's never tried to contact me. I'll never understand."

"Poor dear Andrea..."

"So tell me, have you become accustomed to widowhood? It must be hard after so many years together."

"Hank and I had fifty-one good years together. I was a lucky woman to have found a decent kindhearted man my first time up to bat. Hannah, Larry and their families are good to me and they live in town, but they're all so busy. I have friends too, but the evenings are the hardest. Long and lonely. I surely do miss them, Hank and your mother."

Andrea spoke softly. "I know you do. Would you like to go see a movie with me one night?"

"I'd love to, and maybe an early dinner before the movie?"

"Sounds good to me. Are you free tomorrow? I'll look forward to seeing you again."

Later as she was preparing salad, potatoes and steaks to grill for dinner, Joel came in behind her, slipped his arms around her trim waist and nuzzled her neck. "It smells great in here. How was your day, honey?"

She mockingly slapped his hands. "Hey, you better be careful, my husband's due home any minute and he's the jealous type!" Then she turned to face him and teased. "Ohh, thank God, it's you, Joel! You're early today."

"I'd finished up everything that had to be done and it's such a gorgeous day, I decided to take my chances and come home."

Andrea kissed him tenderly. "I'm glad you did."

Tiffany and Thomas returned noisily from their afternoon at the Country Club pool.

Thomas looked at the dinner preparations and grinned. "I'm starved, how long till dinner?"

Joel answered, "About an hour. But it's your turn to grill so be back down here in thirty minutes, okay?"

Thomas gave his dad a mock salute. "Yes sir."

Andrea called up the stairs. "Tiffany, I need you to set the patio table for dinner...thirty minutes."

When they were alone again, Joel spoke reflectively. "My God, they're practically grown up! Do you ever wish they were small again?"

"Not for more than ten seconds. That's about how long it takes me to remember how demanding they were back then!"

She told him about her meeting that day and her surprise call from Luella. "She sounded so lonely that I asked her to a movie tomorrow night and then she asked me to an early dinner. Will you be here to hold down the fort?"

"No problem."

"Do you realize today is the sixth anniversary of Mother's disappearance?"

He shook his head, "Seems like only yesterday...while at the same time like a life time ago."

During dinner the children chattered about who said what to whom at the pool.

Alexander looked at his very pregnant wife and his two year old son and smiled fondly as he thought of how full and satisfying his life had become.

He jostled Alex Jr. to his shoulder as Jackie and he started out the door for an evening walk. The phone rang as they closed the front door. Jackie turned to answer the phone, but Alex said, "Let's go, the answering machine will take it."

She shrugged, "Okay."

They all loved their after dinner early evening walks that most often ended up at a playground near their home. Alex Jr. laughed when a bird flew into a low resting nest in a nearby tree. "Birds, Daddy!"

When Alex lifted him down to the ground, he took off running for the swings. "Push me, Daddy. Swing! Please, Daddy!"

As he pushed the boy on the swing, he reflected on his life. I can't help it; I melt when that little guy calls me Daddy. It's a phenomenon I never experienced with Cassie, but then she was virtually out of my life by the time she was his age. Except for the child support, college tuition and cars, but now she's graduated and started her first real job. This time I have a real family.

And Jackie...I couldn't have been any luckier if I'd have won the lottery than I was the day I hired her to run my office. Except, perhaps the day she agreed to be my wife. It really does make a difference in a marriage to marry the right person. I oughta' know. Took me three tries before I got it right. But if I hadn't had those first two, I might not have appreciated Jackie like I do. Of course, that's pure speculation. Two more months and Alex, Jr. will be a big brother. I'm truly a blessed man.

When they returned to the house, Andrea's voice spoke clearly on the answering machine. "Hey Jackie, you two Alex's...please give me a call when you get a chance."

"Call your sister and I'll give Alex his bath."

"Hi Alex, thanks for calling me back tonight. I guess I just wanted to hear your voice."

"Are you okay? Joel and the kids? What's up?"

"Everyone's fine...did you realize its six years today since mother disappeared?"

"No, I didn't. You still won't admit she's dead, will you? Lots of water under the bridge since then."

"Alex I don't want to argue with you, but I know I saw her when I was in New York City a year and a half after she was gone."

"I know you think you saw her."

Andrea's voice started to break. "I did see her and I miss her Alex; I wish she could've been here to see her grandchildren grow up. I'm taking Luella to dinner and a movie tomorrow night."

Alex sighed. "How's she doing? Please tell her I said 'hi'. And have a good time."

Andrea hadn't seen Luella since Hank's funeral and was surprised by the sudden onset of the aging process. She'd gone from a spry senior to a frail elderly lady. Widowhood had not been kind to her. She used a walker, was very hard of hearing, and had difficulty with her short term memory. Yet, Luella was full of stories of adventures she and Mother had shared throughout the years of their very long friendship.

Andrea made a vow to herself to stay in closer touch with dear old Luella as she drove home later that night.

CHAPTER NINETEEN

And the Years Went By

OLIVIA...TEN YEARS AFTER THE ESCAPE

I HEARD HIS FOOTSTEPS WHEN he entered the garage and I could smell the heavenly scent of the red roses even before opened the door.

He thrust the bouquet toward me, "For my dear Dorothy."

I felt myself blushing. "Oh Ray, they're lovely! What's the occasion?"

"Ya really don't know, do ya?" He shook his head in mock disgust.

"Please, give me a hint..."

He folded his arms across his chest and smiled at me, the twinkle in his eyes reminded me of the first time we met, I glanced at the calendar.

"Oh, Ray! You big romantic wonderful man! It's been ten years since our first dinner together! The flowers are so beautiful. Thank you!" And I hugged him.

He held me close. "Ya know, when I look in the mirror, I see this old man, but when I'm with you, Dorothy, ya make me feel like a young man again." He wheezed, and continued, "I'll be damned if ya don't."

Just then a lovely old song, 'You Made Me Love You', came on the radio.

He whispered, "Would ya care to dance, my lady?"

I rested my head on his shoulder as we slowly shuffled around my small kitchen. One of those special fleeting moments that are far too rare.

A few days later I made an inventory of my accounts and I was down to three thousand dollars. I knew it was time I took a trip to the city again. I hadn't been there for more than two years.

I invited Ray, "It could be fun; we could see a couple shows, take a tour of the city, and eat in some nice restaurants."

He stared at me incredulously. "I thought by now you'd have that foolishness out of your system. Ya ain't draggin' me to that damnable city. No way."

"I'm sorry you feel that way. I'll see you when I get back."

Ray glared. "Sometimes I feel like I don't even know ya."

He stomped out and slammed the door behind him.

I left early the next morning, checked into my hotel by mid afternoon, and immediately went for a walk in Central Park. It was a brilliant sunny yet brisk autumn day.

I loved my anonymity as I observed the diverse throngs and felt the exuberance that oozes from that great city.

Of course, as soon as I returned to my room after an early dinner, I called Luella. When she heard my voice, she started to cry, softly at first and then it quickly escalated to deep gut-wrenching sobs.

I repeatedly asked, "Luella, what's wrong?"

She continued to weep for several minutes. I felt a great sadness and even guilt as I waited for her to calm down. Finally, her breathing became a bit more regular as her sobs relented to little more than a whimper.

"Luella…?"

She started to speak in a tight choked voice. "Olivia, where have you been? Hank had his final heart attack almost a year ago. I've needed you. Most of our friends have died off or moved away and with Hank gone, I've been so lonely and angry. What kind of friendship do we have if you can't even give me a damn phone number? Where's the trust?"

"Oh my God, Luella, I'm so sorry about Hank. I didn't realize I hadn't called for so long. I'm truly sorry I wasn't there for you."

With an unfamiliar coolness Luella replied, "Well, what's done is done."

"How are Hannah, Larry and the families?"

"They're all well; busy with their lives. Hannah's oldest is in his second year at the State University, time marches on."

"Dare I ask about Andrea and Alexander? The grandchildren? How are they?"

"Well, I don't quite know how to say this."

My heart was in my throat. "What's happened?"

"That's just it; they're all doing very well. Sometimes I feel sad for you when I think how much you left behind. You wouldn't know Alex. He's so relaxed; he adores his wife and children.

"Cassie finished college three years ago and he's finally done sending money to Lori every month. Cassie has no interest in her half-siblings and rarely contacts her father. Some things never change. But Alex did and you'd like him. Alex Jr. is four and Janie is two. They're totally delightful children and Jackie is a great wife and mother. She still manages his office, mostly from home.

"Andrea takes me to a movie and dinner every month or so. She's finally found the balance she needed for so long in her life. Tiffany is a sophomore at Carnegie-Mellon University in Pittsburgh...of all places. She wants to be a lawyer like her father, I have no idea why she chose that school and so far away. Thomas is a senior this year and also wants to be a lawyer. I don't think he's decided on a college yet. They're both excellent students.

"If only you knew them now ... I know you'd be proud of and actually like both of your children."

I sat there as if in a trance quietly taking in the family news.

"Olivia, are you still there?"

I wiped my face with the backs of my hands as I looked down at my shirt, soaked from my silent tears. I took a deep breath, sighed and in a subdued voice answered. "Yes, of course, I'm here. You know, sometimes I wonder if I made the right choice when I left."

"Well, you did what you thought was the right thing to do at the time. Besides, it's all water under the bridge now."

I took a deep breath; gave her my phone number and one last

apology for not giving it to her sooner.

"Luella, you know I've always trusted you and loved you. Thank you for being my friend."

An hour later, among my jumbled thoughts as I hung up the phone, was Tiffany, in college and only two hours away from Harmonyville!

I took a farewell bus tour of the Big Apple the next day. The following two afternoons I attended Broadway Matinees. Somehow the whole city experience had lost its glow. I made an appointment with Isaac Mayer for ten a.m. on my third day in the city. As always he was professional and efficient.

Before leaving, I asked him, "If I need to sell another diamond, could I send it to you by insured overnight special delivery?"

He answered, "For you, Mrs. Hampton, of course."

I knew in my heart that I'd made my last trip to that great city.

Overall, my life's been good in Harmonyville, the Billy problems pretty much resolved when he went to prison.

We all managed to move on after the water sickness nightmare.

The strange phone calls stopped once they were traced to Irene and she was confronted. Of course, she never formally acknowledged or apologized for her offenses. I declined to press charges. After her Walter passed away, she mellowed and I suspected she'd gone on a long-needed medication. She became far less judgmental, though never truly friendly to me.

Within a few days of my return, Ray had recovered from his tiff about my trip and our lives were back to the pre-New York City status which was good, except I realized there was a superficial quality to my Harmonyville life. The past would always be part of me even though I tried to pretend it wasn't. And I knew the superficiality of our lives wasn't Ray's fault at all.

I noticed even though I'd made my morning walks shorter, I was increasingly tired and breathless. I monitored my pulse and was alarmed that just walking to my mailbox each day brought my pulse up to the rate a two mile walk had just a few years ago. I became short of breath far too quickly.

I decided to write letters to Andrea and Alex and explain why I'd disappeared ten years ago and how proud I was of their lives today. I also wrote a long letter to Ray and explained who I was and why I'd refused to discuss my past with him. After I'd finished all the letters, I tied a blue ribbon around them and laid them on my dresser. I tucked a folded note under the ribbon with a request they be delivered after my death. I felt good about that completed task.

Then my conscience began to trouble me. I asked myself if it was fair to explain things to the children with a letter from the grave. Should I send the letter now, or call them? Should I give them a chance for face-to-face closure? Have I been wrong all these years? Was it too late? I even picked up the phone, twice, and started to call Andrea. But I couldn't go through with it. Ten years.

After several days of soul searching I decided to rewrite the letters to the children and send them immediately via registered mail. I included my phone number and left the decision about further contact up to them.

The next week I was on edge, wondering, hoping and fearing they'd call. What would I say? What would they say?

I jumped when the phone rang Monday morning, and answered on the third ring. It was Luella. Ever since I'd given her my phone number six months ago, she'd called me once a week.

"Hello, Olivia."

"Luella, it feels like old times answering the phone and hearing your voice, how are you dear?"

"Old and feeble. And you?"

"I'm afraid my age has caught up with me and its winning the race."

Silence answered me, though I could still hear her raspy breathing.

"Luella, is something wrong, dear?"

"No, nothing…well, except everything. I hate being a burden to my children and grandchildren. I hate that Hank and you are gone. I hate being old and helpless. My mind is good, but my body's about given out on me. I can't even go to the bathroom without using this damn walker!"

"Luella, I…I don't know what to say. It's hard to grow old and watch our strength and vigor slip away from us, as well as our family and friends. But, by God we had some great times, didn't we?"

"Olivia, I wouldn't trade even one of our memories for

anything."

An hour later we concluded our reminiscing, and promised to talk again soon, yet somehow I knew I'd said my last good bye to my dear Luella. And there was really nothing left to say.

She didn't call me the next week, or the following week. Then the phone rang on a Friday afternoon. It was Andrea.

I sank into the sofa. It was so wonderful to hear her voice. We both cried.

"Mother, I *always knew* you were alive somewhere. And I knew I'd made eye contact with you in that subway. Still I was shocked to receive your letter; I could hardly bring myself to call you.

"Luella passed away last week; she's missed you so much all these years."

I spoke softly and carefully. "And I've missed all of you more than you'll ever know. I followed your lives the best I could by reading the Scottsbluff paper online. Ten years ago it seemed like I was doing the right thing. Now I seriously doubt it although I've had a good life and made new friends here in Harmonyville.

"I was going to have another version of the letter sent to you after my death."

"Oh Mother, that would have been cruel. I know Alex and I were far from model children but we don't deserve that. I'm glad you finally got in touch with us. I don't know if Alex will call, he accepted your passing and he's moved on. This whole thing has muddled his mind and he's, well, he's damn mad at you right now.

"But I want to come visit you."

My heart nearly stopped. "Oh, Andrea, I can't think of anything I'd like more. When can you come?"

"We already have tickets to fly to Pittsburgh to visit Tiffany in ten days for Parents Week End. You're not far from there, are you?"

"Not far at all, I can hardly wait!"

By the following Tuesday, I was becoming progressively weaker and easily tired; I thought I was going through a bout of depression combined with a touch of the flu. Ray brought me the mail each day. He wanted to take me to the doctor.

I smiled weakly, laid my hand over his, and refused. "I'll shake this, don't worry about me, a couple days rest and I'll be fine."

He sat there in silence as the fire crackled in the hearth.

I asked him. "Have I told you how much I cherish our special friendship?"

He looked at me with a rare tenderness, and softly replied. "You've told me a few times but it's somethin' I like to hear agin' an' agin'."

We watched the fire dance and shared a comfortable silence. Ray got up to add another log to the fire and fixed two cups of hot tea with honey.

I sat up to sip my tea and rested my head on his bony shoulder. "You know, Ray, I'd never have wanted to miss our time together."

He heated two cans of chicken noodle soup for our dinner. I forced myself to eat a few bites. Ray offered to stay the night but I declined.

As the final embers flickered, Ray kissed my forehead, "Good night my precious ol' girl. Sleep well; I'll see ya' in the morning."

I left the door unlocked; I barely had the strength to get myself to bed. I took the photograph of Andrea and Alexander from the dresser and held them over my heart and prayed for them and their families in Nebraska. I prayed for Luella and Ray too, even for Billy. Then I asked God's forgiveness as I drifted off to sleep.

In the wee hours of the morning Olivia/Dorothy's heart fluttered for the last time and she died...alone, in her small apartment in Harmonyville, Pennsylvania.

Ray knocked on her door three different times before he reluctantly entered her apartment the next day. An ominous sense of doom hung over him as walked through her door; it was only the second time in ten years he'd entered the apartment without her standing there to greet him.

"Dorothy, it's eleven-thirty, are ya' okay?"

No answer. He warily entered her bedroom, and hesitated for a few seconds before he cautiously touched her cold hand to check for a pulse.

Time stopped for Ray as he collapsed on the bed beside her.

A few hours later he called the number she'd written on his letter to notify the folks out west. The distraught girl, Andrea, had seemed like a nice enough sort, they'd made arrangements to transfer the coffin to a place called Scottsbluff, Nebraska to be buried next to her long dead husband.

Which of course was only right, after all, one of these days he'd be laid to rest beside his Sophie.

Days later when the shock began to wear off a bit and he'd read her letter for the tenth time, he shook his head and thinly smiled through his tears. "Miss Dorothy, ya' truly were one of a kind."

THE END

RUNAWAY GRANDMA

READERS DISCUSSION QUESTIONS

1. Can anyone truly escape their past and start over? How would *you* react if your mother ran away at the age of seventy?

2. How did you feel when Olivia said in the first paragraph, "... I chose freedom with uncertainty over secure entrapment."? How important is autonomy to you?

3. Did you most identify with Olivia - the one who went away, Luella - the one who stayed behind, Andrea, Alexander, Ray or Billy? Who was your favorite character? Why? How and when did you most identify with the character?

4. Were Olivia's perceptions of Andrea and Alexander accurate? Was she perhaps clouded by grief from the loss of her sister and sister- in-law? Did you ever doubt Luella would break her promise of secrecy to Olivia?

5. In what ways were Andrea and Alexander's perception of their mother accurate or inaccurate? How did Olivia's disappearance from her children's life affect them in the short and long term?

6.   Did the story cause you to question assumptions about someone you may have been taking for granted in your life?

7.   Did you like Ray? In what ways did you or did you not find him charming and believable? Olivia had not been romantically involved with a man nor did she expect to be at the age of seventy… since her husband died many years ago. How did you feel about Olivia and Ray's blossoming friendship?

8.   Have you ever met someone like Billy? Do you believe there are some people who are incapable of change? Were there too many *bad* adult children? In what ways did Olivia and Ray enable their adult children to be self-centered?

9.   How did you feel about Olivia's steely resolve to leave the past behind? How did you feel about Andrea's refusal to accept her mother's death? Were you satisfied with Olivia's attempt to reconnect with her children at the end of her life?

10.   At what point does strong personal determination cross the line …and become stubborn pride? One of the reasons Olivia left was because she didn't want to end up living in a small apartment and dying alone. Did you find this ironic?